Rain On A Tin Roof

From the Co-Author of *In Search of Eden*

by

Gabriel J. Christian

Pond Casse Press

Upper Marlboro, Maryland ◆ Brampton, Ontario ◆Roseau, Dominica

D1595685

*For my wife Joan and
children Samora and Makonnen*

❀❀❀❀❀❀❀❀❀❀❀❀❀❀❀❀❀❀❀❀

Copyright ©1999 Gabriel J. Christian

A Pond Casse Press Production.

Publisher's Note

These are works of fiction and any resemblance to actual persons or events is entirely coincidental.

Fifth Pond Casse Press Publication, 1999

First Edition: Rain on A Tin Roof

Pond Casse Press, 4711 Cashill Court, Upper Marlboro, MD 20772

E-Mail:Gabrielchn@aol.com

Cover designed by: KDL Graphics

Desktop Publishing by Hard Copy Management, Inc., (www.hardcopyinc.com) and Cartiann Allen of GJC & Associates.

Manufactured in the United States of America by Bookcrafters

Library of Congress Cataloging in Publication No. 99-95666

International Standard Book No. 0-9668454-1-2

Christian, Gabriel J.

Rain On A Tin Roof

Glossary p.

Caribbean Literature (Dominica, Society)

Rain On A Tin Roof

ACKNOWLEDGEMENTS

One can never give thanks to all those who contributed to the writing of a book. However, by this "Acknowledgement Page" I give thanks to all those whose names are not mentioned.

Specifically, I thank my Mother, Alberta and Father, Wendell for having given me a start. All of my siblings played a role: Christalyn "The Guardian Angel;" Lawson "The Incisive Critic;" Samuel "The Keen Analyst;" Esther "The Motivator;" Hildreth "The Reviewer;" and Wellsworth who urged me to submit a short story for the National Independence Competition in 1982. I did. "Sure Bet Cecilia" won first prize that year. I must also, thank Irving Andre for encouraging me to be part of a new wave in Dominican literature of which he is part creator, part progeny. Also, Cartiann Allen who worked the computer like a piano to make this happen. And, of course, all the comrades who said: "Do it Gaibu! Just do it!"

I cannot forget Aunty Floss, Uncle Henckell and Uncle Lemuel "Steward" for being beacons of knowledge. The teachers at the Roseau Mixed Infant School, Goodwill Junior High School, Dominica Grammar School and Sixth Form College, all laid a base for me. And much praise to the stalwarts at Frontline Cooperative Bookstore, who have kept the fires of literary consciousness burning.

Last but not least, I thank my Wife, Joan for giving me the love and support, while explaining my late nights and absent Saturdays to the puzzled duo of Samora and Makonnen.

Rain On A Tin Roof

TABLE OF CONTENTS

Carib Basket

Aaaah! Good! Good! I mean to say Auguiste, this thing, it *bon*, as all you does say. This is good quality rum," says the uniformed man in hobnailed boots, black twill pants and a gray flannel shirt, as he purses his lips and withdraws the ex-whiskey bottle from his lips.

"Hmmmp," he goes on, wiping his mouth with the back of his hand. "But, I don't think it's ever seen the inside of customs though."

It is late August 1930, and Corporal Elijah Mathews of the Leeward Island Police Force has just had a drink in John Auguiste's yard in the Carib Reserve. The reservation is where the Carib islanders, encountered by Columbus in 1493, were confined to by the British who came later. It covered three thousand acres of hilly terrain on Dominica's northeastern coast overlooking the Guadeloupe channel. On a cloudless day, the faint outline of the French colonies of Guadeloupe and Marie Galante can be seen across the sparkling blue water.

Corporal Matthew's is from Antigua, an island further north; a land where a Carib presence has been extinct for at least one hundred years and French Creole is not spoken. At this time, Dominica is considered part of the Leeward Islands, a colony of Britain with a governor who presides from Antigua. With its looming green peaks and its French-Creole speaking blacks and Caribs, Dominica is still a strange place to the officer. But the corporal likes his grog and at the reserve he throws his weight around to get it for free. After four years with the Reserve as his beat, Mathew's begins dabbling in trade to pad his meager income. His favorite trading piece is the prized Carib made basket, well known for its resilience and good resale value.

The corporal hands over the bottle to the brown-skinned man who goes by the name of Auguiste. Auguiste does not smile as the muscles in his wiry frame coil and uncoil, swiftly, as he springs from his perch to grasp the bottle. Auguiste acquiesces in his name, as it was what the priests told his parents they should name him at his Roman Catholic baptism forty-five years prior. The presence of such names have not been with his people long; it is no more than a one hundred year old relic of the former French colonial presence. It is a name that, like all the others in the reserve, mocks any memory Auguiste's people may have of their Carib past.

Brushing off the tattered seat of his khaki pants as he goes, Auguiste takes the bottle around which a reed wrapping has been woven and hands it to his young wife, Doreen. Doreen, the nipples of her firm young breast pressing against the thin cotton dress she is wearing, shakes her long, blue-black hair away from her sweating brow and arranges it so it hangs low on her back. The corporal's eyes move with her, she notices and bends her head, avoiding his stare.

She jumps quickly over to a pile of *vert-t-vert* reed in the backyard and hides the bottle. She picks up some reed and returns to plaiting a mat, which she must finish for the corporal before he leaves. Next to her a blackened pot holds a simmering broth of dasheens, white yams, green bananas, and mackerel. It is Sunday and Peterson Ferdinand - the fisherman - is having a christening fete for his first child this day. Money is tight and Doreen's gift will be the food.

"Okay! Auguiste, I have three cutlasses for you. And I got this cloth, it could make nice clothes for you pickney them." Corporal Mathews pulls out several yards of red shiny cloth from his canvas knapsack and hands it to Auguiste. Attracted by the bright cloth, Auguiste's little girl and boy, mud spattered yellow-brown feet padding atop the beaten earth of yard, come nearer to look.

"*Negre! Negre,*" the children, giggling, call at the man with the shiny red cloth. He returns their attention with a gap-toothed smile.

"What they saying Auguiste? I black? Is that what *negre* mean?" he inquires. "It sound like negro, anyway."

"Don't worry officer, they is just children. As you know, already is two type of people who not from here we know, *negre* and *blanc.* You is not a *blanc*, so you bound to be a *negre*. Anyway, I find your Creole knowledge coming to come. You must try speak it more and more."

Auguiste fingers the cloth. "Officer, you think that strong nuh? It look like it can tear easy... it look like *soosoon-*

clayway. Mondieu, that is a *kochonni* cloth oui …them stores in Roseau too like to sell that to Carib people." Auguiste pouts.

"Don't worry man, I not charging you for that…before long Christmas will be here. That is just a little extra for the wife and children. Believe me, Doreen will look nice in this." As the corporal explains, his eyes dart over to Doreen and he scratches under both armpits in turn as if red ants had gotten up his sleeves.

"Alright, let me give you this," Auguiste says, as he rises and enters the hut. He returns with four baskets, woven with fine alternating strands of dark brown and light tan reed.

"Officer, you see this," Auguiste points to the bottom of one of the baskets. "It can hold water for a little bit. If you carrying load across the river and it fall in … just pick it up fast and nothing inside will wet. You can put your *farine*, cocoa stick and saltfish in this, and it will never spoil. The vine it make with bitter, so rat stay far away from this."

"You think so, nuh boy," the corporal looks at the baskets, his eyes squinting in the early morning sun.

"Anyway, I getting the mat your wife finishing too ... and the demijohn, right?"

"But officer, I need more than what you giving me if you want the demijohn ... that demijohn go through a lot of trouble to get, oui. I had to row quite across the channel to get this thing... you never see how tall those waves be? Plenty water was getting in my canoe, last time I make the trip...I nearly drown. And you know things tough all about...money tight...none of our baskets fetching good price in Roseau. The shop and them not giving credit."

Auguiste looks away toward where he has placed the little pile of cloth and the three cutlasses he will get in exchange. He scratches his right forearm. This is the forearm which weeds the garden, chops the gommier tree, hollows out the raw log to fashion a canoe, caresses his wife, comforts his children and beats the tikki drum. But, whenever he is nervous, Auguiste's right forearm itches like it has rubbed against the stinging zuuti bush.

"Okay," mutters the corporal. "I have a couple shot for you." Peeling out his pants pocket, the corporal hands a fistful of shotgun shells to Auguiste. They bear the tall tale blue casing of government issued cartridges.

"Careful with this now chief. If word get back that I give you this, I dead, dead, dead, you hear me? This is his majesty's own bullets I giving you, you hear? Anyway, I hear Salybia and down Castlebruce side have plenty wild pig. If you shoot one, make sure I get me smoke pork for the Christmas," the corporal says with a smile.

"Wild pig, eh? Who say about wild pig? Is people pig they thiefing in their yard at night and calling it wild pig. Anyways officer, you eat manicou? If I get manicou, you will take it? Take a taste?" Auguiste is speaking of the rabbit-sized marsupial common to the island.

"Yah! Why not? But don't waste my shot on no manicou, you can catch those in trap, right? Don't waste the shot..." as he speaks the corporal goes behind the pile of *vert-t-vert* reed. Without waiting for Auguiste to make a move, he parts the pile and pulls up a demijohn: a big bottle with a cork filled mouth and a plaited reed base.

"But this thing almost finish, chief?"

"Officer, I always split my rum. I never keep all in one bottle. What if it break? All my labors gone!" Auguiste looks at the corporal, his face is marked with the discomfort of a man losing his treasure.

He wants to take back his prized demijohn, but the authority that reposes in the officer has him frightened by the minute. After all, he reflects, this is contraband. Corporal Mathew's could beat him up and toss him in jail. At least, he got a little something.

The corporal walks to his horse, which has been tethered to the rickety fence fronting the yard. It snorts and stamps its right front hoof as the corporal approaches. He slips the demijohn into a pannier on one side of the horse and struggles to fit the baskets and reed mat into the other side. Scratching his forearm, trailed by Doreen and the children, Auguiste follows the corporal out the yard. The horse tosses its head and jangles the brass buckle adorned reins held firmly in the corporal's left hand.

Several young Carib men loiter near the fence which separates Auguiste's yard from the rutted path which leads back to Marigot. They have been observing the corporal as he prepares his horse.

"Morning gentlemen. All you behaving yourselves?" Corporal Mathew's smiles at the nearest Carib who has one plait falling across his shoulder, a red bow twisted at the end. He doesn't smile back.

"*Chien lawen*!" the Carib spits out, under his breath.

"What you say?" Corporal Mathew's cranes his neck, backward, towards where the words have come.

"Oh, he say: take care. Take care of yourself," Auguiste trots up to the officer and explains. "Is Creole. I know all you Antiguans don't know Creole, but I'll teach you. The more we do business, the more you'll learn."

"Okay, Auguiste. Keep an eye on things for me. If any trouble, let me know. And too many cooks spoil the soup...if you sailing the channel I can watch for you," the corporal motions to Auguiste to come closer.

He whispers in his ear, "But if everybody and his brother starting to do business too, Sergeant Maynard will know. Before you know it, Inspector Branch will know. Is only so many shops in this place. If you selling rum and you don't have a receipt to show where you get it, you will be in big trouble. I can't help you then. Remember French rum smells different from local rum. So do your business, quiet, quiet." Auguiste nods his agreement.

Soon, the officer out paces Auguiste. At a little distance, he grabs the knob of his saddle, places his left foot in the stirrup and swings his right foot over. Firmly settled in his saddle, he canters off towards the settlement of Marigot.

As Auguiste walks back to his yard several of the young men who have been loitering around run behind him.

"Chief, why the hell you give the man my rum for free?" says the young Carib with the red bow in his plait. He had made the channel crossing with Auguiste, and helped him row the canoe.

"Frederick, you too *fou!*" Auguiste shouted.

"What you talking about? Just because I bring you with me, don't mean we in business together. Anyway, the man have a gun, he have the power over us. At least, I got something for it." With that said, Auguiste goes to the pile, picks up one of the cutlasses and hands it to Frederick. Frederick grabs the cutlass and runs his thumb along the edge. "This thing here look dull, chief," he says.

"Okay! Okay," says Auguiste. "Hold these shots too. They can fit that French shotgun you always boasting about." He reaches into his pocket, pulls out a bulging fist, and hands Frederick the blue casing cartridges and turns towards his yard. But Frederick is not pacified.

"You know how much trouble we had to go through to cross the channel, ...now this *chien*, this damn *negre*, this *chien lawen*, you giving him everything. You only giving away, giving away, eh? Next time he will take your damn wife." Frederick follows Auguiste into the yard, the veins in his thick neck popping.

"Yes! Is true!" shouts a bareback Carib youngster.

"Yeah, they only want to walk about here playing big and putting their hands on what not theirs. Just because they put a boot on their crooked foot or carry a gun, they think that make them a *blanc* too," Frederick goes on.

"Them fellas too like to *tate* our girls. We need to teach them to doh touch what ain't belong to them," snaps a slender Carib, with anger welling up in his eyes.

"Is true Fredo, them police like a damn freeness too much!" yells an older companion, who is part of a loose half-circle of males in front of Auguiste's yard.

The part about his wife grates on Auguiste and he spins around suddenly and screams:

"Okay, boy! That's enough! Leave my damn yard for me." His face turning red, Auguiste pushes Frederick out of his yard.

"Ma Titroy! Ma Titroy!" Auguiste is calling over the fence. "Come and take your son from here before I *blese* him."

"Auguiste, you? You *blese* me? You and who? I will *kweve* you first," Frederick flings his threat to Auguiste's face, as he raises a balled fist.

"*Blese,*" means to cripple with blows. "*kweve*" means to beat into submission. They are the fighting words of

Dominica's French Creole and they cause Doreen to leave the broth in the back yard and rush out front.

"Leave him! Leave him!" Doreen tells her husband. "He don't know better. If he want to fight police, let him go by himself. He think he alone can overthrow England. Since he drink a little rum, he getting hot and want to fight everybody. The boy just ignorant." Doreen tugs on her husband's right arm as she speaks, pulling him deeper into the yard.

"Yes! Let your wife save you...you should give her the sash and staff to wear. From today on, you not my damn chief again!" Frederick moves his head backward then forwards quickly, ejecting a thick glob of spit in Auguiste's direction as he does so. He walks back to the group of younger Carib men who have been urging him on.

Auguiste shrugs off Doreen's concerned grasp, vaults up the back step and enters his hut. He can barely control his anger, as he flops into his hammock and lays his right forearm across his forehead.

Inside Auguiste's room, hanging on the wall next to the hammock where he sleeps, is the silver headed staff and red velvet sash emblazoned with the words, "Carib Chief" inscribed in gold thread. These symbols of authority, given to the Caribs by the British Administrator Heskeith Bell in 1902, have been passed on to him. These symbols should mean respect for the Chief, but even the most lowly police constables boss him around in his own yard. Auguiste's symbols of office speak, dimly, to the glory of the Caribs brave defiance against early European invaders. Now, education has opened the eyes of the young Caribs and they are restless and tired of years of submission. The British, to avoid fraternization and the pull of national sympathies, have purposefully staffed the police force with Antiguans, Barbadians, and men from St. Kitts and Montserrat. The men from these older British colonies are non-Creole speakers. Ever suspicious, they treat the Carib Reserve like enemy territory. Auguiste has to walk a fine line in his role as chief to the Caribs and official headman to these representatives of the British crown. His constant battle is to remain within the good graces of the lawmen that sometimes run roughshod over his people, while putting up some resistance. It is a vexing seesaw battle that leaves him tipsy with indecision.

The 1929 Wall Street Crash had depressed prices for island exports and brought harshness to the land. Auguiste thinks of how little he got for his baskets. When he ventures into Roseau to buy provisions is the same low price he fetches while saltfish and flour expensive like hell! To survive, many Caribs delve deeper into smuggling. It is now August of 1930. In July, a hurricane had damaged the food crops and made things even harder. The crops are slow to claw their way back to vitality from the recently assaulted earth. To bury their woe, many despair and take to drinking. Now, police will deny them even the bottled spirits with which to mellow their hurt? Such harshness stirs Carib blood and anger comes quickly in this season of want.

All this swirls through Auguiste's mind. And as if his burdened mind was not draped with enough woe, the darkness of the hut presses close, fixing him to his hammock. He looks again at the dull knob of the staff of office, which hangs on the wall near him. The staff is frail, incapable of even knocking a man senseless without, itself, splintering. It's a constant reminder of the Caribs loss of their martial heritage. He stares up at the ceiling, searching for nothing in particular, desperately trying to seek some ease. He covers his face with the palms of both hands and rubs vigorously. Suddenly, he jumps out of his hammock and goes back to his step. The sun bathes his body in warmth and he sighs, heavily. Fatigued by this tumultuous moment, he fishes for the clay pipe in his pocket. He leans beneath the step and extricates some cured tobacco nestled in a plain wooden box. Methodically he tamps some of the dark brown plant into the bowl of his pipe. On the large tobacco box, printed in red stylized letters on its cover are the words: *Produit du Guadeloupe*. The corporal missed that.

"Look Doreen, see what we can do with this. Sell it, whatever..." Auguiste hands his wife the box of tobacco, cutlasses and cloth, as he draws deeply on his pipe.

Corporal Mathews whistles as he enters his room at the Marigot police station. He bends to hide his haul beneath his bed. However, all cannot fit beneath the low-lying bed, so he drags a tarpaulin from the verandah and brings it inside.

As he tosses the tarpaulin over his pile, the sound of leather boots crunching against concrete reaches his ears. A very British accent startles him.

"Well, hello," says Inspector Branch. "Corporal Mathew's, I presume! Sergeant Maynard here was telling me about your wonderful work with the Caribs. I see your labors, this day, have not gone unrewarded." The inspector moves over to Mathew's right, and raises the tarpaulin with his brown boot, which sits atop well-polished leather leggings. The demijohn comes into view.

"Rum, by golly! Looks like you got some smuggled goods here, eh? I didn't know you'd launched any recent raids?" The British Inspector looks at the sergeant, who stares hard at Mathew's.

"Ma, Ma, Ma Mathew's!" the surprised sergeant stammers. "You got a report? You, you, you docket this seizure in, in, in the charge book?" Sergeant Maynard's mouth trembles as he looks at Mathew's.

He knows Mathew's is close to the folks in the Reserve and has heard that Mathew's keeps women there. In the past, the sergeant has observed Mathew's dealings with a wink and a nod; even sharing a nip of traded contraband grog with the corporal on occasion.

A little Carib boy squats by the door and listens. In the tension of the moment, the officers are oblivious to his presence. His name is Dudley Licente and he is, virtually, Mathew's adopted son. He runs errands for all the policemen at the Marigot police station and they fondly call him "Little Contraband." His father, a friend of Mathews' died in a channel boating accident and Mathew's has been helping Dudley's mother with a little codfish, salt and sugar from time to time. On his days off, he has slept over at her house.

Dudley's little round face is smooth, and his lips are shiny from the oil of the New Brunswick sardines some constables had shared with him from their breakfast table. The men at the station are entertained by this eight-year-old boy's intelligence, as he can recite his times table up to seven and tell the names of all the kings of England since 1800.

Dudley rises from his squatting position, concerned.

"Yes, sir! Yes sir, Inspector Branch, sir... I just come back. Sergeant Maynard know, I always docket my seizures. But I does wait until the day is almost over, then I write everything one time. I don't like to waste ink. As, as you, ... you can see here, I was only doing some rounds when I came upon this contraband. You know I always suspected that I would get something one of these days. But I was unable to effect an arrest... the Caribs, their skin's oily. And you know, they don't wear much clothes. So I make a grab for the man but I lost my grip. The fellar who I got this from, he slip out of my hands and he run away ... but I got his rum."

The inspector, hand under his chin, takes in the corporal's recitation. His face wears a quizzical look.

"Well, sarge, it looks like you will have to go back with Corporal Mathew's. Right away! You see you got to move when the trail is hot. Without showing these wild men the importance of the king's laws, we will lose respect of the people here in Marigot and all over the island. These Caribs cannot run all over us. If we let this go, people in La Plaine will want to smuggle. Grandbay and Delices will follow. Before you know it, there will be no taxes collected in this island and things will collapse. We can't have that, can we?" The inspector whacks his riding crop against his breeches, turns away sharply and steps outside.

"Yes! Yes sah! You... you right! I'll take care of that, sah! Those Caribs don't like to work, all they believe in is a freeness here and a freeness there! But... but... if they cannot hear they will feel!" The sergeant, fidgeting, salutes the inspector in acknowledgment. He turns on Mathews, fire in his eyes.

"Okay Mathews, saddle up! Let's go," he barks. "Call out Constable Joseph too. Also, wake up Hammond. Draw some ammunition from the stores. Make sure everyone carry their revolvers."

As Mathew's hustles to execute the sergeant's orders, Dudley slips outside, silently. As the officers step further into the station to gather their saddles and equipment, Dudley takes off. Before long, he is dashing through the woods in the direction of the Reserve.

Back in the Reserve, about two dozen people mill about Peterson's yard. Inside and outside, women scurry about with calabashes of Doreen's broth. It is also pear season, and several have their calabashes filled with mashed avocado pear and cassava *farine.*

Inside older women and children crowd around and coo at a naked baby girl squirming in a reed basket and laying on a piece of shiny cloth forming a cushion beneath her. It was Auguiste's gift.

Auguiste had accompanied the French priest, Father Lafleur, out to his horse. As the man in charge he had to meet all-important visitors. It was a time to walk around with his staff of office and he relished such meetings. The Roman Catholic priest could not stay for the fete, as he had some more babies to christen in the nearby village of Castlebruce. Ever the gracious host, Auguiste had made sure that the priest had taken a stiff shot of grog before he hit the road.

Sitting on stones, hammocks, and stumps of fallen trees in the yard, the men are locked in the solid grip of their liquor. Peterson is beating a tambourine, Auguiste's hands are flying as he beats the tikki drum, and Frederick - having cooled down - is blowing an instrument called a boum-boum - a piece of hollowed bamboo.

Peterson has had a tough week, having cut two gommier trees and hewn out two canoes from the harvested hardwood logs. In celebration of that effort and his baby, he has decided to sacrifice the half a demijohn, which remains of his last trip to Guadeloupe. Some of the men take swigs of the grog straight from the demijohn; others pour their share into calabashes. Some chase the fiery potion with coconut water from nuts picked off a dwarf tree in the yard, most take the warming liquid straight. Suddenly, a cry pierces through the yard from a woman in the house and Auguiste jumps up.

As eyes turn in the direction of the scream, they see Ma Titroy's body filling the frame of the backdoor. Held, tenderly, between her palms is the tear-streaked face of Dudley Licente. His little chest bursting with the exhaustion born of his dash through the woods, Dudley can hardly speak. Ma Titroy will speak for him.

"Peterson, oh Peterson! Police *ca vini!*" she shrieks in Creole. The police are coming she says. A stunned silence throttles the music and gaiety.

"Is Dudley... Dudley saw them. He heard them planning a raid. They coming to look for contraband..." as Ma Titroy speaks, Dudley nods his head frantically. Right at that moment, the sound of rapidly approaching horses is heard.

Peterson leaps up and his tambourine spins towards a goat nibbling at some zebgwa grass that rims the yard. He raises the demijohn above his head and smashes it against the stone on which he had been sitting. The plaited reed bottom of the demijohn collapses as the rounded bottle splinters into jagged bits of glass.

Blad-da-dap!

The fence falls with a crashing noise, as Sergeant Maynard, along with Constables Joseph and Hammond tumble through in a rush. Corporal Mathews is hanging behind, his mouth wide open. Stricken with embarrassment.

The women scream in a hundred Creole curses at the intruders.

Sergeant Maynard rushes to the shattered remains of the demijohn. He quickly scoops up some earth and raises it to his mouth and nose.

He extends his tongue, daintily, and tastes the moist soil. He sniffs at the small mound of moist red earth in his palm.

"Pure taffia!" he shouts with grand self-assurance. Taffia is the Creole name for a particularly notable brand of smuggled rum from the French islands.

"Corporal Mathews, this is Peterson's yard. This here is contraband, arrest him!" commands the sergeant.

The corporal is locked in place as if struck down. He does not move. His glazed eyes do not even search for Peterson. The Caribs all know Mathews and their eyes meet with his, pleadingly.

"But sarge, I mean... the, the, the, evidence done soak away. Let we give the man a break... I mean, is a christening party they was having," he implores.

"Yuh don't hear me boy? I order you to put the bloody man in handcuffs, or consider yourself on a charge for disobeying a lawful command!" The sergeant, his eyes blazing, rears up in the corporal's face.

Auguiste steps forward, nervously scratching away at his right forearm, "Sarge, you know my people. Ask Mathew... You, me, all of us is one in this place, don't let this make a big *commess*. Let me handle this..."

BOOM!

A loud explosion fills the yard. And, for an instant, all is still. A dramatic quiet born of shock congeals the blood. In a gap between the fence a wisp of bluish smoke curls up from the dark hole at the end of a black pole-like protuberance. Amidst the thinning smoke the leering face of Frederick takes shape.

At that instant, the corporal feels like a swarm of voracious hornets have stung his left buttock, all at once.

"O lawd, me gawd!" screams the corporal in an accent heavy with the roots of his Antiguan home.

"Me muddah, me faddah, look a Carib done kill me," the wounded corporal cries, as he falls forward, towards Constable Joseph.

"Is bad all you bad, eh? Then see if you can arrest this..." Frederick shouts. He is drunk and as he stumbles back, unsteady on his feet, ...

BOOM!

Another shotgun blast thrashes from across the fence.

The pellets spray wildly across the yard, nicking Chief Auguiste in the forearm, where he had already been nervously scratching away. Peterson and the other men in the yard scatter for the safety of one side of the house. Constable Joseph scampers for safety under the three feet of space beneath the floor of Peterson's hut and the pillars that raise it from the ground. Sergeant Maynard whips out his Webley .38 revolver and fires towards the fence. Constable Hammond fires too.

When the officers lower their pistols, there is blood on the fence, but there is no Frederick. Lying at the base of the blood- spattered fence is an unspent cartridge.

In the distance, the sergeant hears conch shells blowing. On the island the conch shell is blown at times of trouble to rally people, to summon reinforcements. The hollow hoot of the conch shell was usually a prelude to insurrection during the days of slavery. The sergeant has been on the island's police force since 1914 and he has heard stories of the La Plaine Tax Riot of 1893. To avoid a full scale outbreak of bloody passions, he signals a retreat. But, not before quickly examining Mathews injury.

"Raise yourself Mathews, is just a few pellets in your backside... we got to get the hell out of here. Men saddle-up and head for Marigot! I'll cover you." As he speaks he walks backwards, his pistol pointing towards the jeering, threatening, crowd which has now taken courage.

Corporal Mathews, held up by constables Hammond and Joseph on either side, makes for his horse. As he limps out of the yard, he looks at the pained face of the chief and then, towards the sergeant who retrieves the cartridge dropped at the base of the fence.

As they scramble towards their horses and mount up, Sergeant Maynard eyes the spare cartridge. Quickly, he twists it around in his grasp. Suddenly, he turns on Mathews with dread in his every word.

"Mathews, all this is your fault. And you pretending is only basket you buying, eh? What the devil have you been doing among the Caribs, boy? Are you confused? You always have Carib around the police station, eating, sleeping, drinking and maybe stealing? These are not your people, me boy. Anyway, you think your tail on fire now? Hah! Let's just wait until we get back to the police station."

Corporal Mathews' emits a pitiful moan. He winces and ducks as a few stones sail past his head. With the angry Carib voices dwindling in the distance, he fears what the morrow will bring. Police reinforcements will come. He does not want to be present when the full force of empire will be made to strike back. After all, he is close to some of the Caribs. He fears for his friend, the Chief. The thought of what will come of the Chief and his family sits heavy on Mathews. He wishes the thought away and hopes that he will be nestled between white sheets at the Roseau hospital when official retaliation occurs. After all, he is wounded and a wounded man shouldn't be in the saddle. The corporal's mind is in turmoil: What of Dudley and his mother? Would he see them again? Would he be branded as a Carib lover and lose his stripes? Would he be sent back to Antigua, condemned as a failure? No easy answers come forth.

Over, to his right, the Caribbean sun is setting in a flash of blazing red and orange streaks. With a growing realization that his days of easy trading are over, the corporal urges his horse into a gallop to separate himself from this bitter moment.

❀

Rain on a Tin Roof

On Dominica the rains come suddenly, swiftly, and often. It is a kind of rain that can sweep away the heat of an otherwise cloudless day, with scant forewarning. So whenever we commandeered Didier Lane for quick pick up games of cricket or football, we were wary of the valley in the distance.

That valley, which reared up in a majestic sweep to the lush, dark bluish-green mountains that bounded it, had no name. There were too many such valleys on our island for each to have a name. But we knew this one well. In the summer, we would cast a frequent gaze in its direction, looking for signs of rain while we went about the business of a game. Whoever was first to spot the rolling white clouds as they descended the valley would shout, "Fellas! White man coming down on his horse!" to send us scampering for cover.

If we were lucky, it would be just a passing drizzle that would disappear as the rain cloud drifted out over the open Caribbean Sea. Then, with an all clear, we would scramble from the temporary shelter beneath some concrete step, mango or tamarind tree where we had sought refuge.

But if the rain came in big fat drops and showed no sign of easing, guys would begin making that brave dash for home by jumping out into the downpour and sprinting down the street; bobbing and weaving as if to slide between each driving droplet. You see, one had to attempt to get home at least half dry because our parents did not take kindly to our arriving home wet and splattering their drawing rooms.

Those drawing rooms, with stuffed settees, throw rugs and center tables with pretentious vases over-filled with plastic flowers, were for show, not to be idly splattered by sodden bodies. So, the mothers of the lane were keen to avoid the mildewing of their finer things in life. Not to mention those wet clothes made them worry their children would catch some rapid pneumonia or a thousand other varieties of the local cold.

We were conscious of the plight of those of us on whom our clouds had poured. But would keel over in riotous laughter as we observed the antics of any one of our soggy friends trying to gain entry through toilet windows, back doors, cellar entrances - anywhere but the clout-at-the-back-of-the-head-stop-messing-up-my-place front door.

Today, we are on the Harris' porch. We gaze out at the sheets of rain in silence. Earlier, we had picked a side, - one wicket up the east side of the street, a homemade bat and *kaka rubber* ball. The rain had caught my side just as we were about to take our first turn to bat. It was coming to the end of August of 1979 and my six-person side had been broiled under a blazing sun for the better part of the afternoon. As a particularly dark cloud swiftly swaddled the sun and let loose its dammed up weight in rain, we had made for the Harris'.

Most of the guys hung out on Ma Harris' porch. She and her husband were a relatively young couple. Her husband was a warder at Her Majesty's Prison at Stock Farm, a renowned football player, long distance runner, and cricketer. He was about the only neighborhood father who would hold court with the boys. Now and again, he would even kick a ball with us or bowl a few hours in a game of street cricket. Because of his easy-going nature, most of the neighborhood boys would dash to his porch at the first sign of rain. Ma Harris thought that he "encouraged" us too much. In the past, as the shadows lengthened and trails of muddy feet marked her linoleum floored porch, Ma Harris had been known to yank her boys inside, douse the lights and wail about "wayward" neighborhood children who always messed up her place. At that point we would scatter.

But something is different today. As the rain beats a steady tattoo on the tin roof of the house, everyone is lost in thought. We are getting on in age. For most of us, high school graduation had come that June. Some of us are waiting for the examiners at Cambridge University in England to send us the final results of our General Certificate of Education (GCE) "O" Level exams. Those at the Sixth Form College had done "A" Level exams. We had taken the various tests in June and the results, which would shape the rest of our lives, would come in September. We would move on. With summer's passing we would soon give up the things of youth like street cricket.

As I listened to the melodic beat of the rain I thought of childhood nights of snuggling between warm sheets while listening to creepy zombie stories from an island past. Also, it was on nights like these that my family would be fed some memorable corn meal porridge, thickly spiced with nutmeg and cinnamon sticks. Or thick cocoa creme tea with hot, homemade bread lavishly spread with some Glow Spread margarine that would melt into golden rivulets and run down one's palm. The pre-sleep ritual of prayers would follow. After the prayers, we would squeeze tightly around our parents as they would blow our minds with scary stories of children bought and sold by knapsack-carrying dealers in human flesh or of the *lougawous* and *ladjables* who cavorted around our thickly forested island home, thirsty for blood. Scared, we would retreat to our rooms, frightened that the glinting lights of the fireflies flitting through the inky dark of night were really the eyes of *lougawous* and *ladjables* lurking near.

On such occasions, I would almost welcome my brother Sami pounding me with one of those thick cotton pillows we used. With my head ringing, I would stumble onto one of my other brothers, Lawson or Wellsworth, trying to enlist them on my side in a pillow war. If successful in my recruitment campaign, a pillow fight would ensue. Such down-to-earth engagement, a game of cards, idle talk of the day which had gone by, or the company of a good book would distract one enough from eerie tales and quicken the onset of drooping eyes.

Then, rain on our galvanized tin roof would elicit yawns; presenting a cool and calming evening backdrop; blurring that divide between sleep and wake so effortlessly that it was always welcomed, even though it may have stalled grand plans earlier in the day.

A shout pulls me back from reflection.

"Reynold! Reynold!" Ma Harris called out to her husband. "Radio Antilles is saying that a hurricane may skip Barbados and hit Dominica instead, you know."

She stood at the front door in a colored cotton dress, curlers in her hair, a flour encrusted-fork in her hand, looking at her husband as if in shock. The spiced air that pours out the door tells me she has been frying bakes and ackra. Her entrance snaps us out of our reverie.

"Hurricane? What Hurricane?" Mr. Harris mutters. "I didn't hear anything about that? Put the radio louder!"

Ma Harris goes into the drawing room and turns up the volume on their stereo, or what we call gram, full blast.

"...degrees latitude. Hurricane David is traveling north, northwest at approximately 150 miles per hour and is expected to miss Barbados. Hurricane warnings are posted for Martinique in the south to Guadeloupe in the north. The National Hurricane Center in Florida expects that it will strengthen during the night. Small craft advisories are in effect from Antigua, southward to St. Vincent..." The announcer's voice trails off.

"What! I never heard anything about that on DBS today," chimed in Dave. Dave was a friend who lived in the lane next to mine. We discuss news all the time. Had he heard anything he would have told me. DBS stood for the Dominica Broadcasting Corporation. It is our local radio station. I hadn't heard that report on DBS either. Radio Antilles was on an island to our north called Montserrat and seemed to always be ahead of events. Excited chatter breaks out.

"Calm down, calm down!" says Mr. Harris. We haven't had a hurricane since 1930. But even if we are to have one, our mountains will break its back. Don't forget, we have big mountains like Diablotin and Trois Pitons, you know. Remember fellas, we are still the most mountainous island in the Caribbean, even though they scraping up our mountains to send to Puerto Rico." It was Mr. Harris trying to reassure us and we all manage tight grins.

The "scraping up of our mountains" part had to do with the square mile or so of a yawning canyon gorged out of the red hills above our lane. We called it Tarish Pit. A construction company had created the pit by mining the fine pumice in that area for export to Puerto Rico. There, it made its way into the numerous hotels which sprang up during that island's sixties tourist boom. We lamented the loss of such land to the steel claws of foreign owned bulldozers. Their work had left a tarnishing scar of exposed red and gray rock atop Dominica's green breast. The gorge formed was a desolate echo chamber that sometimes filled with fetid pools of rainwater. In the idleness of summer, we would run around the cavernous pit and scream; waiting, thereafter, for the echoes which came bouncing back, in waves.

But even though we worried about the "scraping away," we knew that Dominica's Diablotin and Trois Pitons Mountains both exceeded four thousand feet above sea level. Together they are the backbone of a giant range of mountains, which run down the center of the island from north to south. Those dark blue/green massifs had been the source of many of the showers that had come charging down to spoil our games. But now they gave us a warm, reassuring hope.

"Turn to DBS!," Mr. Harris shouts to his wife. As she does so, we hear the local DJ nicknamed Baga-Laga put on a hot number by Calypsonian Short-Shirt. Short-Shirt is singing about cutting a lady's grass with his cutlass and getting on about how she likes it so, that she keeps bawling for more cutting. We shake our heads. Perhaps Baga-Laga believes in the resilience of our mountains too, or had just not gotten the news.

Suddenly, the rain eases up. A stillness descends which silences even the normal chirp-chirp of the crickets. We all say our hurried goodnights and scatter to our homes.

As I burst through our front door, I see my father slouched on the couch, sleeping. He has been watching television, but the screen only shows jagged lines.

"Wake up Old Talk! Wake up! Wake up!" I shout. He always had stories of ancient history, his World War II years, so we call him Old Talk.

"There is a hurricane coming! Hurricane David. I was at the Harris' and I heard it on Antilles." my father props himself up on his elbows, from where he had been slouched in the chair. He looks at me cock-eyed, quizzically.

"What?   What the dickens you telling me boy?   I didn't hear anything about that.   You always talking some foolishness.   You better be careful, you know.   You're are a bloody alarmist!" He rubs his eyes and looks at the straggly lines on the television.

"What the hell you do with my TV, boy?   I was looking at *Quo Vadis*.   You know how much rushing was going on at the cinema when that movie came to Dominica?   I tried four times before I got in to see it, you know.   In fact, to get in the last time, I had to put on my uniform and tell the manager that I was there to conduct an emergency fire inspection. Now, why the hell you change my station, eh?" he said.

My father was a fire officer on leave and I was messing with his beauty rest.

"I didn't touch the thing.   I didn't change your channel.   I just came in the house, I tell you.   I bet the transmitter must be knocked off the air.   This hurricane thing is near Barbados," I say.

Our local television comes courtesy of the Caribbean Broadcasting Corporation on Barbados.   I twist the dial through to the channels that usually pick up the French islands of Guadeloupe and Martinique, but now they too are blank.

"What the hell am I hearing? You mean you can't pick up anything?" He is on his feet now and staring at the blinking box.

With talk now filling the house, my mother comes out from her room where she had been doing some sewing, scissors in hand. She snips at a piece of cloth in her hands and looks me up and down, with suspicion.

"Boy, check the phone," she says. I guess she figures if the winds are already lashing the other side of the island lines would be down. I check the phone. It is okay. Then, it rings. I pick up.

It is Sami, my older brother. He is in Rome, Georgia. A couple years ago he had gone off to college there on a scholarship from Mr. Jennings, a kindly, southern, funeral home owner who shared Sami's Baptist faith.

"Yes man, this thing look bad, *oui*," Sami was saying. I saw this whirling red blob of nasty weather on local TV and it looks like it's heading straight for Dominica. You all need to secure the place. Now is batten the hatches time," he went on.

"Naw, man. We alright," I say. "This sort of thing happen before. It does look like some storm heading for us dead on, but when they see the big teeth our mountains have staring in 'em face, they duck out the way and gone hit one of those flat sandy islands like Barbados or Antigua." I went on.

"Man I talking sense to you, you talking *makakwi*! Put on Old Talk," Sami sighs.

I hand the receiver to Old Talk. He is silent, for a while. Then he starts talking.

"You sure about this boy?" he says. "This is a hell of a thing *oui*, and I just was thinking that I need to change a few of the sheets of galvanize on the roof."

"I remember the hurricane of 1930," with that Old Talk took a deep breath and his eyes widen.

"That time I see my mother in petticoat when the wind lash the side of our house. At the first lick of wind, the house capsize one time. We all had to hurry out and make for Tommy's shop. Tommy was a fella with grey eyes who did marry Magdalina for your mother's grand uncle Hyson. And lemme tell you Magdalina was a pretty, pretty church girl and hard to catch. But Tommy, he had plenty gold teeth and had made his money in Cayenne and Venezuela. The gold over in those parts real rich, yellow, almost orange, pretty gold. He had gold ring, gold chain, gold watch.... I think, in fact I hear people say he was *mounted* on gold. Anyway, as I was saying, mister was the only fella in Delices with a stone basement, that's where he stores his barrels of salt pork and flour for his shop. Boy, when we reach the place it was jam wit' all kind of people. The wind outside making like judgement day come. In the meantime, Tommy busy trying to hide his gold. He even put his gold teeth in a glass and place it on a shelf, high up, so much itchy hand pack up in his place, so sudden." With that, Old Talk laughs, but it comes out more like a nervous titter.

"Anways, as I was saying when we was passing under the rain, the thing sting my skin, force it have so, even though I had an old jacket on," Old talk shakes his head, worriedly, as he speaks.

His voice drops into a low zone of worry. If Sami is in the U.S. and saw it on TV, it had to be true. I was listening in and Old Talk seemed to have forgotten the part about our mountains. So, I shouted something defiant about our mountains, past his ear, into the receiver. He gave me a bad look and asked whether I wanted him deaf. He condemned my slipping manners, and how I was getting too big for my boots.

Mother stands by, telling him not to stay on the phone too long. "You all think long distance call is a freeness, eh? You all should know Sami is a student. Ten to one, he maybe using somebody's phone to make a quick call. Give me the receiver," she says, as she firmly reaches towards Old talk.

"What time is the hurricane expected...," we hang our ears close, waiting. "Between seven and nine tomorrow morning? Hmmp! Marie Josef, mother of God, pray for us sinners. At least, it won't be at night," mother bites her lower lip and looks at us. We stare back. "Anyway boy, don't worry yourself, we'll make out. Just pray and look out for us."

She delivers a few motherly niceties and hangs up. She brushes past Old Talk and me, as we smile sheepishly.

"You all had better go to Hayden tomorrow to get a can of crackers. Get batteries and candles too." It is my mother getting on with her practical self. Hayden is our regular grocer in nearby Pottersville.

"You mad, Alberta?   We still have things from the party. Bread, cake, Ritz crackers, cokes..."

He is right, sort of.   My parents 25th wedding anniversary had just come and gone that weekend. There was even some black cake left. It sits on the cabinet where all the breakable dishes are kept. I eye it. As my father directs his attention at my mother, I break off a big piece, with icing, and stuff it in my mouth.

My mother throws something back at Old Talk about whether he intends to use the tiny cake candles when electricity goes out. He seizes on that to start up about all the torchlights he bought over the years that he can never find and follows her into the room arguing. I go into my sisters' room to alert them to the approaching peril.

Hildreth is twelve and Elizabeth seventeen, they behave like big women who are increasingly dismissive of my intrusions into their grown lives by the minute. They are in bed, sliding into deep sleep and my entrance barely stirs them. They wave me off, after looking at me, bleary-eyed and commenting that they would wait to see what the morning would bring. Perhaps they think my dramatic intrusion on their tranquility with this news too incredible; another ploy by me to direct their script.

Oh well! So, off to my room I go. There, my mind races ahead, trying to glimpse morning, as I shed my street clothes. I fall back on my bed. For a while, I listen to the usual sounds of the night: Frogs croaking. Crickets chirping. A barking dog. A speeding car in the distance, sounds like its making its way toward Rockaway Beach, maybe to Canefield and beyond. In the neighbor's yard, a cock crows before its time, maybe waken by a shaft of light from a passing car. The palm fronds of the coconut tree in the Rolle's yard rustle in the light breeze of this muggy night. I am waiting to hear something...something different, then I drift off into sleep.

It is now morning. The night brought no added rain, apart from what had earlier forced us onto the Harris' porch. As I look through the window, I see Dave running past the house in combat boots and a police cape. His father is the police chief and he sometimes filches his old man's supplies to parade around with. I wave him a quick hello. He does not stop to chat at all. Other guys from the street zip by my house in galoshes, oddly rigged raincoats and hats. They purposely stamp into the rain filled potholes to test how waterproof they are. All of the guys my age are having a great time as this, the first hurricane of our lives, bears down. It seems like a big game for which we all have to dress the part. So, I quickly don a leather jacket made up of pieces of different textured leather patches that my brother brought back with him from his studies in Nottingham. I slip on a pair of black, calf-length, lace-up boots. I am getting ready too.

I go to the back of the house. On my way, I fasten every window to the side of the house. I ease open our second story window at the back and look into the yard. Our dog Spiky is frantically trying to squeeze itself between a bag of bananas and the upright butcher board in the yard shed. Its feverish whimpering sails up to the bedroom window above, as it labors at finding a niche.

Elizabeth and Hildreth, squeeze into the window frame with me to take a look. The early morning sky has turned a grayish red. The sun's red orb is nowhere to be seen. From over the mountains to the east, birds of all sizes and shapes are streaming out to the Caribbean Sea in waves, flying in dazed patterns as they are buffeted by the winds. Others abandon the wind swept sky and squat atop the fence that separates our yard from Mr. Rolle's garden and still others mill about the pavement of the adjoining lane.

Back there, in the east, is the Atlantic Ocean. That is where the hurricane is coming from.

Over to the west the normally gentle Caribbean Sea is already churning; frothy white caps topping its waves. In the distance, I can see people returning home, hurriedly, from work even though it's 9:00 a.m. The government has just declared a hurricane emergency, sending everyone home. But the official notice has come late and most people had already gone to work as if it was any normal day.

At the front of the house Old Talk, cutlass in hand, and wearing full khakis, lingers. He was on his way to loose the cattle. But Mama begged him to stay. He looks up to the hill above the house, longingly, thinking about our cattle and what will come of them. Already, the green mulch reeds which grace the hill above the house are bending low. Gusts of wind slam into them, only to ease off, causing them to spring back into place. Suddenly, a crashing sound jolts us.

BOODOOM! BOODOOM! RAANNG! BADANG!

The sharp crashing noise splits the air. We stiffen. Mama, concern creasing her face, calls at us to shut the windows, but not before I see a broken wooden beam with a piece of tin roof still attached to it crash into our yard. It looks like a part off one of the country homes that dot the islands winding rural roads. We quickly shut the window at the back and I run to check on those that face Mr. David's house. On the side of the house facing the Simeon's, are white aluminum louvers. They are opened and closed by a rotating handle and I shut them with frantic whirls of my wrist. Now, the house is caught in an unholy shudder. The feeling vibrates my teeth. We all look at the white tiles of our ceiling, fearing that we will see sky any moment. Outside, a dark mist has descended so that I cannot see the walls of our next door neighbor's house anymore even though it is not more than ten feet away.

WOOW! WOO,WOO,WOOO! WHOOSH!

This thing is now a howling monstrous wind. My breakfast of bread, cheese and grapefruit juice is doing somersaults in my innards. I dash from window to trembling window, as the roaring wind squirts little jets of water between the space where the shut windows meet their metal frames.

RAT-TAT-TAT-TAT! RAT-TAT-TAT-TAT! Comes the sound of the driving rain atop our roof, like a hail of machine gun bullets from some desperate war movie where the bad guys are sent fleeing. Will we have to flee too? I am torn with dread.

RIK-TIK-TIK! EEEEK! EEEEEK!

This infernal creaking is a new worry and comes from above. We can hear the wind straining to get beneath the galvanized tin sheets that layer our roof. Are the nails lifting? Did the carpenters remember to bend and flatten the nail ends on the inside of the roof boards where they had penetrated? I am sure we are all wondering the same thing. I remember that our ever-so-resourceful mother had demanded that the builder bend the steel rods from the four walls over the rafters. That way, the walls would have to come along if this angry wind wanted to take our roof for a ride.

TING-A-LING-PING-A-LING!

Now, the rain is drumming at the glass panes on the front door. Mama is at the stove, stirring a pot, trying to appear calm, cautioning against over-excitement. Elizabeth and Hildreth are removing portraits, the clock, and other bric-a-brac from the walls. I assist. If the roof goes, we must be ready. My father, both hands grasping the shuddering handle of the front door, peers out intently.

"Leave that one alone, " he shouts. He is craning his neck backwards and tells Elizabeth to leave a framed Biblical saying which she is about to take down from the wall. It read:

As for me and my house, we will serve the lord.

It is one of the few things to remain in its position. As Old Talk returns his attention again to the outside, he says: "Let us pray."

Old Talk now charges through every hymn, every Biblical verse of consequence or relevance and we strain to keep up.

"Onward Christian soldiers, marching as to war, with the cross of Jesus..."

BANG-A-LANG! BOOM-DEEE-DOOM!

When the sound of debris falling on the roof, causes us to pause, Old Talk switches on us to:

"The lord is my shepherd I shall not want. He maketh me to lie down in green pastures. He leadeth me besides the still waters..."

BOW-DOW! BOW-BOW.

With such devilish crashing I cannot believe our roof will make it through this day. There is a bubbling pit in my stomach that prayer seems unable to fill and which neither food nor hot cocoa tea will settle. I stumble in prayer and warn, loudly, that we will have to get ready to make a dash for downstairs.

Downstairs is an entirely new house, patterned on the top floor. It is rented out to another family. Our floor, of steel-rod reinforced concrete, is the roof to downstairs.

"The tenants are as safe as the Bank of England," says Old Talk, while I wonder how we will make it down, if we dare try. There is no internal staircase to get downstairs and we would have to go outside and enter a side entrance to make it. And outside sounds like death afoot.

I hurry to the back window to look and what I see is even more frightening than what I have been hearing.

What horrid moment is this that I have chosen to look? The roof of the Princess Margaret Hospital is peeling back, now airborne, in slow motion. That is where I was born. A constant to the skyline on the hill above home, I have known it no other way, but its solid self. Now, in a flash, it's unhinged and a swirl of white clutter follows the roof skyward bound. In horror, I realize it is escaping hospital linen. I shout to those at the front, running excited commentary on what I see. Everybody rushes to join me, except Old Talk. He holds the fort, as he likes to say, up front. I can still hear him, faintly.

"Oh lord, our help in ages past, our hope for years to come. Our shelter from the stormy blast and our eternal home..."

As snatches of lilting verse drift back to me in the rear bedroom, Mama fixes her madras head-tie firmly, in tight loops. She is getting ready for whatever must be.

"Look! The church!" It's Elizabeth and she is looking straight out the back window through an opening where the mist has parted. Over the flattened banana trees in Mr. Rolle's yard, beyond the now roofless house of the soft drink seller from Barbados we call "Bajan," the St. Alphonsus Catholic Church's roof is writhing. The church is an everlasting place, so we can't accept that its roof is now twisting like a snake whacked across its back with a big stick. Slowly the long, dark, shingled roof quakes, shivers, and then peels back in layers. The shingles lift in disorderly clumps towards the sea. Suddenly a white mist, as if to sedate us, blocks off what we care not to see.

PAPA-TAP! PAPA-TAP! comes a new sound. Assorted greenery of mango leaves, grasses, breadfruit tree leaves, pieces of paper are being slapped on the windowpanes by the driving wind. They stick there and obscure our view. Suddenly, it is quiet.

"The eye of the storm is passing," shouts Old Talk. Then there are voices at the door.

First, Ehrelin and her near dozen sons and daughters tumble through the door in a soaked tangle of muddy limbs. Her barefoot lover, Toteeyeah, follows. His name is Creole for "tied-up" or "twisted-into-knots." And this is what he looks like, literally, at this moment with his arms tightly clamped against his body. Wild eyed, he keeps murmuring in French Creole, "*Mondieu! Mondieu! Lapli diable! Lapli diable!*" My God! My God! Devil rain! Devil rain!

This group is more than soaked, their torn, muddy, clothing clinging to their shivering skin. They are in the middle of our drawing room, puddles of water forming at their feet. They smell of freshly cut grass, or that scent of leaves once crushed in ones hands. Ehrelin is blind and works with my mother at the Work Shop for the Blind. Her home had given up at the first lick of wind, she says. That was the most I could catch from her, as we wrap them in blankets, sheets and hand them cups of tea. The rest of her story of how she crawled on her belly to get to our house is cut short by the entrance of Agnes and her children.

We do not know Agnes. I have never seen her before. But, by the looks of her, she seems to come from one of the modest houses across the ravine. Old Talk had seen her struggling against the last gusts which preceded the lull; a line of six children, in descending order, behind her. He had called her in. She stands, forlorn, in our drawing room. Suddenly, she plumps herself on Old Talk's prime couch. She has not asked. Old Talk looks at me and shakes his head. I put up my palms in that almost universal sign of resignation.

From her entry, a wave of chatter pours forth. Between gulps of Red Rose Tea, a mug of which my mother has handed her, she alternates between moaning and recounting her close encounter with death. She is a medium-sized woman, and you can see the red right down her throat as she sobs and wails out her woe. As she cries, she frightens her children and so they cry with her. When she sees them crying, she cries even harder. Her children look at her and ratchet up their volume too. The warmth of the house, hot tea and dry clothes does not dissipate her terror, nor soak up her flood of talk.

Lights have been out for some time and even though it is just mid-afternoon it is almost as dark as night. Mama lights a few candles as she moves around to make space for those who have sought refuge with us. More people stream in, warmed by Old Talk's generous face, which is peering through the louvers.

Outside, tree limbs, clothes, and sheets of twisted tin roof, litter the lane. Immediately in front of the house, the rear windshield of our Singer Vogue-Sunbeam sedan lays in a shattered heap on the trunk. It had been smashed by a wooden post which still protrudes through where the windshield had once been.

Just as I thought the so-called "eye" passing meant a lengthy reprieve, a strong gust shakes the house. The air that makes it inside the house blows out all the candles. The wavering tongue of light in our venerable hurricane lamp, which has seen many a storm, flickers, falters then fails. It becomes so dark that I cannot see my hands when I hold them in front my face. A sickening moan goes up from what is now a full house, with standing room only in the drawing room. Outside, a howling wind-driven rain dashes against the eaves, tearing through the narrow concrete alleys on both sides of the bungalow, threatening to burst through to our living room at one moment, whispering away in another direction, the next.

"*Mondieu*! *Mondieu*! *Nou mort*! *Nou mort*!" Agnes, spurts out loudly in patois about how we are all dead.

"Shut up, Agnes! That's enough! And no more patois in this house! " Old Talk barks out, taking charge and rallying the household. Agnes stops as immediately as if she was a radio being turned off. Not a whimper, or sigh comes from her thereafter. Even at this dark time Old Talk holds tight to his intolerance of patois; fearful it will hinder our standing in society. Quickly, he resumes his prayers and, with the added voices, he has a choir to back him up with the hymns.

The rest of the day is frightful but, incredibly, does not cost us our roof or, even, a broken window except for the car.

Sandwiched between our neighbors bungalows, we are protected. But our neighbors are not as fortunate.

Mr. Simeon lost his roof. First, however, he had tried to lasso the restless cover with some strong cord tied to the rafters and the help of his brawny sons with which to anchor the valiant effort. But the roof had bucked and kicked and almost dragged the men of the house into the heavens. They had let go and made for their basement.

As the winds die down, I make a dash for the city with some friends from the lane. The neighboring suburb of Pottersville has been torn asunder; its modest houses a jumble of splintered wood and tin, with their entrails laid out in the street. Hopping across fallen lamp posts and trees, skirting twisted coils of electric cables, I cross the Old Bridge over the rushing Roseau River, which greedily laps at the creaking iron span. It is higher than I have ever seen it. The roaring sound of the boiling brown mass of river is rushing along. A donkey being swept out to sea brays pitifully amidst coconut trees, odd pieces of painted housing and an upturned Volkswagen Beetle.

On Queen Mary's Street, the main thoroughfare into the city, the shattered glass facade of Banque Francais

Commerciale carpets the wet asphalt with a thousand glinting slivers. My feet crunch the shards of glass and even though I see a cash register with several wet bank notes sticking out of its broken drawer, I do not stop. Down by the bay front, the waves are still high, soaring twenty, foamy feet or more, threatening to swamp the land. Behind the Bata Shoe Store through which the waves have rampaged from end to end, boxes of shoes bob in the roiling water. The houses along Old Street lean against each other where their pillars have been knocked askew by the wind. The walls of some stores on Cork Street are bared of cover for all to see the torn curtains and other tattered clothing heavy with wetness and moving limply in a more tentative wind. Already, a few hardy homeowners have hammers in hand, scavenging among piles of debris for that rarity: a piece of straight tin roofing.

At Baron's and a few other general stores, the looting has begun. On my way, I come upon a pile of sweet biscuits lying just beyond the shattered glass display case of a city store. They are English tea biscuits, McVites, or some such brand. The display is now strewn about, where it has been knocked down by the wind. Those glossy red and gold colored packets connect me to a time of more genteel afternoons laced with cricket, soccer, lime squash and rough cake. This is also a place where I had bought apples and grapes at Christmas. A store where I had bought my sandwiches at lunchtime break from my job as a grocery bagger at Gabriel's Cash n' Carry just down the way. The biscuits look vulnerable. I look around. Everything, every one, has gone into a state of helter-skelter. By the look of things, Roseau looks finished. Maybe food would soon be short? It was now every man for himself and the devil take the hindmost, I figured. Frantically, I scramble past the sharp edges of the broken plate glass display window. I jettison upbringing, descending into this frightening moment where survival seems a slippery slope. Quickly now, I slip down the zipper to my rain jacket and squeeze in some of the biscuit packets. Then I zip all up, spin around and take off.

At home they are waiting for my report, so I head back at a trot. I zip by the blurry images of the constants in my life, which now lay ravished. Swinging up the lane, the valley looms ahead in the distance. But now, it is different. The clouds have shifted some and I can see that the mountains to either side have been denuded of their green cover; scraggly trees show here and there, with reddish-brown gashes where the land has slid into the river below. Our mountains have not been barriers enough for this Hurricane David, which has rolled over us like some Goliath.

At that moment, as I tear towards home, my ears soak up the reality of a different sound. On so many houses that line the lane, now bared of cover, there is no rat-tat-tat of rain as on a tin roof. Rather, sickening splat-splat sounds reach my ears from where fat raindrops connect with exposed wooden rafters.

A shivering hand clutching the nylon collar of my jacket close to my throat, I leap onto our porch. Daddy swings the door open, his eyes pregnant with the expectation of news. Breathless, I pause. They await what I have to say. Now, in this split moment of stillness, I listen. At a time when all seems lost, the pitter-patter of rain on our tin roof is more than a reassuring sound.

❁

Sure Bet Cecilia

His double chin trembled as I inched up closer to him to get a glimpse at what he was looking at. The man was laughing because he had been able to catch Cecilia with a packed straw basket on her head, wading through the muddy water in the ravine we called "Gutter".

Earlier that morning, a tourist ship had docked at the nearby harbor and a thick ribbon of awed islanders had stood at the sea's edge, necks craned upward at the hundreds of pink faces staring down from the huge multi-leveled ship. The profile towered over the skyline of the modest houses, which hugged the beach. Such ships were rare because, unlike the Bahamas and Jamaica, Dominica was not a big tourist destination. From their elevated perch, some tossed coins into the clear blue water near the ship. At that, only certain kinds of people moved. Ecstatic urchins, what locals called *kawants*, dove into the sea to retrieve the coins. As the scantily clad boys beat their hands and feet against the foaming water, cheers rose from the faces above.

A motorcade of local drivers, eager to rake in some U.S. dollars, had made for the pier. There had been a big scramble among all those who owned a jeep, truck, car, or bus to service the tourists who had streamed down the gangplank of the dazzling white ship. That stream, for the most part, had emptied itself into the various conveyances. Some would go to the open-air market in the capital, Roseau. Big groups would head for the Trafalgar Waterfalls and the Emerald Pool. Others would be satisfied with lying under the coconut trees at nearby Rockaway Beach, catching a quick rum and tan before the boat departed later that day. But this one guy had gotten away from the beaten path.

As I stared at him, I wondered what had caused him to lose his compass. You see, he had not exactly walked down tourist alley. It was a wonder he had not had his heels gnawed at by any one of the half-a-dozen mangy dogs, which prowled the grass-lined verge of the road. This was our neighborhood; a place where yard fowl picked at leftovers on the roadside, and children ran around in dusty yards with bare bottoms. Rows of majestic tamarind trees which girded the road concealed the modest houses with rusting corrugated tin fences separating the various yards lining the street. Perhaps, if seen at an angle, it would look scenic to a visitor? Maybe so, but further down the street, before Goodwill Junior High School, was the visual blight of Dicky's Bike Shop. Not much there to look at. Really, it was an unsightly jumble of old BSA motorcycles, along with scrawny looking, weed-entangled, Honda and Yamaha dirt bikes whose black and gray mechanical entrails marred the green foliage. Nearby, the Public Works Garage compound reposed under a ravenous sun that glinted off the chromed hydraulic arms of assorted, idled bulldozers. To regulars like me it seemed that was all there was to see around here.

So, this one guy had broken away from the pack. I first noticed the tourist when Mano, one of the lords of Tamarind Tree Row, gave him a shout. An area of welcomed shade, the row got its name from the collection of rickety wooden benches nailed three levels high into the stout tamarind tree trunks. It was the rendezvous point for most of the school guys during the long summer holidays and a permanent perch of the area's unemployed that cared to watch the world pass by and offer comment.

"Columbus, where yuh going?" Mano shouted.

The visitor kept on walking, as if he hadn't heard a thing.

"Aye, dude! Is you I calling!"

Spurred into action by what seemed an airy disregard of his call, Mano became animated and was trying to call the tourist by the cool names he had picked up from the movies.

"Take our picture man. Discover us!" He went on.

The group under the trees roared with laughter. Mano stood up and did a gym man pose. Dicky, roused from where he had been performing surgery on a bike, gazed in the direction of the action. A group of Public Works road workers laying macadam on the sidewalk paused, looked at the tourist, and waited for his response.

But the tourist paid no mind. He had sprouted a quick grin and trotted over to the ravine as if to get away from the attention coming his way. It was there that he had found Cecilia.

Standing erect, a middle-aged paunch bulging forward, the tourist in his Bermuda shorts and multi-colored shirt fingered the Japanese camera slung around his neck and readied himself. I was close enough to smell the tourist. The antiseptic smell was like that one picked up when passing by the lotion counter at the Dominica Dispensary downtown. As the man moved his head into position I noticed that the exposed skin at his neck had already turned an almost lobster-like red from where it had been seared by the lancing rays of the Dominican sun. But his well-fed calves were almost the color of milk. Then, I heard a click.

I immediately thought that Cecilia would have a problem with this. Cecilia was hot-tempered, or as we say "ignorant." She had not noticed the tourist and hadn't she realized that she had been captured on film. In haste, she now stood at the edge of the ravine, her basket on the ground, wringing her skirt and putting on her slippers. She was mumbling away to herself, perhaps cursing the fact she had gotten her dress wet. It was a Saturday and already nine o'clock. She was already late and it would now be difficult to get a choice spot on the Lagon sidewalk where so many other women competed with each other selling vegetables and other ground provisions. Ground provisions meaning what grew below and not above the soil.

"Hey, maybe ah should give this a movie shot as well," the tourist mumbled. He searched his side bag and produced a sleek looking, compact movie camera.

As the American began targeting Cecilia through the eyepiece of the instrument, the camera whirred softly.

"Mister, you looking for trouble," I half whispered. I didn't want Cecilia to embarrass the visitor and I was trying to shoo him away, quietly.

"You can't just take pictures of people around here without asking," I told him. "You better watch yourself."

He turned towards me and gave me a swift grin and then yanked it back. It was the kind of grin that was too abrupt to convey much warmth. I bared my teeth at him too, so we were even. Then, I fastened my gaze on Cecilia.

People like Cecilia - a middle-aged, street-wise vendor- now wanted money for any pictures taken of them. In days gone by, tourists would be lords of all they surveyed; waited upon hand and foot, giving little in return. But islanders were cutting back on freeness. Why not? Tourists looked like they could afford most anything. Or that's what islanders believed. They were always walking around crisp like just-issued paper currency. Their sunshades, shoes, bags, frocks, shorts, money - everything about them - spoke of plenty, looked brand new. That, even when their skin looked wrinkled.

The market was near the pier. When the once-in-a-blue-moon tourist boat came by, the occupants would spill out of the massive ships into the open-air market. Roving around the vendors with their piles of fruit displayed on groundmats, some would pick up a mango, take two bites and throw away the rest. Imagine that! A Dominican would have eaten the whole damn thing, right down to the surface of the seed. And then sucked the seed too!

Some of them must have thought the fruits displayed were a freeness put on by the tourist board. I remember once when Sophia, a street vendor, had waded into the Roseau River after a tourist lady who had taken an armful of her fruit into the river with so she could pose for pictures. All the while the tourist's husband was splashing about in the crystal clear river, shades and all, not advising his wife to pay her way. Afterwards, both husband and wife started sampling the fruit and Sophia had not seen any green Uncle Sam's yet. Finally, Sophia had enough. She had told them how they were brazen and that she wanted her money quick, sharp. The tourists had dug into their pockets and given it up. Market-mouth-radio had it that she scored well. News, that the well-dressed visitors had not cowed Sophia had set the market ladies buzzing. After that, a couple vendors took courage and started jacking up their prices.

Anyway, the visitor's presence stirred up interest by the minute. A group forms: Tamarind Row members up front and Public Works guys who were doing some Saturday overtime, looming large over the group, at the rear. Taking a front seat at the feet of the onlookers were a several notable area canines like Tojo, Fraid-Stone, Broken-Muffler, and Hard-to-Dead. I knelt near the tourist with a handful of smaller boys.

We called ourselves the Rolling Stones and had been rolling sec. A sec is what we called disused bicycle rims, minus the spokes. Along with that, we had short sticks with which to "beat" or guide the sec.

We are about eleven of us altogether and we soon begin to argue as to what Cecilia's response would be once she realized that she was fast becoming part of the tourist's private home movie-collection. Hardface argued that it's not right that magazines in big countries make fame and fortune from pictures taken without permission.

"Man, remember when they put Big City in that movie they take out at Emerald Pool last year? Man, they say that thing fetch big dollars in the states you know? Big City face was lighting up the background behind the tourist lady, teeth shining and all, but he eh get a black cent for that," he went on. Several in the group nod in agreement.

"But why mister want to only take picture of our mess, nah man? And the ravine so dirty today, eh? He couldn't catch a taxi to Trafalgar Falls or the Botanic Gardens, man?" muttered Blagar, a Public Works employee.

"I find some of them tourist too like to catch us when we not ready. I bet you he go back to his place and show this off as if is so we really is," he added. "Anyway, Cecee go sock it to him, let him skylark with that camera still."

Others lament that pictures of the Gutter area will reflect poorly on our proud island. Still others suggest that, perhaps, it's just the thing to do to pull-in a U.S. dollar or two.

Cecilia isn't new to us. In fact, we know her so well we called her "Ceecee." Often times, we amuse ourselves by giving her the "shout," usually some rude commentary about her character.

While still in kindergarten at the Goodwill School, a boy had found a broken tooth in one of Ceecee's coconut candies. Rumor had it that she had dispensed with a grater and, for speed, had shredded the coconut meat used in her candies with her teeth. We also had it from a good source that Ceecee would salt her *bakes* - fried biscuits-with sweat. Such talk, running wild, had killed her school recess sales. So she had moved from selling snacks at recess time to peddling

·vegetables and provisions by retail on the Lagon sidewalk, the main street into the city.

As we grew through the school system some of us began making detours on our way from the public library. The intention was to give Ceecee a "shout" on our way. We even had a song on her:

"Ceecee bakes hard and bumpy, her fingers always dirty."

A quick rush to get out of her firing range would follow as she hurled rotten tannias or cucumbers at us. In fact, she once dashed fish water on Mano, who then had to walk home, smelling like a fish vendor, with scales glistening on his forehead, arms and even on his library books. The name Mano Mermaid stuck with him after that.

"Mister is bound to get a lash *oui!*" Mano whispered.

I nodded.

"Aye, Aye, what is that nuh?" Her eyes squinting against the glare of the sun, Cecilia looked up to the embankment where we stood. The small crowd even caused curious motorists to slow down and look at the scene.

"Look here, I not in no freeness you know! Mister-taking-pickcha make sure you have big money or is trouble *oui*!" Cecilia, hands on her hips, head thrown back defiantly, flung her remark in our direction.

"What's that? " The tourist replied, "Money? What money? The value of this photo is the publicity you'll get ma 'am. All my friends will see it. More people will see it than you'll ever know. You'll be big time in the fine U.S. of A." The tourist looks up from his camera, eyebrows arched, puzzled, and waiting for Cecilia to react to his point.

"Publicity? What publicity? I can't eat publicity. I know all you well. Next thing my pickcha in big books, magazines, postcards and I get nutting, eh? No! Is money I taking today. Dry cash!" Cecilia retorted.

"I've got money. What do you mean? I could pay you anytime! But what about some more live shots huh? Hold up that basket again!" The tourist had no heart for bargaining. Surprisingly the basket is up in a flash, with Cecilia beneath, spreading a grin wider than the ravine.

We are amazed at the transformation of both Cecilia and this unlikely scenery. I mean, the ravine had seen a big summer rain just the other day. One of the usual summer tropical depressions had come through. The deluge it brought had washed away heaps of waste. Really, with the few hibiscus bushes which dotted its edge, the ravine now looked rather decent when viewed from where the tourist stood.

"Cheese and bread, that take me *oui* pal," Zozeo muttered. "Ceecee is a changed woman." Carl was called Zozeo because he had a "chicken" chest, with each rib competing with the other for prominence. His surprise that Cecilia would bargain, and did not explode, was shared by all.

The photo session over, Cecilia strode up to the stranger.

"O.K. mister pay me now!" Cecilia said, her arms akimbo. Bounded on all sides, the slightly nervous tourist dug his hands into his pocket.

The knot of people grew tighter. The dogs shook themselves. Hard-to-Dead rubbed its dull gray coat against the tourist's legs, with an odd familiarity. The Public Works mechanics working on a dumper nearby drew near, peering intently. Some of the boys bent down and attempted to peer through the camera's eyepiece, as the device hung loosely off the man's shoulder.

Meanwhile, Tony-*Toutouni*, whose name literally means "Tony- the- naked" in French Creole, squeezed his bare butt self through, right into the center of the steadily contracting circle around the tourist. A five-year-old busybody from the housing scheme nearby, Tony regularly walked around with only a white cotton vest on. He liked to hang around bigger guys. We all teased him as "Tony-*Toutouni*, independent candidate for the Gutter constituency." He was excitedly clasping and unclasping the pocket strap of the tourist's camera bag. At that, the tourist started feeling crowded and is waving his hands around as if to shoo flies.

In the meantime Mano and Zozeo almost exchanged blows over whether, dollar for dollar, a camera like what the tourist had would cost more in downtown Roseau than it would in the States.

Slowly, the tourist pulled out a wad of bills, and counted out four U.S. dollars.

"I guess this will do ma'am." The words are spoken in limp resignation.

"Yes, yes is enough. *Ca bon!*" shouted Cecilia as, with a smile, she counted the money while affirming that the deal was good.

Sweating profusely the tourist whips out a handkerchief and dabs his forehead.

"Thanks Sir," Cecilia said loudly, her eyes still on the money.

"Sure! Sure bet, sure bet. Nice thing meeting ya ...".

The tourist spun around, squeezing himself through the crowd, which parted with difficulty. As he ambled off towards the town of Roseau, Cecilia shot a piercing glance at us.

"What all you was crowding the visitor for eh? All you mother eh teach all you manners? Is first time all you see white people, eh? All you think tourists come here to see knock-abouts, running the streets like a lot of litter with hole in their pants behind? Is all you so who does make the island shame."

"Aw shut up! You's just glad you get a dollar, so you singing for your supper!" The words spat out the mouth of one of the mechanics that had drawn near. With that he sauntered away, towards the motorbike he had been working on.

Arms flailing as she spoke, Cecilia's eruption broke up the crowd. Tony scampered away, his tiny exposed member jiggling in the wind, as Cecilia missed his head with a downward swipe of her hand.

The other bigger guys sucked their teeth at Cecilia and walked back to attend to whatever had earlier commanded their attentions. A few dared her to try them. One Public Works guy told her to haul her tail to the market - quick, sharp. But Cecilia really wasn't talking to the grown-ups, she was aiming her sting at us.

"Bloody pestilence is what all you bringing here, running people away from the island. Tourist didn't come here to see all you face! A tourist can't land in the island before all you sticking up to them, skinning your teeth. Is scamp like all you that does shame the island by diving after tourist money in the sea. Some of all you playing hungry, like all you mother doesn't cook food. All you think the tourist them owe all you? Get outa my sights before I squeeze one of all you piggy!"

She pointed her gnarled fingers to that hollow formed between her neck and clavicle. We all believed that if you squeezed someone's piggy when they were young, they would stop growing.

We made ourselves scarce as Cecilia, pushing the money into her bra, bent to pick up something to fling at us. But we were in luck, as only easy- to-crumble tarish stones were in the area.

A shout went up from one of the guys as we scattered:

"Nasty Ceecee

Go have big fete

because a Yankee tell her

Sure bet!

Looking behind as I ran, I could just catch some of Cecilia's words as they came to me faintly:

"All you... mother... cannot... get... money... like ...that ... though... mind...you... say... I... nasty. I didn't have to go... by... the bay and sell nutting... to sailors... to make my money...". Her voice trails off.

Far away enough, I removed the sec from under my right arm where I had held it, so I could run faster. Now, as I rolled it along in the direction of the harbor thoughts of what had just happened tumbled through my mind.

This was a quiet country. People from afar came around to stare, take pictures, talk funny. We had to smile at them, please them, my father always insisted. One of the high school guys on Tamarind Row had said tourists were food for the 'conomy. If so, it wasn't much since I only saw tourists giving out chewing gum and stuff a couple times, not any serious food like pig snout or drumsticks with rice and peas.

Anyway, I know they lived where it was cold like ice, but nice places though, like we would see in the pictures out of magazines and in the movies. Places with tall buildings and roads that went on forever. Our tallest building went to five floors and, except for a one mile stretch of the Imperial Road, most of our roads were *kochi*. My uncle had returned from England and said he never knew his neighbors and how life was so fast in the big city that a man would fall "boo-doop" and die right there on the pavement and pedestrians would keep on walking. I didn't know whether that was true, but I still wondered what the heck the tourist man saw when he looked at the ravine?

Maybe our leaves had something in them that we couldn't see. It just looked like a lot of bush to me. Maybe where the tourist lived was all concrete or - perhaps - those flowers that dotted the ravine's edge didn't grow in his home town. Next thing they would come take the leaf, bottle it and sell it back to us, I thought. That's what they did with pictures such as Ceecee's: Put them in postcards and next thing she making fame without the fortune, or that's what the fellas under the tamarind tree were always arguing about. But what did the man see in Ceecee? Was it the way she balanced stuff on her head? The clothes she wore? I had never seen anything in Ceecee that needed a picture taken.

Yes, that was tourist for you; always looking at things different and acting like they never see big bush, river, sand, sea and sky. Just lying there under the hot sun, doing nothing. As for me boy, when it's hot, I hug the shade long time.

In the distance, toward the wharf, I could see a few more straggling tourists. Sightseeing beckoned. When I got there I could stare at them too. Or maybe point them towards the beach, away from the ravine, for a fee.

Rum In An Essence Bottle

"**S**lade! You have the rum?"

"Yes!" I said.

Vincent was speaking to me, his eyes like slits under the glare of an early afternoon sun.

It was 1969 and I am an eight-year-old schoolboy with carnival ecstasy causing my belly to growl with the sweet tension of this my first jump-up. Sweat on my brow, still panting, I had just run into one of the dusty yards that jutted off from Virgin Lane.

Vincent lived with his mother in Pong, but he had us meet him at his father's house in Virgin Lane. His mother was a Seven Days. Seven Days belonged to the Seventh Day Adventist Church. My father always said that they pretended as if they were more Christian than Jesus himself. Seven Days people didn't believe in carnival; they thought it was of the devil. So Vincent's mother was against carnival.

My mother was Roman Catholic. Her church was the most powerful on the island. The Catholic priest who had married my parents had instructed that their offspring follow Rome. So my mother had brought us up as Roman Catholic. My father was Anglican. On some Sundays he would carry some of us to his church to take up space, as it was always nearly empty. Anyway, Anglicans were just like Catholics. Only difference was that their mass was longer and you got wine with your host at communion and had a little plastic cushion to kneel on. At the Catholic cathedral we knelt on rather rough boards and the priest and his acolytes hoarded the wine for themselves. In those days a dry wafer posing as the body of Christ is all we got. Other than that, the differences didn't count. Anglicans rolled around and jigged their waists in the street, come carnival day, like most everyone else. As for Methodist, it looked like they were half-and-half. I didn't know any Methodist, so that didn't count either.

Virgin Lane itself was the same street that ran in front of the pastel-colored bishop's palace. Next to it was the huge Roman Catholic cathedral which stood guard over the city's skyline. The Catholic Church didn't mind carnival. It wasn't like Pentecostal, Christian Union Mission, Church of God in Christ, Seventh Day Adventist, Deliverance Baptist, or what we called save-soul churches. On carnival day save-soul people fled the city for beach picnics or some other country side distraction. But if you were a Roman, you could jump in carnival and drink your rum. On Ash Wednesday you could still go to the Catholic Church, clasp your hands, close your eyes and pretend that hard drink and bad words hadn't crossed your lips. With a knowing smile, father so-n'-so would bless you and then put a cross of ashes on your forehead. The ashes on your forehead made everything right again and that was that.

Vincent and I had eaten communion before our time. When I say eat communion, I mean eat the flour wafer you got once you went to receive communion. We had not yet made our first communion vows after which the church allows one to eat of the tiny communion wafers. But the ritual had entranced us. So one Sunday we joined the communion line, accepted the host and stuck it in our pockets' after getting back to our pew. We had prevented the wafer from disintegrating in our mouths by puffing our cheeks and holding it in an air pocket. All day that Sunday, I remembered looking at the sky, wondering whether God would come down and kill me for putting a piece of his body in my pocket without permission. The following Monday my fear had dissipated and Vincent and I brought the, by then, clammy wafers to class and showed them off. I even gave Tessa a piece of mine. She sat next to me in class and I liked her. I wanted her, but I didn't know what to say to get it started.

"Where it?" Vincent asked about the rum.

"Here. I put it in a little bottle. A vanilla essence bottle. I didn't want my mother to see," I said.

With that, I whipped a flat, five inch, crystal-clear bottle from my back pocket. The rum in the bottle was still swirling and frothing from my dash through the yard. It had been my duty to get the rum for our little group. Along with the music, rum set the mood for carnival. Rum itself was soaked into carnivals past and present, an inextricable embrace born of necessity. How else could you get someone to dance on and on in the hot sun? We had come to expect that rum would give us the wings to soar above the straightjacket of our everyday lives. With rum in our heads the drums sounded ever closer, their pounding beat drilled through our very being, putting fire under our feet.

Vincent's father was a carnival man, a regular drinker. Upon the approach of carnival, he had hidden all his rum so as to secure it from Vincent or guzzling visitors who didn't bring their own.

"In an essence bottle? Man! You foolish or what? The rum going to smell and taste funny now. You couldn't have gotten another bottle?" Vincent was looking at me, angry like. He was just nine, but was a boaster. Always playing like he was a big man.

"What happen to you Vincent, you stupid or what? You want my mother to slam me for taking her rum? I didn't want her to see. You wanted me to take a whiskey-sized bottle? I had to use a bottle I could hide man!" I shouted back at him.

It was my mother's rum. She bought that rum to make cake or for visitors like my uncle Isiah who drove his red Ford Cortina like the devil was chasing him. I had gone with her a couple Saturdays ago to Shillingford's near the Old Market. There, a skinny lady with always-near-sleep-eyes, sunken cheeks and flapping lips, had taken an empty bottle from my mother and ladled the rum into it from a barrel. It was white cask rum, the kind that could feel like hot coals in your belly when you drank it straight. Or, creep silently to your head, deaden your lips, make the tip of your nose tingle, and make your ears hum. All of that, even if you lessened its bite and slowed its sting with some lime juice, grated nutmeg and sugar.

Essence or not, Vincent was looking intently at the flat bottle. He shook it. He opened its top. Sniffed.

"Hmmmp! Anyway man, is carnival day. Rum is rum!" He muttered.

With that Vincent flicked his head back, brought the bottle to his lips, and swallowed hard. He squeezed his eyelids tight and grimaced.

Vincent had to taste the rum. Of all of us Vincent knew the most about rum. And girls too. He used to try hanging out with big fellas. Fellas like the Ebonies who used to go to Sunday cinema at the Carib. They would dress all in black, with black belts encrusted with metal knobs and black pointed toe ankle boots. Their girls would dress the same way. These fellas used to drink a deadly Bagatelle Rum at their afternoon gatherings near the deep, azure green pools of the Roseau River at a spot called Under Power. They would drink the rum, chased by the water of coconuts freshly picked off nearby trees. Then, they would plunge into the pools naked and soap themselves. Sometimes, us boys would chance upon a gathering of Ebonies perched upon the stones that dotted the river. We would park ourselves amidst the Roseau reeds nearby and silently squat and watch the men wreathed in pungent soap lather. Enthralled at the sight of the naked, well-muscled bodies. Astonished at the size of their bent manhood.

It was carnival day. Carnival Monday to be exact, and the town was on fire with people, color and calypso music. The Mighty Sparrow, King of Trinidadian calypso, had a hot tune that year: "The Lizard Run Up She Leg and Disappear." This was Dominica, but we listened, via Radio Rediffusion, to

Trinidad's tunes too. "Lizard" was about a teacher named Mildred who brought a lizard to a science class only to have it escape into that most private part of person.

But we had our calypsonians too; guys like Tokyo, Spider, Spark, The Saint and Caterer. One of them had belted out a popular tune that year which went:

Madoh sock it to me,

look my water falling down.

I feeling sweet in me waist,

look my water start to waste.

From the proper standpoint of a boy my age, the song was about somebody whose bucket might have been leaking. In those days most people still fetched water from public stand pipes. Sometimes a leaking bucket meant that all one's water could be spilled before one got home. I figured Madoh was the sort of kindly neighbor who could help out with a spare bucket, if need be. So that's what I thought the song was about then. Later, I knew better. Calypso could be so rude.

"Leroy! Leroy! Yes sir! You is a boss!" Vincent shouted. He had seen a cloud of dust approaching, heard galloping. Just like in the Clint Eastwood movies we saw at the Carib.

A human form exited the puff of yard dust. It was our Leroy entering the yard with a red velvet cape and a red bandanna around his head. Leroy lived on Bath Road, where a lot of steel band men lived. Rain or shine, he was always smiling, his big eyes aglow as if planning some mischief. He pranced, swinging his legs high. Not missing a step, he handed me a green bandanna. Vincent got a yellow one. Our bandannas would go with our white T-shirts and baggy pants cut out of cotton flour bags. We would jump together. We were ready to hit the road. Quickly, we passed the rum around. Then we heard a commotion.

"They playing Madoh! Hold me somebody! Somebody hold me!" It was Taste Me.

Taste Me lived in the yard and we knew her as an ice cream vendor. Normally, she would wind her way through town with a wooden ice cream tub balanced on her head, shouting "Taste me! Taste me!" So the name stuck with her. If her pitch swayed you, she would swiftly ease down the tub and scoop out some coconut, vanilla or peanut flavored ice cream into a cone. That was in normal times. Today, however, she was sweating, had a mask on, and a huge green cape. She had already been jumping in the carnival and the drink in her head had her bouncing off the corrugated metal fences that lined the entrance to the yard.

"I want to pee pee! Aye! Pee pee!" She cried. Laughing and weeping at the same time, she gripped her belly with both hands.

Taste Me was an older woman too. Ordinarily she was an upstanding woman, who would have said some things like: "Vincent you drinking rum? I will tell Mr. Winston." But today, rum had her in a *jouboum*.

She could still hear right though. Indeed, the faint strains of the song "Madoh" drifted into the yard. The tune was soaring on the wings of blaring brass too. Madoh with brass! The tune went straight to my legs. I wanted to jig that way, and then this way. I wanted to raise my arms in the air, shout, and then twist my little waist this way, then that way. I could squeeze myself on Tessa now, now. RIGHT NOW! I thought.

Tessa sat next to me in class. She was shy, had a nice looking face and long hair. I loved her, but held it inside. So, I only talked homework with her, nothing more. However, one day, I asked to read her palms, pretending that I knew how. It was something that I read about Archie doing to Veronica in a comic book. It had been a good move for Archie as it allowed him temporary possession of his prize. However, Tessa didn't let me have her hand for long. Once I held it, I had gotten tongue-tied, forgotten my lines. Soon, she had yanked her hand from my sweaty palm grasp. Since then, she had avoided me in class. Just last week, she had watched me "cut-eyes" and sucked her teeth when I called her "baby." I had been trying to soften her up for carnival, but it seemed that I hadn't made the grade.

The distant tunes were growing louder in my head and I shook off further thoughts of Tessa. A mixture of rum and music had me hot and I was ready to fly down the road.

My impatience was growing, as Vincent was trying a quick sweet talk on Madonna, a neighborhood girl from the Holy Redeemer High School who was bigger and older than Vincent. He had been trying her for a long time, but I knew she was taking him for sport. That chick was already in the land of big men, I thought. Fellas from the St. Mary's Academy, like my older brother Wello. Ebonies, perhaps. Or perhaps Dominica Grammar School guys. Forests of a different stripe. Forests of significant wood.

"Shoo! Fly!" Just as I thought. Madonna gave her answer to Vincent. It was a wonder that she didn't say, "March! Dog!" That used to be one of her favorite parting shots to unwelcome advances.

An impish smile on her face, Madonna slammed shut the window through which she had been leaning. She had to get ready to jump in the carnival too and was going to squeeze into one of those tight three-quarter pants in which she loved to wag her behind. Vincent turns toward me. He is a light-skinned fella and his face is red with embarrassment.

"Don't feel too stink, man. She easy for all kind of big man, but when is one of us, she playing fresh. Don't mind her Vincent, I think she is a *sea poom* anyway." I try to cheer up my partner.

"The band sounding good. I bet you we go find plenty chicks in there," I add.

"Fellas! Lewwe go!" I shouted. I was saving Vincent's pride. He could "try-out" on another day.

"Let's take one for the road," Vincent shouted. Quickly the essence bottle was passed along.

The music I was hearing meant that Swinging Stars was going out on the road. Swinging stars had a hefty brass crew: trumpet, saxophone, trombone and French horn.

Quickly, we squeeze past Taste Me, who was already sprawled senseless in the yard entrance almost blocking the way.

We hit Virgin Lane. Then we took a sharp left and headed towards the pulsating crowd surrounding a truck in the bed of which the Swinging Stars Orchestra is jamming.

We picked up speed like on wings.   With the rum churning my stomach, I soon outstrip Vincent and Leroy.

The crowd drew closer. As I ran, the wind tugged at my bandanna, making the tails flap. The rum sloshed around in the near empty bottle in my back pocket.

Vincent caught up. He gripped my belt from behind. Leroy gripped Vincent's belt too and we move like a train headed to a Zion of twisting and turning joy nestled within the warm embrace of calypso and color.

"Fellas! Watch your toes! I see some people jumping with police boots! They'll mash your toes!" It was a warning from Leroy.

One had to careful with this carnival business. My mother and father had stopped jumping-up in carnival after a mysterious fire in 1963 had consumed three masqueraders whose *sensay* costumes had been set alight. My brother Wello had been in that band and one of the men, engulfed in flames, had almost fallen on him. In carnival, people could get on ignorant and if you pushed someone too hard they could jack you. Then a fight would start and someone could put your belly out in the street quick, quick with a blade or some broken bottle. In the thick of the band bad men like those in the Que Pasa and Howlings gangs often tussled for dominance. We had to avoid that.

I glanced at my soft tennis shoes and fretted some. But mashing toes is part of carnival and you couldn't be in this thing if you 'fraid people touch you.

Arms outstretched, palms clasped like I was ready to dive into one of the pools at Under Power, I aimed for a safe part of the crowd. Maybe Tessa was in there, somewhere, I thought. If so, I would sneak up behind her, do a quick wriggle on her behind and quit before she knew what hit her.

Rum in my head, the piercing sun rays ricocheting off gleaming saxophones, trumpets and trombones, I plunged into the mass of twisting arms, prancing feet, bottoms, perspiring breasts, powdered bosoms, perfumed and unperfumed under-arms. Writhing flesh!

"Hold strain!" I shout, breathlessly, to my partners.

We hung on to each other as we swirled away in joyful abandon. As we were carried along in the crush, I tapped my back pocket. Essence bottle or not, our carnival fuel had done its work.

Our Cross To Bear

I t was on a Friday afternoon after school that I really found out how long our cross was. I had hurtled round the bend in the street near my house with three classmates chasing me. They wanted to be the last to slap me at the back of the head. I had just given one of them a solid *kalot*. It was understood that he wouldn't take my "last" *kalot* and that he had to do me too if he was to salvage any pride. Two of his partners wanted to clout me too, so I had made myself scarce. Negotiating the warren of alleys near my home, I had outstripped them.

As I came to the straightaway that led to my house I saw a crowd of St. Martin schoolgirls in front of my yard. They were all well dressed in their white tennis shoes, white shirts and blue sleeveless dresses. Laughter rippled through the group knotted around the low gate in front of our house as they pointed their accusing fingers at our front door.

I slowed my pace but walked with a defiant, yet heavy-hearted, deliberateness. St. Martin's was the school to which my mother had sent my slow-to-learn, mostly silent older sister. It had led to trouble.

"Moo-moo! Moo-moo!" The crowd shouted, the cow call with a vicious slant. Moo-moo was the insult of choice hurled at any one considered slow or retarded on the island.

I had brushed past the girls, all bigger than me, and made for inside. When I got to the door I spun around, glared at them with all the rage of my wounded soul, and banged the door shut in their faces. Inside stood Dorothy. Next to her was Catherine, my darling oldest sister. Little beads of water, glistening, dripped down both her legs and a puddle of piss formed at her feet. A trembling right forefinger pulled at a corner of her lower lip as she stood looking at her reflection in the mirror. I ran to get a mop.

"Moo-moo! Moo-moo!" The shouts from the schoolgirls were only faintly muted by the thin wooden walls of our modest house.

"All you better don't bring her back to our school again, we don't want to get dunce like her," one of them shouted, her words lashing into me like a whip.

"Yes, all of you too damn doltish in that house," another chimed in.

"Yes, that's right! I don't want no doltish person rubbing up next to me on the same bench! I will catch it too! Ha, ha, ha," boomed a loud voice.

I recognized that voice and it belonged to a particularly boisterous, hairy-legged girl who was notorious for Friday afternoon school fights.

"Thank you, Dorothy," I said. "Thank you for bringing Catho home." Catho was our fond home name for Catherine.

"Is alright Slade, all you is family to me. When I had just come to town to go to school, is your mother who had give me money for my passage. I can never forget what Tanty do for me!"

Dorothy called my mother aunty or "Tanty," as she held Catho by the arm, protectively. Either she was a distant relative or my mother had gone to school with her mother. After the war, when everyone was heading for England, Dorothy's mother had left her behind. So, whenever my mother visited St. Joseph she would cast a caring eye on

Dorothy. She encouraged her, gave her hand-me-down clothes and persuaded her grandmother to send her to school in town. My mother's advise that Dorothy go to school in town had been followed. Now, she had become Catho's protector.

"Bad-dap!" the door was opened and shut in a flash. It was my older brother, Wello. His nostrils flaring, his presence coincided with the quiet that now muffled the street side noises.

"They better be careful with me," he said. "I didn't have a chance to sock it to 'em. As they see me coming, they scatter."

From his right shoulder and slashing diagonally over to his left side was a khaki cloth school bag sewn by Ma. It was chock full of his school books. He wore the blue of the Roseau Boys School. In his right hand was a thick piece of stick he must have picked up off the roadside. The stick was gripped tightly in his hand, brimming with threat.

He swung his gaze at Catho.

"Catho! You couldn't have *jook* one of them girls in the eyes, eh? You couldn't have scratched one of them face, eh? Look at you, letting those girls pinch you and scrape you." His lips twitched violently as tears came to his eyes as he spoke.

In the subdued light of the setting sun which filtered through the rearward facing window curtains I could see several bloody streaks on Catho's arms and face. Cowardly nails had gorged those patterns of hate into her skin. A patch of dried spit was clearly visible at the nape of her neck.

Mop still in one hand, I quickly went into the kitchen to get a rag. I dipped it into a pail of water and came back to Catho. I started to rub at the congealed patch of spit, curling my fingers carefully away from Catho's skin as I did so, afraid that I would catch the germs that dwelled in the unknown spittle.

"Don't worry boy. God is good! He will give them theirs one day. Since morning I had to stop a girl slapping her at recess time. In the afternoon, Sister Borgia put her in the front seat to protect her from those vermin in the back, but when the Sister wasn't watching, they were pricking her with hair pins or pulling her skirt," Dorothy said.

"As class was over, I hold Catho by her hand and start bringing her home. A pack of girls start following us. Who not spitting, throwing thump. Who not thumping her, calling her all kind of dunce that have. I couldn't block all the blows, but believe me cousin, I tried." Dorothy sighed, deeply, as she gave an account of the afternoon.

"And you know in all of that mess, is only one man that tell them leave us alone. It was the crippled man that making cups out of tin can next to where Tanty does work. Nobody else come and help or say a damn thing." That said, Dorothy grabbed the mop from me and started mopping vigorously at the puddle.

"Go get some water to put here boy! If you don't water this down, this spot will stay sticky. Before you know it will stick in the wood and smell. I don't want Tanty to know I was here and allow this to happen to her floor." With Dorothy's instructions flung at me, I relinquished my role as an eraser of spittle and scurried to the kitchen to get the pail of water. I returned with it and, with my cupped hand as a ladle, poured several handfuls of water at Catho's feet.

"Well, move aside eh, Catho? Move, so we can clean this up," I tugged at Catho's sleeve gently. The embarrassment of the moment had her rooted to one spot. She glared at me and muttered something hostile. Now her stubbornness was showing.

"Okay, eh Catho, Tanty coming just now. When she come you will tell her what those girls do you. She will be good for them," Dorothy's coaxing soon had Catho mobile. She edged away from her wetness of place and moved to peer out the window. She looked for her tormentors and discovered that they had disappeared. She looked back at me, Wello, and Dorothy and muttered, "Co-cosh! Hmmph!"

Co-cosh was her word for foolish people. I never knew how she came to devise that word, but everything and anything stupid was a "co-cosh" happening; some silly human slip into idiocy. She was okay, *they* were just co-cosh! I smiled at Catho's small realization of victory. Co-coshing her opponents was her only stab at a response to those who had defiled her with their tongues and deeds. But this wasn't good enough.

I always wished that *they* could be made to pay, one at a time in some dark corner where the numbers of a cowardly mob did not bolster them. But *they* always scattered when my older brothers came to the rescue. When *they* had gathered in front of my house, I had the courage to brush through the mob. If *they* had caught me in the open space of a street far from home, all I could have done was grab Catho by the arm and run from the jeering mass as I had done on occasion. Much too often Catho was a drag and didn't run fast enough to avoid my shame at the circumstance of such unwelcome attention. But one day, oh one glorious day, we would show *them*.

Oh, how I wished she fought back as much as she was stubborn. But Ma had cautioned us to accept God's will. This was our lot, she had said. She had gone on and on about how, in life, you had to allow for a mix of both good and bad. And how God never gave one a cross they couldn't bear.

But we could never ever accept that Catho was born feeble of mind, because, to do so would be to concede the fight to everyone who thought that if Catho was retarded from birth so were we all. To back up their acid clad comments, some teachers added that our tongues were too large for our mouths, which was why we couldn't speak up in class. They said that if Ma knew what was good for her, she would have Dr. Malintyre, the local surgeon, slice away that excess flesh from our over-sized tongues so that we could better speak the Queen's English.

Such insult was heaped upon degrading remark, until we knew our place and hung our heads low in the class. We bunched together in a protective group at outings and stuck around the house far too often, forsaking the closeness and gaiety of other children running around our house and yard, becoming a close, brooding brood. It was the curse of our family, a so-called den of the dense. Our house marked out as the one with the "moo-moo" sister peering from behind the curtain. To an unkind world, Catho was the queen of dunce personified.

They knew nothing of how she had helped Ma clean us up when we were young. How she could be so wise in things small, remembering where things long lost could be found. Tending to her chores like the rest of us, or laughing off the silly lot of those who stared at her, after they had turned their backs. Her smile and warmth was saved for us, within our four walls.

Ma took it all in and clad us in her faith. She went on pilgrimages to different Roman Catholic saints -- little marble statues of white women mostly, nestled in nooks carved out of the island's granite bedrock. At the saintly places of reckoning we, whomsoever was selected that day to accompany Ma, would kneel carefully on the rocky ground, anxious not to scrape our knees. At the feet of the saints we would plant long candles.   With bent heads we would accompany Ma's recitation of the rosary.   Hymns, then more rosary sayings layered upon layers of plaintive requests to the coldly staring saints, all of whom stood with hands outstretched at us as if asking for more collection than we had already placed in the glistening brass plates the Sunday past.

Made strong by her call to a higher being, Ma would sweep away from her bowed position and raise her head with renewed strength. At night Daddy and Ma would gather us in prayer around their bed. More bowing of heads lifted our spirits as Daddy went on praying forever. He meandered to minute details as he thanked God for the birds of the air and the air that we breathed, the fish in the sea and the beasts of the field, the food that we ate, and the beds that we slept in.

He would insist that we respond, all of us, by saying, "May my prayer come unto thee." If we were slow, he would throw us a dreadful look and upbraid us by saying, "Look, don't play the fool with my prayers, eh."

And then he would always remember to ask God to help Catho get well one day from that rotten injection she had been given when young, or the fall she had taken as a babe which must have shaken her brains.

Collectively, we asked God our souls to keep, and that we be protected from the hurts of a small place. Our call gave way to a strength which, drop by hopeful drop, entered our pores like a salve to a wounded consciousness. Until one day the barbed words merely stung, but didn't cut great gashes in the heart any more.

There came a time when Ma had enough of St. Martin's. She thanked Sister Borgia for the opportunity to have had Catho there, but the pressure of the place was no good for Catho. If ever she had a chance to assimilate into normalcy or speed up her slowness, Catho would never know. The stabs of hairpins to her back and catcalls had stolen her innocence until the curtain of the window become her protective shroud, protecting her from malicious eyes and deeds.

"Berta," Sister Borgia had said in her heavy French accented English. "Truly, you are a child of God. I did my best for Catho, but Dominicans do not understand God's work when they see it in a soul like your daughter. She is here for a purpose. A test. She is your cross to bear. Bear it strongly and it will be a challenge for others to follow."

"Yes, sister! I know my cross is long, but I will bear it. I have no choice. This island has no school for those like her. I will have to be her school and companion," Ma had responded, as she kissed the old Belgian nun.

In time all of us, Catho's heavy tongued brothers and sisters, left home. We traveled afar, away from our island home. We had gone on to show that we could speak after all. Soon what seemed like the everlasting shame of our youth was seemingly replaced by a sheen of acceptance. Ma, prickly stares bouncing off her pride, brought Catho along to work at the Workshop where she worked with the blind. There, Catho sand-papered trays, and arranged straw for baskets and other craftwork, laughing and working alongside others who had endured the hurt of being outcasts in a small place. A place where hurt was always around the corner.

At carnival time, Ma and Daddy chipped-chipped behind many a carnival band with Catho's hand slung across their waists. No shame intruded to limit her exposure to the sun, the beach or a trip to the garden. As our lead cross bearer, Ma's defiance freed Catho from the cage of her limitations. All the while Ma gave praises to God and, soon enough, Catho became a regular companion to Ma's prayer partners in the Legion of Mary.

Time went on and then one day I visited home after being abroad for some time. Then, one Sunday I went along with Ma and a slightly graying Catho, to church. Slowly I scanned the church and noticed that in front of us was the, now much older, hairy-legged girl with the hurtful laugh. Towards the end of the mass the local priest, Father Thomas, urged the worshipers to engage in that new practice of a more spirited Roman Catholic Church where, in times past, people kept their hands to themselves. It was time for the handshake as a sign of peace. As my mind flitted back into time the hairy-legged lady spun around and shook Ma's hand then mine, though I hesitated. Then she looked at Catho, whose head was slightly bowed.

"Remember Catho," she said. "Remember all those good times we had back at St. Martin's?" she went on. Not to be limited by the dry handshake she bent over the back of her pew and slobbered Catho's left cheek with a moist kiss.

"Co-cosh," Catho muttered with a smile, as she raised her head and smiled at Ma and me.

"Aye aye? She can speak then?" fretted the former St. Martin's student, as in surprise she slapped her right palm to her breast.

"All the time I think she... she am...you know what I mean," she was lost for words.

"I guess she was only playing shy then? She only had to come out a little bit more in public, get some exposure, eh? Boy, I tell you, you never know! But Ma'am, you do well to bear your cross, eh? Don't care what all those people say, you bear it well," she said looking at Ma.

Ma looked back at her and smiled.

As the priest asked the congregation to join hands in worship, Catho grabbed the hand of the former St. Martin's student and raised it high.

"Co-cosh," Catho repeated, smiling – broadly - as she did so.

To that hairy legs responded, "Amen, sister! Praise God!"

When the Corpse Wore Socks

"**D**rink boy, drink! A gnarled hand shoved the big enamel cup with a much-chipped rim into the man's mouth, past the soggy cotton balls between his lower and upper teeth. That hand belonged to the man's father. Those craggy hands worked the cup, pleadingly, between the man's bluish lips. Yet the guy remained stiff, unmoving. I peered, intently, from behind a gently swaying woman, to see if he swallowed. All the while, the sparsely furnished room hummed with low moans, interspersed with snatches of the hymn "Abide with me."

As I stood there a woman, bent with age, covered the mirror which hung on an unpainted wooden partition with a white sheet. At both sides of the solitary bed atop which the man lay, two candles burned quickly into uneven clumps of melted wax. From behind the wooden partition came lively chatter, broken up by the sound of metal plates knocking against each other, and the clanging of tin cups. The commingled smell of broken flowers, smoked pork broth, cask rum and Dettol disinfectant hung thick in the air.

Reposed on a white sheet, with starkly green ferns laid carelessly about him, the man made not a move. It is the stillest man I had ever seen, at least from close-up and personal. And his disbelieving father was trying to put water into his mouth, again. I moved closer for a better view.

First, the reluctant water gathered in a glistening film atop the man's barely bared teeth. Then it hesitated, tried to find a balance. Then it streaked down both of his cheeks. Tiny rivulets descending into a puddle which had formed in one of his distended ears.

"Alas, but he shouldn't have done that!" The lady who had covered the mirror with the white sheet cried out and wrung her hands. As the eyes in the room swung toward her she grabbed a bottle of Limacol and started sprinkling some of its scented contents around the room.

"Such a nice boy. Just 'cause the girl leave him and gone England, he gone and drink Gramoxone," mutters an old lady nursing a glass of rum on the nearby wooden step

"And they say she was pregnant too. But not for him," A wizened man, stick in hand, whispered to the old lady who now had her drink to her lips.

So far, everyone had been talking in whispers. Now a loud raspy voice stirred the hush of the place.

"But, if is Gramoxone, where the damn bottle? Nobody can find a bottle! As for me self, I think is bad hands that kill the boy. People around here too damn wicked. And everybody know is who, but I eh calling no name." Her point made, the thin lady standing next to the entrance, sucked at her ruddy lips.

"And Alexander, you must to accept the boy gone. You only humbugging yourself by trying to feed him still and give him water," the thin lady with the high strung voiced directed her words at the father who was approaching his son with a loaf of bread, his eyes brimming with tears.

"Leave me, leave," he said, as he faltered and then stumbled into the outstretched hands of a burly man who had stood, silent, against the partition.

"Alex, come with me outside," the man said. "You need some breeze and you must take a good shot. Somebody, get me a drink," he called out in the direction of the kitchen.

Soon, he held a bottle of Bagatelle Rum to the father's lips. "Is so God make it be, Alex don't kill yourself. Take a drink man," the burly man urged. "Whoever do it will get theirs," he went on.

The father somewhat consoled, the mourners turned to look at the lady who had talked of "bad hands." But she avoided their eyes, flipped her head back and took a quick drink out of a flask that was making the rounds.

Felicia and I watched, mesmerized. Caught within a bind of curiosity and fear, we soaked up the images of this, our first funeral. Out of respect for this neighbor, either our mother or father had sent us. To be frank though, I can't quite remember, really, which one did. Perhaps mother, because she had more of a feel for exchanging courtesies. They chose not to show up themselves. Or perhaps they were both working that day and we were the only ones the family could spare.

Felicia and I were in infant school. The official name for it was The Roseau Mixed Infant School. Our Aunty Floss is the headmistress there and we get pinched, in retaliation, by whomsoever sits near to us whenever she takes a strap to their behinds.

It is my guess that Mix School got its name from the fact that they mixed boys and girls in the same class rooms. After school ended at three in the afternoon, there was really nothing grand or important to call on our time. There was no serious homework at our school. Classes were mostly about reciting the arithmetic tables, or singing rhymes like:

The grand old Duke of York

he had ten thousand men.

He marched them up to the top of the hill,

and he marched them down again.

And when they're up, they're up,

And when they're down, they're down.

And when they're only half way up,

They are neither up nor down.

Ms. Cuffy and Ms. Joseph never told us why the old Duke of York marched his men so mercilessly. Maybe old York could afford to do that in foggy England. It snowed there. But, the sun was really hot on my island. I know that we wouldn't have wanted to march up and down hills for nothing. If old York tried that here, I thought, we would toss him all over the place. Come to think of it, maybe we were made to sing about York so it could breed some British backbone into us. But such rhyming was easy stuff. We didn't have to do homework on such subjects. We would sing rhymes about how "London Bridge was always falling down." Now and again we would hit on "The Cow Jumped Over the Moon." Or, perhaps, "Dan, is the Man, in the Van."

Our older brothers Wellsworth, Dawson, and Tyrell were at high school and we had left them at home engrossed in the homework clutter of geometry sets, slide rules, and exercise books. As Felicia and I had walked out the house heading for the funeral, I almost tripped over one of the brass-lock adorned leather book bags at Wellsworth's feet.

High school was a big deal and they couldn't spare their time going to that funeral, I guessed.

Yes! They sent us to represent the family. One had to send somebody, that is if you wanted peace. If you did not attend the funeral of a neighbor, or send some representation, it would be remembered for a long time. That could lead to adults exchanging bad words over the fences that divided their respective yards. Soon enough, the children too would not speak to each other. This could go on for generations, until people couldn't remember what had started it. Our parents knew that. They couldn't take that risk.

We obeyed their orders and put on our Sunday-best clothes. By the way, we used our Sunday-best for going to the movies, the botanical gardens, first communion parties, the merry-go-round, any such nice place, or event. But this was a funeral! Our first funeral! The one thing I'll always remember is that the corpse wore socks!

Man that was wild because I knew those socks. They were sold by Nassief's store downtown, and they were close in color to the blue ones I had on. As matter of fact, I knew more than that. I knew the guy who was lying there, refusing to drink. Furthermore, I had known that body when it was alive, too. That body once belonged to the neighborhood woodcutter and he had been cutting the branches of the Kenip tree that towered over our yard just a couple weeks before.

Kenip trees produce a, grape-sized, green-skinned fruit, beneath which is a succulent layer of sour-sweet pink flesh. In season, they were great treats for us. There was a huge tree in Ma Elvina's yard next door. When the kenips on that tree looked nice and shiny, we would tie a rope to a stone and throw it over the lowest branch of the tree. If it caught that branch we would tug it down, real close so that we could pick bunches of kenips. They grew in clusters, just like the grapes we saw in movies about Romans and gladiators at the Carib cinema downtown. Felicia and I did the rope trick.

Hah! But, if "Wello" - as we called our big brother Wellsworth - was home, he would just scramble up the trunk of the tree and pitch clusters of kenips into our cupped-hands as we stood behind the security of our fence. Sometimes, Felicia would hang around on the verandah as a lookout to make sure Ma Elvina wasn't coming.

Ma Elvina was an old lady who had looked like she was a hundred years old from the first time I saw her. We feared her wrinkled face and sharp tongue. She would howl out curses in Creole that we couldn't quite understand and we were fearful she would "spoil" us. You must understand that in Dominica, at least back in those days, you could spoil someone by cursing them with obeah. But you would have to be an obeah woman, someone who dabbled in necromancy. For one thing, Ma Elvina never turned-on the lights in her house, though she had electricity. More suspiciously, she always used long crooked church-candles to find her way about a night.

Sometimes at night I would peep through the jalousies of the boy's room and see the haunting flicker of her candles roaming behind the thin curtains of her next-door window. On nights like that I would burrow as deep as I could beneath my brother Tyrell, who I called "Tyso". People thought she was a *soukouyan*: a witch who rolled off her skin at night and flew around in a ball of fire. My reasoning was if she ever took to the air to suck the blood of anyone in their sleep, she would take Tyso first. If that happened, I figured that I would have enough time to alert someone with a piercing cry and then disappear as fast as my legs could carry me.

But how did she come to figure in all this? Well, she had hired that woodcutter to trim the branches that had spread over to our side of the yard. The tree's natural growth had made our kenip-eating spree easier. So Ma Elvina got the woodcutter. In seven days and seven nights of whacking away at the branches with a cutlass and an axe, he was done.

All the neighborhood had grown annoyed with the whacking all day, and late into the night. The cutter had even cut up till midnight by flambeau, causing people to lose sleep. Everybody agreed that the job had been, at most, a two day job. But the cutter had gone on whacking, whacking and whacking away. What was worst, he was consuming kenips faster than you could say "Jack Robinson!" That hurt Ma Elvina real bad. Those Kenips were the sweetest in the town and Ma Elvina made a killing selling kenips to passing schoolchildren.

Everyone thought she had put a spell on the tree to make its fruit so sweet. I wondered about that too, until one day Wello came back from school and got to the root of the mystery about this sweet kenip tree. He told us he had learnt about urea and how urea was found in urine. He went on about how urea was a good fertilizer and that he had seen Ma Elvina hoist up her dress on several early mornings to piss in the roots of the tree.

Anyway Ma Elvina was mad as hell about her now, almost bare, kenip tree. Some people said that seven days and seven nights relate to the Bible and that the woodcutter's Biblical work routine had tied up Ma Elvina, thrown-off her tricks and caused her to come unhinged. That especially since the cutter's late night whacks caused Ma Elvina to be grounded.

On the last day the cutter stood beneath the now narrowed spread of the once mighty tree, splintered tree limbs at his feet, looking up with satisfaction at the completed job. As he wiped his brow with the back of his left hand, he was feeding kenips into his mouth two or three at a time. After all the kenips he had eaten, some people said that the payment he asked of Ma Elvina was highway robbery.

Personally, I thought the cutter did a good job, since the pigeons that slept in the kenip tree branches overhanging our yard would no longer shit on our concrete front step. At the same time, I wished he hadn't performed. But Ma Elvina wasn't pleased with the job, or so I found out. Next day, the guy drops dead.

People said he ate something that had "hurt" him. Maybe, it was the fact that he failed to eat his Kenips one at a time. Or, worse still, he might have bitten into the soft bitter core beneath the kenip's thin shell. God forbid that he ate any pineapple or avocado pear after eating the kenip. You see, if you mix the two that is slow poison. That is what we young ones were taught.

On the island, anything you ate could hurt you according to the time you ate it, or what you ate with it, or if you had an empty stomach that instant. Food on the island had mysterious qualities. In America and other faraway places, I read that people ate damn much what they wanted, when they wanted to. But when I was small, growing up on Dominica meant that you ate by a different set of rules.

Just a few months before the woodcutters' death, there had been a big funeral for a pretty and popular girl who died after drinking a hot coke while on lunch break at the Astaphan supermarket. That's how I heard it, so that's how I'm selling it: A coke had bubbled up in her stomach and forced the air out of her lungs. Coke in those days was powerful! Ascribed with mystical properties, it could - under the "right" conditions - cure asthma, headache, and even settle people with bad nerves. I had even overheard Flora the fish vendor, say that Magee, who hung around sailors at the harbor, had gotten rid of her embarrassments by washing herself with hot coke and holy water.

So I stood there transfixed, staring at the socks that looked like mine. Hell! I was vexed. One could feel so pumped-up with pride if one owned the only copy of something. Especially if it meant you were in "style."

Anyhow, I looked at the socks, puzzled as to where the hell he was going to walk with it, to show it off? Wasn't that a waste? I hadn't yet understood that wearing socks gave people style. And style was class.

Poor people wore shoes without socks. Those people had no "style," according to the rules back then. Perhaps they didn't have family who were "away" in one of those places over the horizon where the tiny silver specks of aircraft, which overflew the island at great heights trailing vapor, were going to. That world usually conjured up Snow. Castles. Kings. Queens. Teeming sidewalks and loads of large cars clogging traffic. Traffic lights. "Away" meant fields of golden wheat swaying in the wind. Cowboys chasing Indians. Apples all year round, not just at Christmas. Tall buildings. Rivers as big as our Caribbean Sea, over which spanned serious bridges that went on and on. People who wore their Sunday best all the time. Simply, places out of movies and glossy magazines.

Places where you could get lots of things, like nice clothes and food, so cheap it was close to a freeness. That was what "away" meant.

The "away" to which this guy was going, was not too far. I had seen his "away" one Sunday morning after church, and it was not too far away at all. That Sunday, I had decided to leave the church from the back, just to see what lurked behind the Cathedral's massive rear door. As the door swung out on its huge squeaky hinges, I saw a field of crosses, dazzling in their whiteness against individual mounds of raised earth carpeted with wild grass and flowers. The scent from the graveyard had come at me with a rush of tangy air just like that given off by the frail green ferns and wreaths in that room. But it was time to go.

The burly man eased up the father who had given up on feeding his son and was under his liquor, both hands covering his face. Someone whispered that it was his only son. But I wasn't listening. All I thought of were those socks. Older people saw socks as making someone important, decent. Even in death, you could confound the style-setters and be what society refused you while you were alive.

But how did I know all this complex and fashionable stuff about stiff toes and socks? You see, in a place like Dominica, there weren't any funeral homes then. So people who died were laid-out for viewing at their homes. Though I had never gone to a funeral except for this first one, I knew about dead people. After school, it had been habitual for groups of us to pass next to a house where someone had died. All day we would have most likely discussed it.

That was normal to do, because people did not die often. In those days Dominicans died in ones and twos. And then you never really knew the people that well anyway, it was always someone unconnected to you, and very old. So there was no grief on our part, only curiosity. One would scamper pass the home of the dead and peep quickly through the door because you didn't want your eyes to drink up too many images lest they returned to haunt you that night. The still figures we saw on their beds would sometimes have an enamel basin on their stomachs filled with rough chunks of ice. The ice was to keep them from getting fat in the heat of the place, while clumps of grass scattered about them struggled to mellow the air.

Relatives and friends would do food and hammer together the coffin while a heap of others would crowd the entrance to the house, chatting about the deceased. Lively chatter of would-be mourners wreathed in that musty aroma of funeral flowers is a strong recollection from that time. Yes, there were special ferns and flowers used only at those occasions which could be picked off the street side. And be assured that the rum and wine would always flow hard enough, so that one of the neighborhood characters like V-8, Axe-You-Ras, or Suzie-Muzie would start dancing or cause some other ruckus.

The stiffs I had glimpsed through open doorways always had on their socks. They may have come from relatives working in England, or from packages sent by family in Brooklyn or Ontario. Or perhaps, still, from a cheap selection at one of the Lebanese stores in the city where people complained of having to pay double. They may have been of cotton, or more likely old fashioned nylon with designs of the Empire State Building on the side, the Tower of London, Mickey Mouse or perhaps a knit in thread of Lady Liberty-torch held aloft. No designs of rivers, of our sunset, or any place the wearer had seen or been; the designs were always really far out.

Peasants feet, for the most part, they resided within those socks seemingly dignified for the journey to the other side of their sunset. I heard it told that richer dead folk went as far as to wear their shoes for that final passage. I would never waste my shoes like that, I thought. I would have saved it for a christening party, or something.

Yes, one would more than likely go beneath the loam the same day your maker called you home - just before sunset - since no big enough freezers were around to hold you till the next day or week.

No one was coming from England, St. Croix, Aruba or Curacao. We had to go. The sun had begun to dip behind the trees and the file of mourners trickled out of the house.

As the corpse was raised into the purple cloth covered box, I thought I saw movement, like toes wriggling? I had already become known, through Ma Elvina's gossip, of causing *daybah* - what one called trouble making in Creole. I didn't want to stop the procession as it filed out of the house and bawl out that they were going to bury a guy who was perhaps in a deep state of booze. After all, there hadn't been any autopsy.

In those days any Dominican who slept tight could be in big trouble. As a matter of fact, one carnival a notorious scamp of a merchant had gotten hold of some cheap-but potent- Spanish wine. Everyone who had feasted off it had their teeth and lips stained red for weeks and people came to call it "Vampire" wine. A carnival reveler by the name of Barabas who had fallen into a deep sleep after drinking it had been carted off to the mortuary. When he awoke on the cold slab at midnight, and realized where he was, he had gotten crazy with fright and burst out the door. When the door had crashed open, with Barabas bursting through at breakneck speed, the poor night watchman guarding the place had gotten a heart attack and died.

So, I kept my thoughts to myself. Wearing socks that looked similar to the pair that had just been boxed was enough for me. Figuring how style can lead to a dead-end, I remember vowing never to wear those particular socks again. As the somber procession shuffled down the street, I got a bad case of the creeps. Because of all this business of socks, I would have to burrow deep under my blanket, way beneath Tyso, come night-time.

It's Six O'clock and Roseau Boy Can't See

Over the top of the gray, barb-wire edged, wall which formed one part of the enclosure to my yard were several hundred square yards of green rectangle called the Windsor Park. Windsor Park was Roseau's main park for soccer; what we called football. Also, around carnival season, the calypsonians would sing there and the carnival queen contestants would prance around the prefabricated stage on stiletto heels and answer heavy questions, a wrong answer to which could blight one for a lifetime. During the carnival show-nights, calypso-loving zealots would vault over the tall barbwire topped walls. In the morning, the strings of vicious wire would sprout a new crop of multi-colored cloth flags, with odd-shapes: the residue of sliced pant bottoms caught in the night when the stowaways jumped the fence to get in free. Torn pants or not, islanders loved a freeness. So, it was an honor to perform some sort of daring stow-away that one could boast of in the future.

Later, cricket would be played there too. The idea was to give the cooler, more genteel Botanical Gardens a break from the scurrying feet of cricket spectators that would often mash its exotic flowerbeds.

But in 1969, it was football that drew the crowds to Windsor Park. The high school competition between the Dominica Grammar School, in burgundy and gold tops, and its arch rival the St. Mary's Academy in white, yellow and blue or the real hard football teams like the Spartans, Saints, Celtics, and Santos, battling it out for the national football cup. Football players like Jose, who could cut his opponents' boots with his sideswipe or bowl them over on a dribble. Or Pitchie John Baptiste of Celtics, swift on the link, pouncing with the ball, cat-like, straight into the goal mouth of the opposing team. Perhaps in the goal, fellas like Stallion doing a Gordon Banks in emulation of England's famed World Cup goal keeper. While Dewhurst and Souse Rene, made as if Pele of Brazil had come to town and was playing within their own bodies, guiding their every artful feint, and darting pass of the ball. But no matter how superb to the eyes of the ecstatic onlookers, no matter how flashy, no matter all the emulation of overseas talent, that was all local football fare. But to us, it was super.

Now and again, the crowd would revel in a victory of local squads over visiting British or French naval officers on a friendly port call. The sailors were almost always trashed soundly because they were more eager to eat the fresh luscious tropical fruit of the island, or bury the loneliness of martial sea duty in island rum punches. But we were playing for real and would roar over the lopsided 10-1, or 12-0, victories in our favor, as the best football legs on the island filled the baskets of the opposing sides with goals. We would joke about how these white men couldn't stand the sun and talk on and on about what we thought was gospel.

But these easy victories were deceiving. They were lulling us, young ones especially, into being mesmerized by our players who appeared so fleet of foot, so swift with the corner kick, so resilient on the defense, so hard with legendary goal kicks which could tear those cotton goal nets, which existed before the advent of nylon. So went our football dealings with sailors, most-perhaps-still unsteady on their feet after months at sea. But the *real outside* came in one day and spirited those illusions away in a puff of football field dust. But first, I must tell you about Roseau Boy.

Roseau Boy was a big fella. A young fella, but big and tall. People had given him the name of the city as a nickname because he was one of the smart country guys who had done well enough to get into a city high school. After high school, he had stayed in town and become a city regular. During the week, Roseau Boy was a serious looking shirt and tie-wearing office worker, sunshades on at the right angle, a row of sharp-looking Parker pens always in his breast pocket. On the weekends, Roseau Boy was an action-seeking dandy, with spring in his every step. For sport, he was a goalkeeper.

Since the island wasn't big enough to support a man on sports, everybody who played football did so part time. Some fellas hung around the field more than others, but it was still a part-time thing, this football business. For instance, Barry Beard, a white fella who held the top job at Honeychurch Supermarket played part time, after work. And then, he was like a cat on a hot tin roof in that goal. He would be pouncing here, and pouncing there, punching that ball out his net-even after it may have scored. He would wear these tight shorts, and he would bruise fast on the rough grass, but he was good, good, good. When Barry was in goal, only breeze was allowed to pass. Now and again, when the sun had tired and roasted him well, he would allow a few goals to score. But only now and again.

Roseau was like that. Only sand fly and perhaps a couple mosquitoes could pass by Roseau when he was in his element. Otherwise, he was like a dragnet, catching anything that come his way. What too hot to handle, he kicking out of the way. What too high to kick, he cuffing it over the bar. If his hands or legs embarrassed, Roseau's healthy chest barring the ball, deflecting any shots that mad enough to come near him to the outside of his goal net. All that time Roseau would be serious, serious, only shooing-off the young fellas like me who would hang around his net. We would be behind his net; shouting advice; holding conversation, trying to call the outcome of the game. All that, while the action would be intense in the area of the opposition's half of the field. But when the opposition was approaching, Roseau was like a caged lion within his goal. He hoisting up his short pants even shorter, fixing his black gloves, dusting-off his jersey as if making sure he has no extra load before he takes flight on one of his saves. Yes boy that was Roseau Boy in his element! But there was one problem: Roseau Boy wore glasses.

Our big stadium, our fancy football stadium, was splendid to our standards. For instance, we didn't have floodlights. I mean, we knew Gordon Banks and Pele and these big football stars played in all kinds of weather, under lights and all. Some of their stadiums even had roofs on. But we only had the unadulterated blue of our island sky and the fiery Caribbean sun. This was an all natural affair.

The games would start sometime after four in the afternoon. Roseau Boy's fame was made in the first half, which came to an end around five. On the island, night falls swiftly at about six. But between five and six, the sun's rays will begin to show its tentative ways. Sometimes, the clouds would begin to tease the sun, barring its glow off and on. At times, even the sun would play shy and try to hide behind some big tamarind or mango tree on the hills of Goodwill, which overlooked the park. Once the sun dropped behind the heights of Goodwill, Roseau Boy would begin to fade fast. His face would squeeze up as he seemed to force all his energy into his tiny eyes, behind those thick glasses he wore. It was then that Roseau would begin to move by instinct, but mostly away from the ball.

But Roseau was still one of the best. For that, he was made the substitute keeper for the Dominica national team. The regular keeper, a sometime calypso crooner with the Jumping Stars Orchestra called Stallion, was the real deal. Stallion walked on the tip of his toes, all the better for him to be always leaping high to push a ball over the bar. He was a prim and proper fellow with a welcoming face. A lot of girls would hang around his goal and go "Ooooooohhh!" and "Aaaaaahhhh!" when Stallion made a big save. After some spectacular move, Stallion would always brush himself slow, slow, slow, with his white kid leather gloves, put his hands akimbo, and flash a big set of ivories for the mini-skirts behind his net. Now and again, one of his female admirers would slip him a piece of orange, grapefruit or even a Guinness stout. The man had appeal. So, in any big match against the outside, Stallion would go first. But for us fellas, Roseau Boy had character.

Then one day, as I knew it would happen, the outside came visiting. It came visiting in the form of a football team from Suriname. Now, for those who don't know, Suriname is the place the Dutch exchanged for New York. Imagine! The same New York called the Big Apple these days, with all those overgrown buildings that trying to peep into heaven. In 1600 or something the Dutch saw more fortune in Suriname, what with cane sugar made sweeter by black labor at 100% discount and so forth. Then, New York was not prime real estate as it produced nothing as valuable to European trade as West Indian sugar.

The news came that Suriname was going to play Dominica. Bam! Everybody excited and in a fuss. From the back window of my house, we could see Windsor Park and for weeks our national team could be seen practicing late, late, late. Sometimes way past six in the evening, to the degree that fellas with cars around would ride up near the goal post and put on their headlights to help the cause. No matter their batteries run down, they had to help the cause. After all, Suriname coming!

To understand the anxiety caused by Suriname, you have to understand geography too. Suriname is in South America. What with the history of football as religion in South America, that was bad enough. But wait a minute, Suriname wasn't just anywhere in South America. It bordered on Brazil. Brazil, the place of legend, where all the football gods reposed; where Pele could full a goalie's basket just by looking at him hard. Suriname was next to Brazil. Even worse, Suriname was still a Dutch colony and we knew that Holland could play football. We considered ourselves British too, but it was cricket that really called forth our best.

So the day dawned bright, because that's how it usually is in Dominica anyway, except if it's raining. The day itself didn't know Suriname was going to play Dominica, it just dawned like it was accustom to. But it was the afternoon that was important to us, not dawn. By four o'clock Windsor Park is full. The governor and the bishop are in armrest chairs, high up in the only set of permanent park stands available. They were both busy fanning themselves, now and again bending heads into each other's ears like they conducting hush-hush matters of state. The premier was there too, a regular fella looking studious with his glasses, newspaper in hand; surrounded by a lot of shirt and tie civil servants.

So all these folks were on the stands looking down on the big crowd, a shimmering blaze of colors in afternoon. Here and there a few ladies have parasols to ward off the sun which is beating down. Around the field, vendors like always-in-a-short-pants-Charlie Mo and others made a brisk trade in peanuts, Max chewing gum, and frozen joys. Earlier, the prisoners from her Majesty's Jail had put up a couple prefabricated wooden stands for the anxious population. Those were already creaking under the unaccustomed weight. Long before the game started, everybody was busy giving advice to the players. Others had transistor radios listening to pre-match analysis, the wonders of Surinamese football prowess having them more frightened by the minute. All that time I am a stow-away as I had jumped the wall earlier that afternoon. Tickets expensive like hell today and I couldn't afford to pay.

The game starts and Stallion is in goal. From the outset, my head was sent swimming by the dazzling speed of the Surinamese players. It's like our guys were laden with lead boots. Our fellas stumble, the passes don't connect, our shots at goal go high. All that time, I walked the sidelines jumping, screaming encouragement, cajoling. Soon, a rain of shots hits Stallion's net. Our defense had collapsed; the Surinamese were pouring through the breach, raining shots at Dominica's goal. Stallion is moving around in slow motion as if he is in the pictures the same way those cowboys fall off the rotten roofs in the western movies I used to see every Sunday. His muscles stiffened, he ceased to take flight. He isn't smiling anymore. He lost one glove during an attack upon our goal. Bad news. The pressure of Suriname has his mouth dry, his wings are cut. A clutch of mini-skirt ladies behind his net, collectively, put their hands between their knees and screamed. They flailed at the limp air with their wrists and browbeat Stallion. Now and again, Stallion stole a backward glance and attempted some smiling reassurance. It didn't work. The girls trembled, their faces sagging in disbelief. No fruit passed. No Guinness Stout through the back of the net today. Then it's half time.

The patriotic crowd mobbed our players, offering grapefruit, oranges, soursop, mangos, and all kinds of fruit to rescue the flagging juices of our home team. Advisors who'd never been on a football field since the beginning of creation, scurried to and from giving advice on passing, dribbling, and goal keeping. The whistle blew. We are back on. It's after five. Wait a minute, Stallion didn't come back on. A low shot must have caught him in the gut, I am told. He has a cramp, real or imagined. I imagined that the coach must have rubbed him down with bayrum, but that didn't work. Whatever the reason was, Stallion is sidelined and Roseau Boy was substituting. He did a few press-ups; jumped feverishly in place and adjusted his glasses.

God man! Roseau has the sun to his back. The red orb of light is lazily beginning to dip below the Goodwill heights. With the sun to his back, Roseau was in the shadowed area because the goals are switched at halftime. We held our breath.

Dominica pressed the attack. The deluge of crowd advise, the bishop's prayers, the cajoling, the cursing, plus girlfriend talk with promises of "tonight," not forgetting the grapefruit juice, all must have had an effect. We scored one against the fearsome outsiders. The premier dropped his newspaper, opened his collar and cheered our boys on fervently. They retaliated. Roseau Boy was now our Churchill of beleaguered 1940 Britain facing the advancing Germans. Roseau was our man-o-war, a kind-of-sea-wall, fronting the raging tidal wave that sought to swamp our land. He back-flipped and cuffed a shot at goal aside. Time and time again, Roseau Boy pelted cuffs and kicks at the oncoming ball all over the place. The crowd roared. We loved it. We were saved. Or were we?

Our treacherous sun gave us not a minute's saving grace. True, it had dawned brightly that day. But the sun was just behaving as usual now. Nothing special about today's sun, just that its timing was criminal in this instance. Game or no game, Roseau Boy or no Roseau Boy, the sun was going about its craven business. It was playing us nasty, by slinking back to its rendezvous with some watery lover in its nightly lair 'neath the Caribbean Sea. As the fingers of dark extended over the field, the rays of sunlight retracted, as if to throttle our island hopes of football glory come.

Roseau Boy was now valiantly diving in the opposite direction away from every shot at goal aimed by the Surinamese. They smelled blood. I even think they noticed when the elastic band that anchors Roseau's glasses to his head snapped. With that snapping of the elastic band, all was lost.

Bam!

A ball shot towards the net at face level. Roseau Boy pelted away with his balled fist. His glasses went flying. Even today, on a quiet afternoon years afterwards, you can still hear the big "Nooooooo!" as the Dominican crowd deflated. But Roseau doesn't hear that. He kept on pulling up his sleeves, hoisting his short pants even shorter; giving his bulging thighs room to work with. Now and again, when the Surinamese gave him an ease-up, he went scrambling around in the dust searching for those glasses. Picturesque futility.

The final whistle and now all you could hear was the shuffle of departing, disappointed feet. Only a few regulars like me who lived close to the park hung around to watch our boys as they changed their clothes in a daze.

Damn! We lost that game. And we knew that we were good... Maybe. Maybe if nice man Stallion was the substitute instead of Roseau we could have had a chance. Maybe if Roseau Boy had been put on first, when there was still light, it would have been better. Maybe, maybe, maybe.

But a late start did it to us, and so we could excuse the loss to Suriname. So, over a beer or rum punch a hundred years hence, we will have a reason for that defeat. It is legend now on the island. Whenever fellas talk about football, when football was football... before steroids. We have an explanation for the Suriname game. Man it was almost six o'clock... and you know... at six o'clock Roseau Boy can't see. And that's the plain truth.

❀

And the Seat Turned Twice

I t's 1969 going on 1970 and the beads of Dominica's sweet fresh water are clinging to my young forehead. I am ecstatic with pre-cinema fever, fighting to get my clothes on, my own water, sweat, already pushing through my pores, edging away the globules of sweet freshwater in this anxious moment. It's almost four o'clock and I am running kind of late.

I've just exited the shower in the backyard. Yes, the one right next to the chicken coop and rabbit cage. The same shower stall, with green moss within it's cracked retaining walls, with a blue Caribbean sky for its roof. I've just slithered out of that misty cubicle of soup suds, jumped onto the concrete step, grabbing my frayed bath towel off a wash line while in dripping flight.

Big show at the Arawak cinema today: *The Good, The Bad and The Ugly,* starring Clint Eastwood. It's showing at the Arawak Cinema not the Carib. I have the benefit of nearness with which to ease my lateness. You see, my street, Boyd's

Avenue, is just about half a mile from Arawak. All I have to do is swing a right on Bath Road, then hang a left on Kennedy Avenue. Arawak is right there, new plate glass front and all, with a soaring roof of steel.

It will be only my second movie there. The first was *The Bible*, or was it *The Ten Commandments?* Was that Charlton Heston or Richard Burton starring? It was the same picture that caused the Millingford fella to die of a heart attack, when God said, "Thou shall not commit adultery." He frothed at the mouth and drop dead right there in the Balcony.

Mr. Millingford was a good Catholic. He had attended the St. Mary's Academy and all that. But he liked to tangle with different women, especially those who worked on his father's estate. It was known that he often used his position to wangle a quick rudeness under the dark cover of low-lying cocoa trees. He had about twenty children, all of them with different colors: some dark some light skinned. All over the island now you can find different kinds of Millingfords. Not like before when they almost all were of planter stock and near white. But I'm getting ahead of myself here.

The Balcony held one of the most expensive seats, near the rafters. Just adjacent to it was Box which held the most expensive seats, where esteemed folks like the British appointed governor, the bank manager, bishop and other such "high-ups" would normally sit. It held seats with padded armrests, where shirt-and-tie big shots smoked highbrow cigarettes and drank whiskey in breakable glasses during movies. Below were the House seats. There, you would find office clerks, school principals, people with steady jobs, mostly. The Pit was for the masses or overflow. When one looked up towards the Box, the Balcony and the House seats, the complexion of the faces got lighter with the rise. In the Pit, ebony hued faces reigned; a sprinkling of light tan sometimes interspersed with a yellow-brown Carib descended face here and there.

Right now? Man, I'm chucking my shirttails into my short pants, fastening my belt crookedly. Doing it and undoing it several times, before getting it right. I am feverish with excitement. First, putting on shoes without socks. Then quickly flipping them off with my bare toes behind each heel as an opener, and putting on my red and black nylon socks. Decisions! Decisions!

"Elizabeth! You going? I ready, you know!" I shouted to my younger sister, panting, almost out of breath, and I haven't even left the house yet.

"Sambo, what about you? You coming?" Sambo, my older brother, had been at the river all day playing around on an inner tube. He had just returned from Under Power and Silver Lake; his regular Sunday watering holes. His black skin had paled some, from his soaking in the river all day. When you were that complexion, people would tease by shouting, "Hey, look at a *bekay layvye*!" Literally translated that meant white man of the river. The noise of clothes being whipped on in the other room convinced me that he was coming anyway. It was supposed to be a good movie and there would be rushing. Sambo would be in front pushing. Elizabeth would be in the softness of the center. I would take up the rear guard. One had to fight seriously for tickets to any hot movie.

We were ready. Mama gave us a quick look over. Then it was out the door and down the street past Bowsie, the hunched cobbler with a thousand brilliant ideas. Yes, the same Bowsie who swore that he could have seen Armstrong and Aldrin when they landed on the moon with the help of his ancient pair of German binoculars from World War... something; I or II, I couldn't remember. After Bowsie's cobbler shop, we hang a quick right on Bath Road and dart across the street to the fire station, or what we sometimes called the fire brigade. Our father was a fireman. However, children and older people who followed their lead called firemen on the island fire brigades.

"Good afternoon Mr. Challenger! Good afternoon Mr. Robin!" We exchange hurried pleasantries with the officers leaning across the guard desk. The guardroom was fronted by huge louvered windows of glass through which the guys at the fire station would look at the Convent High School girls during the school week. It was a time of mini-skirts. During the weekday lunch break, the Convent girls would stream down the hill that swept by the station. As they sashayed along, bookbags swinging, the eyes of the idled firemen would ignite and make as if to undress the more comely girls running commentary on their thighs and looks. But it is a quiet Sunday. The sun is pelting down and the streets are almost empty of people or car traffic. Most people were probably at sea or river picnics or at home eating their best meal of the week while listening to oldies but goodies on local radio. Except, of course, those of us who were on the way to matinee.

"S.O. Christian! S.O. Christian. Look, Zap, Elizabeth and Sambo come to see you, sir!" S.O. stood for Sub-Officer. Robin was shouting to my father who was somewhere within the dark concrete recesses of the station. Soon the crunch, crunch of his leather boots on the concrete floor would signal his approach.

Zap was my nickname. It was corruption of the word Jap. When I would amuse the fire brigade fellas with second-hand World War II stories passed down to me by my ex-soldier father. Jap would escape my lips with a zzzzz - a kind of hissing sound. I had a lisp, because I'd lost my two front teeth. They were my baby teeth and they were slow in growing back. So Jap became Zap and German, became Zerman. So the fellas at the Brigade called me Zaps n' Zermans.

"So Zap, what you going to see at the pictures today? Something about Zaps and Zermans, eh?" It was Robin speaking as he leaned against the burnished red of No. I, the biggest British made fire engine on the whole island. When people like Mr. Robin spoke of "pictures" he really meant movies.

"No sir." I replied. "Is a cowboy movie I going to. You know Mr. Clint, the cowboy? He really bad you know! I giving war pictures a break for now. I wanna see what happening with westerns these days." I was talking big, hands in my pocket. I was pacing excitedly, kicking up my heels.

Sambo was with Elizabeth, negotiating cinema money from Daddy. I had asked him, and gotten money from him earlier in the week for pictures. So they were in front, I wasn't going to ask again so soon.

"Okay! Let's go!" Sambo spoke with the assurance of a mission accomplished. Maybe he even got money for ice cream and peanuts too.

"Zap! Come here boy. Don't make me cut your tail eh?" Daddy said. I fidgeted. Was he going to bar my cinema plans? True, I had gone earlier in the week to see a desperate piece of action with Klaus Kinski in *Where Eagles Dare*. Maybe he was going to hold me back, thought I was going too often.

Daddy stepped up to me.

"You mean your mother let you leave the house with this kind of bush on your head?" he passed his big soft hand atop my curly hair. It was still wet.

"Boy, your hair isn't combed, you know?" He grabbed me by the wrist and half pulled me to his bedside within the barracks. He flipped open the lid of his glossy black trunk and took his hairbrush from amidst the bric-a-brac of post cards, *Jet, Plain Truth, Awake!* and *Time* magazines, Limacol, Listerine, Kiwi shoe polish, Brasso, badges, epaulets and other big-men stuff. Soon the hard strokes of the bristles were furrowing the hair flat, slicked back. Quickly, he dabbed on some Vaseline jelly, then a little amount of green pomade. He rubbed the mixture on. Brushed hard again. Soon he had perfection, but not before my scalp was throbbing from the hard strokes. I passed my fingers atop my head lightly. I felt waves. Undulating rows. Sort of felt coolie-like, just like Carib Indian hair feels. Daddy smiled approvingly and put his mirror before my face. My hair was glistening, just like some stars one would see in the cinema.

"Thank you Daddy," I murmured and I rushed for the door, out the station, into the bright sunlight of the afternoon. Sambo and Elizabeth were ahead of me, walking quickly down the street. They were already past Ken Ko, the first restaurant to serve Chinese food on the island but which had been shut down after people couldn't recognize the meat they were serving. I caught up, breathless.

Soon, the Arawak was in front us. A huge crowd in their Sunday-best church clothes milled about. We hesitated and cast our eyes about. Here and there we could see people giving professional rushers their money to buy tickets for them.

Fellas like Zincock and Axe-You-Ras, all big and brawny, could rush to get your ticket for a fee. When movies like *The Sound of Music*, John Wayne in *Green Beret*, or Audie

Murphy in *To Hell and Back* came to town, a professional rusher to do ones bidding was essential. Pregnant women had even given birth when caught in the crushing grip of a rushing movie crowd. Just last week a neighbor, had a prized gold tooth knocked out his mouth during a particular boisterous piece of rushing associated with a replay of *The Scarlet Pimpernel.* But professional rushers cost money. Maybe an extra five or ten cents on every quarter spent would be the fee. That was a burden on our meager economy. We couldn't afford it. Our cinema money was exactly budgeted: ticket money and a little something for refreshments. We had to do for self and started forcing ourselves through the thick, roiling crowd in front of Arawak's ticket counter.

The ticket counter at Arawak was in a narrow alley, and was really a window with iron bars through which Anselm the pudgy ticket seller pushed your tickets after taking your money.

I held onto Elizabeth's waist. She, in turn had Sambo by the belt. We held on to each other and pushed, pulled and rocked from side to side. Sometimes the shoes almost got off my feet. My shirt was out one time, next thing my shirt button had popped at the neck. Peoples elbows were poking my ribs, their dripping, smelly, under arms pressed upon my nose. We were small and some big-chested men were squeezing our stomachs out. But this was all part of the rush for tickets. It would be something to speak about in class the next day.

"Mr. Anselm, I know you! Three tickets for pity, please! We have exact change you know!" Sambo said, his face pressing against the iron bars behind which Anselm sat like some lord in his castle, dispensing favors to his minions. Sambo was already in first form at Grammar School and he talked like an educated fella. Respectful, but firm! He was coaxing Anselm like mad.

"Yes sir! Please Sir! Thank you, sir!" Sambo soon had the tickets crumpled in his tight fist. We spun around and squeezed ourselves back out of that ball of writhing humanity and made for the entrance.

Saca Boy was in the door. Everywhere Saca Boy went he had a transistor radio. He would put it to his ear, even when it was off or it didn't have batteries. He was a show-off.

Yes! Even when he was cutting tickets. He tore the tickets with one hand, transistor radio in the next. The management had planned to fire him the other day, because people were gaining entry by giving Saca Boy old half tickets to tear. He so lacked attention to his job. Today, he was only smiling wide and troubling the girls.

Sensing Saca Boy's distraction, my mind was working fast. Perhaps I would save my half ticket and try using it next week to see a Dracula picture or some other horror, I thought. Maybe, *Devil's Bride* - the one with Christopher Lee starring. It all depended on how much of the ticket I allowed him to tear. The less he tore, the better. I held a short stub out and ripped briskly. I think that time I kept more than half. It was a good afternoon so far.

Anyway, we were soon through that door. I snapped out of my thoughts about next week and buried the almost full ticket deep in my pants pocket. Inside, our eyes quickly adjusted to the darkness. Lights were already out. The place was humming with the excited chatter, a standard preface to pictures dancing upon the big white screen. Some high school fellas, like Sancho Burton, were playing "big" up front. They were smoking the minty flavored Kool cigarettes, stretching their necks upward and puffing rings so people could notice. Others were smoking those long brown Phoenix types, glancing at girls as they came in, hoping they could entice to sit close. Some big muscled guys had even backed-off their shirts, twitching their chest muscles in the glow of lit cigarettes and other subdued light; comparing the size of their taut chests, perhaps relishing their recent prowess at rushing. Meanwhile, we were in a scramble to get seats and found some near the back row. Good! We were all together.

Before long the fat lady with the cokes and peanuts tray had passed by. Sambo bought a coke and we all shared it, along with a bag of roasted peanuts. All that time we talked loudly and laughed about the rushing we had just survived.

Next thing you know, the same old lion appeared on screen gave up a lazy roar and the movie was on. A vista of desert scrub and brown mountains unfolded. Clint squinting under his hat, like the sun troubling his eyes bad. His horse, galloping fast, fast, fast after a bad man. The bad man got off his horse and sneaked behind a stone. The whole place erupted: "Look he hiding behind de stone, Clint! Cuff him! Shoot him!"

Before you know it, Clint was off his horse and thumping the Mexican-looking bad man. The crowd roared, happy that Clint was following their advice. Some got up from their seats. Others stomped their feet. The rhythmic chant of "*Higas! Higas!*" went up.

I never got to the root of what "*Higas*" actually meant, what it stood for or where it came from. I just knew that whenever there was a fight on the screen or in real life, Dominicans would start with this "*Higas*" business.

So moviegoers would scream many a "*Higas*" when blows would begin to fly on the big screen. Bolder guys would shout: "*Higas*! Mother ass!" But we had home training and didn't go that far.

All that time, we are sipping slowly on the one glass of coke that we swirled around with the ice. It was in a plastic cup, making the rounds. The more you melted the ice, the more you could stretch the cokes.

Bam!

I heard a crack. It wasn't Mr. Clint's gun or anything like that. In fact, his gun was in its holster. He had moved on and was now trying to kiss some damsel he had just rescued from distress. Clint was just about to push the mistress back upon some upstairs-the-saloon couch when, suddenly, the screen, the big new screen, started to flap, flap as if it was coming loose.

Bam! The screen went dark.

"Harold! Harold! You cut the picture!" The audience screamed, incensed at being denied some action. Harold was the renown projector operator. Even if it wasn't him, people would still shout out his name. The cinema was notorious for cutting matinee pictures where there was kissing or men and women rubbing on each other, about to do something. There was a censor board, which was chock full of priests and nuns. It was a very Catholic country.

Hoots and whistles, intermingled with curses, flew fast and furious around the Pit.

"Harold! Your mother potato!" Shouted a bandy legged guy behind us. He was jumping up and down, looking back in the direction of the projectionist's booth. From the booth two fingers of light - illuminated particles of dust dancing through their paths - cut through the dark toward the screen. In a flash, the two fingers of light were gone. In front of me, a girl who looked like one of those who hung around the bayfront when sailors were in town shouted something about how Harold and the tongue of his mother's potato smelled real bad. The whistling, hooting, and cursing rose to a crescendo. Sambo told us to cup our ears. He wanted to save our eardrums from the cruel volume as well as protect our innocence from the cursers. Still, the screen remained dark.

Bam!

People were now scrambling up and around, getting out of their seats. Some were reaching upwards, groping up the tastefully decorated walls that overlooked the Pit and separated it from House. A Big headed fella sitting next to us shouted, "Boy, I see the seat turn around twice!"

I didn't feel anything, busy crunching my peanuts and sipping coke as I was. But hysteria was infectious. I stood up.

"Fellas! Earthquake!" A loud shout goes up. It resounded.

With that, up went a panic laden roar. People started leaping over seats with renewed zeal. I made for in front, Sambo grabbed Elizabeth. Then I reversed my gears. I don't know how I did it, but I scaled the ten-foot-high wall and entered the House. I didn't even have a ticket for House. I quickly plumped down on one of the padded seats to see how it felt on my behind. I had never sat in the House seats before. In the Pit, the seats were made of polished mahogany benches with no padding.

Anyway, the experience was short lived. There was still, supposedly, an earthquake going on. I made for the exit.

The front of the Arawak was littered with debris. All the beautiful new plate glass windows lay in crunchy shards beneath scampering feet. Hysteria had caused people to fling themselves through the crystal exterior of the cinema. I took off for home as fast as my legs could carry me, with Elizabeth and Sambo somewhere behind. On my way home, I stopped at the brigade.

At the station house, all was tranquil. The engines were at rest, the men idle, gossiping, eating ice cream. No one had alerted them. I ran up to Daddy.

"Daddy! Daddy! Earthquake! Earthquake!" Breathless, I struggled to rouse him out of the sense of normalcy that pervaded the fire station.

"You too stupid boy, what's wrong with you, eh? You not supposed to be in matinee?" He shakes me off. I looked down at my feet, chastened.

"What earthquake you talking about, eh? You see earthquake around here?" he said.

He was right. Everything looked okay. It wasn't like an earthquake was supposed to look. I mean, I knew something about earthquakes. My Caribbean Reader textbook in elementary school showed pictures about Port Royal, Jamaica and the bad earthquake they had there which swallowed Henry Morgan and those other pirates. The Bible too showed pictures of earthquakes, as it would be when God was going to end everything and so on.

But, the streets and buildings looked just fine around the station house. No tumbled buildings, no cracked pavement. In the background, the green mountains which surrounded the city were still standing, erect. The sun still shone. It was only at the cinema that I had just witnessed chaos. The Sunday, with its strolling couples, seemed regular. I had to say something for myself.

"Well, Okay. Go to Arawak and you'll see what I am talking about Daddy. There was an earthquake down there. The new place Mash-up, flat, flat, flat. Everything mash-up!" I implored him, making motions with my hands to describe the scene I had just left.

The firemen gathered around to listen. Some laughed; shook their heads in disbelief. "Boy, I tell you already you mustn't be an alarmist!" Daddy was wagging his finger before my downcast face.

Perhaps they thought Zap was up to his old story telling antics again. The phone rang. Fireman Mason answered. He wiped his laugh off his face. After he has answered, "Fire Brigade, Guard Desk here," the phone message must have startled him.

The station siren wailed. The news was spreading. Soon, No. 2, a small Fire Brigade jeep, peeled off in the direction of Arawak. Something had indeed happened, as I had related. Daddy and the other firemen straightened up and seemed alert, in readiness if need be. At least I had been vindicated. It was to transpire that no one had died, no place had burnt down or sank into the hell I thought existed beneath the earth.

Later, I went home. Elizabeth and Sambo were already there. On the 6 o'clock news, Radio Antilles on the nearby island of Montserrat mentioned there had been a minor tremor. Minor tremor? The big headed fella had said our seat had spun around twice.

Humph! True, I never felt that. But when people running, I was bound to run too. Anyway, up to this day I have never seen the whole of *The Good, The Bad and The Ugly.* Now and again Clint shows up in new pictures and he's still looking serious, serious, squinting like some bad man blow smoke in his eyes. Only that, nowadays, he mostly wears suits and ties. He still carries a big gun though. But even now, with cable TV and all that stuff, when *The Good, The Bad and The Ugly* comes on, I usually walk off and do something else.

Yes! I lost taste for that picture one afternoon in 1969 going on 1970, when my seat turned twice. Or, at least, that's what I heard the big headed fella next to me say.

❀

Common Entrance

Mr. Veritas was striding back and forth, a springy whip cut off a tamarind tree tucked under his arm pit. It is a sweaty Friday afternoon, and he was getting ready to call out the names of the students who are to take the Common Entrance Exam.

"When I call your name, step up the front. Quick! Sharp! You understand!!!???" "Yes Sir!!!" The class responds in unison.

Veritas was a serious man and today was a big day for him and the students in the class. Whether the people who he selected passed the exam would reflect on him. It could put him in line for promotion to principal. The Minister of Education could come to the school and speak with grand flourish. His name could be called out for special mention at the National Day Rally. A high pass rate could increase his reputation for intellectual prowess in the community, and so allow him to give private classes at his home for which he could charge a decent fee.

"Theresa Polydore!"

"Yes so," responds a shy, ebony-hued, thin reed of a girl from the village of Grandbay, way up in the southern mountains. She was a bright spark in the front row, though most everyone in class considered her a *country bookie*. But there she was, edging her way with hesitation toward the front of the classroom, up to the raised wooden platform where the teacher sat. Once in place, she looks over the room.

Theresa is the first to be called and the burden of this moment causes her to bend her head and gaze downward at the big toe on her left foot which is sticking out the front of her torn rubber sandals-or what we call *toeless*. She curls the toe and tries to pull it back into the sheath of torn rubber sandal, but there is not enough of it left up front. Fidgeting, she clutches a little brown paper bag in her hand, a grease spot showing near its bottom. That bag holds her snack for recess. Most of us brought our snacks in such bags. She wasn't leaving hers behind, even for a moment.

Theresa spoke a lot of Creole and her "sir" came out like "so." Her peasant parents had sent her to live with relatives in town because they felt her chances for passing the exam were better at one of the schools in the city. Better still at the new Canadian funded and designed aluminum and red brick edifice of the Goodwill Junior High School.

The school was pretty, not like the barracks-style schools built under the British school administrators. It had flushing toilets, mirrors at every landing, graceful stairs to carry one from floor to floor, a public address system, and even a fire alarm. The windows were made of an inner wire latticework and slanting outer aluminum slats through which the cool mountain air or sweet sea breeze would blow soothingly on an otherwise scorching hot afternoon.

"Fletcher Bully!"

"Yes Sir," clips a brown-haired, light-skinned boy in sharply creased khaki pants and tan shirt. Bully lived up on the hill overlooking the school, in a white concrete bungalow with a drive-in garage. His severe necktie-wearing father who drove a dazzling red Hillman sedan dropped him off every day. He walks up as if it's no big deal. As he makes his way forward, chin jutting in front, the clackety-clack of the steel plate on the heels of his shining leather shoes crunches loudly in the deep silence which hangs heavy in the room. Once in front, Bully folds his hands and stares out at no one in particular. He was as cool as if this calling of his name happened every other day and was fully expected.

"Francisca Letang!"

"Yes sir," comes the singsong of a response from a comely girl whose behind rolls with every step she takes to the front.

Francisca's glistening hair, slicked flat on her head in undulating waves is gathered at the back by a red bow. She is part Carib and part Black. We all knew that she lived with her frail grandmother and went about without a strong hand to guide her from home. I had heard that she hung around the Arawak Cinema at night, asking working guys to buy her tickets to late shows. Around her graceful neck she wore a glittering gold chain with a crucifix that her mother, who worked at a hotel on the nearby French Island of Guadeloupe, had sent her. As she walks up, the guys in the back row burst out laughing.

Veritas spoilt Francisca. He was putty in her hands and the laughter was commentary on her smarts, or lack thereof.

Veritas, a sparse gangly man, peers over his spectacles, which droop low down on his sweaty nose. His lips are trembling.

"Silence! The next time I get anything from the back row, every man-jack will owe me a thousand lines, and will get six of the best!"

As he speaks, he shakes his whip menacingly.

Lines! I hated lines! It was a waste of time and ate up your exercise book in a flash. Earlier in the year a bunch of class "talkers" had been punished and made to write this long sentence a thousand times:

"A baboon, with all its blabber, cannot build a nation. Rather, I must try adhere to the discipline of our Anglo Saxon tradition."

As I remember those "lines," Veritas keeps calling names. Meanwhile, I am a nervous wreck in the middle row, feigning unconcern by doodling in the margins of my exercise books. Yet, the crucial nature of this reality was biting deep.

You see, there was nothing common about the Common Entrance Exam. It represented the do-or-die high point of elementary school education. This test decided whether or not I would move on to high school. Without a pass, no high school would take me. High school places were preciously few. Only a mere third of all exam takers passed. Only a tiny minority of that third got scholarships or bursaries. If I failed, then I would cease to progress with an education. I would go on to what was called standard six, then seven. Guys in those classes had hairy legs and the girls had ample bosoms. Everybody said they were big in people business already. At home, the family shame would be intolerable. The teasing that would follow would designate me a "Grandfather Goodwill School" or simply a dunce cat.

Upon completion of seventh standard one would be given a school leavers certificate. That, if one successfully completed the seventh standard school leaving exam. Earlier in the century parents could accept a school-leaving certificate, but no more. After World War II, islanders could vote. They were able to elect their own. Gone were the days when all the doctors and top civil servants came from England. Now, everybody wanted his or her child to work in an office, be a doctor, lawyer or engineer. University, once unheard of, was being talked about. But the Common Entrance Exam loomed large. It was a forbidding and merciless obstacle.

So I sit there, forcing a daydream to shut out the fear of that moment. I gaze out at the slow afternoon traffic on the coastal road that snaked along the seaside. In my reverie I envisioned myself at one of the Roseau high schools. Maybe the Academy. Yes! That was where all the sharp guys went. They wore real nice blue and gold ties at that school. The guys wore long pants too. My oldest brother was already there, and he was as sharp as a tack. In fact, of all the boys at home, I was the last guy in Junior High. I couldn't let down the side. The weight of that duty wore heavily.

"Gerry Henderson. Tony Charles. Eric Shillingford. Marcus Brampton. Josette Estrado. Mathew Lawrence. Maureen Mark." On and on, Veritas goes down the list in his hand. I remain somewhat hopeful, since he wasn't calling the names in any particular order.

The front row is emptied, almost. Now the mid-section of the classroom is thinning out. Students sat, usually, in order of seriousness. The brainy acts, teacher's pets and those who wore glasses sat up front. The muscle bound guys, with bracelets on their wrists, or razors in their desks and near empty rolled-up exercise books in their back pockets, sat at the back. Now and again, I had played at being a back bencher.

But word had got home about it and I had tasted a piece of my father's leather belt. Now, I was a confirmed middle of the class jockey.

As my panic grows I wonder why my name hasn't been called. Yes, I was poor in math. But in English, English composition, dictation, geography and history I was no pap. Hell! I was constantly engrossed in reading Marvel comics -- *Spiderman*, *Submariner*, or Fleet Street staples like *Lion*, *Valiant*, *Tiger*, *Commandos*. Such reading caused language skill and composition to rub off, or so I argued to my mother who often times grabbed comics from my hand.

"Do your homework boy! Do your homework!' she would say. "All this comic business will turn you into a dunce!"

But I read well. Otherwise, I was a lousy student. In fact, I had a deathly fear about being sent to a narrow room that lay at the end of one side of the building. That room was crammed tight with broken desks, boxes of disused books and blackboards with missing parts. It was a storeroom, really. But it had been serving a dual purpose for some time. It was called: Special. The people who were sent to Special had been given up on. They were the perpetually truant and what we called dunce cats. Once, I had been sent to sit in Special for one day. My name had been put down as a "talker" in class. Veritas wanted to make a point, so he had sent me to Special. That day the occupants of Special were doing their times tables; five times five is twenty five and that sort of exact science. A couple guys had even been caught at the dreadful crossroads of the exact order of the letters that came after L,M,N,O,P in their recitation of the alphabet. They had fumbled, lost their way. Enraged, the teacher had gone whip crazy on their cowering backs. I knew my stuff and wasn't part of that crew, but I had been a keen observer of the event and the message had sunk in, deep. Frightful, I had sworn never to sink so low as to be sent to Special again. Now, I wasn't sure that I had kept my promise to myself.

"Veritas is a real..." I was about to mutter something bad about the sparse teacher who holds forth, up front, as my anxiety builds.

Ah! It comes to me. Not too long ago, there had been one of the traditional Friday afternoon school ground fights. Friday was the best day to pick a fight. With the weekend, the teachers usually forgot about it by the time Monday rolled around.

On that Friday two muscular backbenchers had gotten into it. A pall of dust rose over the Goodwill School savannah as the mob of students egged on the two combatants who were wrestling on the parched grass of the dry season. I was in the thick of it. Veritas had been going home in his sputtering Austin Mini when he spotted the crowd. In a fit of derring-do, he twisted his car down the rough hill toward the center of the cricket pitch to which the wrestlers had since rolled. Upon nearing the edge of the crowd, he jumped out with his whip in hand. He sprang upon the unsuspecting crowd. Their rhythmic shouts of the local fight cry, "*Higas! Higas! Higas!*" had drowned out the sound of his car's engine.

Veritas swung at the backs nearest him. Being in that group I felt the sharp sting that only a tamarind whip, seasoned in brine, can give. The damn thing felt like a swarm of bees had stung me, all at once, on my back.

I cringed and twisted out of the way. The next blow swooshed harmlessly, missing me by a mere fraction.

I felt hot under the collar. Buoyed by my seeming anonymity in the crowd, I jumped behind one of the big hairy-legged guys from seventh standard and shouted out the "Veritas Call."

Veritas,

kaka last

take a cutlass

and cut his ass!

As the alerted crowd dispersed, they took up the chant. Some fellas who were from the Roseau Boys School and just happened to be on their way home even threw some pebbles at Veritas. Nothing big enough to hurt him, just enough to damage his pride. Veritas, having broken up the fight, had retreated.

It was then, I think, he saw me. But I wasn't sure. I believed I had turned my face. Now, as I waited, my stomach churned with the thought that Veritas would keep me off his team.

"Bap!" I feel a clout at the back of my head. The blow causes my ears to ring. I spin around and rage between gritted teeth. It was Lennox Joseph. I tell him a bad word, about his mother. He tells me a bad word about my father then whispers:

"You bloke! Old V just called your name. You sitting on your ears or what?"

"Slade Thomas! I calling you, boy! Get up here!" shouts Veritas.

"Yes, yes, yes sir," I half mumble.

I am stunned. I had, almost, given up. I stumble up and edge toward the front.

Up in front, I eye the classroom. It looks different from my position. At the back, old allies like Lennox, Mano Mitchell, Peck Deschamps, and others give me the thumbs-up.

Soon, I would have to do some serious studying. I would get a new geometry set, as if that could help my lame math. Many parents would spend a small fortune for private tuition. Others would go with musty tradition and rub red lavender into their children's hair, the night before the exam. Red lavender is supposed to seep into the brains, open up its pores, make one bright. That was what many people claimed.

Now, Veritas was launching into a rousing speech. How we were the cream of his crop. That we are the most disciplined and how he is sending us forth to do battle for our school with great hope. Those who had been left behind wear masks of hurt, their eyes glass over. Some in the back row, their hands cupped under their chins in defiance, curl their lips in wry smiles. This is it! The exams were coming and I needed to open a real book for a change.

Julian's Shop

As Ma Bazelique raised the beaked vegetable oil dispenser several inches over the funnel which fed into the empty whiskey bottle and poured, the sun's rays filtering through a crack in the window behind her glanced off the viscous, golden strand of oil, where it hung lazily between the two receptacles.

Behind Ma Bazelique was a big professionally made sign, which read:

No Credit Today, Come Tomorrow.

The sign had a line down the center. On one side was the portrait of an immaculately attired fat man, a cigar in his mouth, a wad of cash in his plump hands. The caption beneath the fat man's portrait explained that he sold for cash. On the other side was a portrait of a pitiably thin man, his scrawny hands pulling at his hair, torn clothes showing his ribs, IOU's scattered on his floor, not a dollar bill in sight. The caption beneath that portrait stated that he sold on credit.

The boy studied the sign, as he always did. It was Saturday morning and ten-year-old Angus was doing groceries. Today, it was fried chicken for lunch. His chicken order was next.

"Four pounds of back and neck please," Angus asked, while placing the bottle of oil he had just received into a recycled, brown paper bag.

Ma Bazelique shambled over to the deep freezer and spoke loudly enough for him to hear.

"You mother don't tired get back and neck? Weekend, is back and neck. Easter is back and neck. August Monday is back and neck. Christmas is back and neck. Carnival, is back and neck? What legs and wings do all you?"

She grumbled about how certain families were too cheap, as she broke the five-pound box of chicken in half at the edge of the wooden counter. The little finger of her right hand stuck out prominently as she pried pieces of the chicken from a frozen tangle and dropped some parts onto one of the copper plates that make up the scale.

In the other copper plate was a four-pound weight. In the middle of the two-part scale is a sharp metal needle pointing to some mid line. When the pointer goes in the direction of your food, then you know that the weight requested has been met. Ma Bazelique coaxed the scale with her fat fingers, alternately, helping the four-pound side up, pressing down the side with the chicken, on the other.

Angus was embarrassed by the comment and lowered his eyes to where he rubbed one dusty foot against the other. It is like that when children come to these shops, he thought, shaking his head. Some of these shop owners always playing with the scale. Always criticizing people's purchases.

The moment Ma Bazelique poured the chicken parts into the bag, Angus slammed the money on the counter and dashed out.

"Dammit boy! All you children don't have any manners these days!" he heard her shout as he mounted the hill back to his home. His mother would hear about this. He was fed up with this shop.

Ma Bazelique's husband was a big clerk in the government. He made enough money doing that to support the family, but the shop was really to keep his wife busy; tie her down while he was at work. Ma Bazelique, fat as she was, was a hot woman. Everyone thought that their third child had come out too dark to have been a genuine Bazelique article.

The Bazelique's are called *pied jaune's*, descendants of French peasants who remained on the island after the British defeated the French in a battle for colonial possession over a century and a half earlier. They had intermarried with descendants of Africans and Caribs, but their French roots still showed in their light complexion and, sometimes, pale blue, gray or green eyes. Ma Bazelique knew everybody business and always wanted to push more expensive Libby's corned beef on customers when is sardine they could afford. Sometimes, if they didn't buy what she suggested, she would dump the groceries on the counter, in a huff.

When things were slow she would lean over the counter and chat up some driver, or the postman, who usually stopped in for a quick bread and cheese or bread and sausage. If she had no customers, she would break open a pack of biscuits and grab a bottle of coke. She would jump from that, to a bottle of malt, along with a thick chunk of ham and bread. Simply, she grazed off her stock and gazed at traffic on the road until someone came in. If she felt particularly bored, she would open a pack of 555 cigarettes and puff away with exaggerated style.

As he hurried up the street, Angus saw Mr. Julian walking into his little shop down the way. He knew Julian and was anxious to give his shop a try.

Before Julian owned a shop, he had always asked Angus about how he was doing at school; always encouraged him to become a lawyer or doctor. Julian had been a bulldozer driver who got injured when his machine tumbled down a precipice after a landslide. Lucky to survive, he had been unable to return to operating a bulldozer. But Julian had a determined wife who strutted around and commanded like a man.   They quickly put Julian's savings and disability payment into a shop and started doing business.

At first, Julian's shop was a little nook under a big step. But he kept a tight hold on things and drove around in a broken down van. He gave credit and sold rum and soft drinks to the truck drivers, road workers and other people who had known him from his bulldozer operator days. Before long he had made some stools himself and placed a fan on his counter. He also erected a plywood partition to separate the area where grizzled men had strong drink, from the counter where other shoppers bought groceries.

For the fellas who couldn't afford to pay for their drinks right away, he kept a Canpad exercise book and recorded what they owed. People said that he stretched his rum with water, but he was such an accommodating man with a smiling face, that people kept coming. Last week Angus had heard that Julian had extended credit beyond the drinkers.

Shopping was mainly a thing for women. Boys were for other kinds of chores like gardening or tending livestock and parents didn't want their daughters hanging around the burly men with their rude talk at Julian's shop. But Angus liked shopping and decided to go to Julian's the next time, whether or not he had permission.

A week later, sugar and rice was needed at home and gave Angus an opportunity to try Julian's. He passed Ma Bazelique's shop straight. She saw him going by with a recycled plastic bag in his hand and knew he was going shopping. As he swung by, he held his head high. Out of the corner of his eyes he could see her glaring at him with a bull face. She saw him headed towards Julian's.

"You scamp! You going to buy flour with weevils? You going to buy rice mixed with stone? You going to buy brown sugar, with black lump of spit in it? Your mother know where you going?" Ma Bazelique had walked to the door of her shop and was shouting after the boy, her fists shaking at her side.

Angus quickened his step. Black lump of spit? His mother had warned Angus about that. She related how her grandfather who had gone to one of the more prosperous - bigger - islands to cut cane in the 1920's, recalled workmen standing on great mounds of sugar and spitting where they stood. That story had upset him much.

At church, his mother sat in the same pew with Ma Bazelique. True, she had sent him to Ma Bazelique. But, he thought his mother wouldn't mind too much, since she thought Ma Bazelique was too hoity-toity anyway. Mother had related how Ma Bazelique had sped by her on a rainy day, with an empty car. She had not even offered his mother a ride, even though they were coming from the same high mass. Yes, Ma Bazelique had a big shiny new car and she didn't even want people to look at it too hard.

As Angus entered Julian's shop he smelled onions and heard the sizzle of the frying pan.

"Good morning Mr. Julian," he said as he walked to the counter.

"Hold on a second son," shouted the shopkeeper as he poked his head from behind the plywood partition. Angus heard sounds of bustle and in a while Julian squeezed from behind the partition, wiping his hands in his apron.

"Hey, little Angus, I haven't seen you in a while. What you buying today?"

"Oh, just some sugar and rice, Mr. Julian," he said, as he looked up at the shelves.

Mr. Julian had a small place but his shelves were neatly stacked to the roof. Row upon row of one-pound brown paper bags of sugar, rice and flour lined the lower shelves. Higher up were cans of Nestle condensed milk, Grace corned beef, cans of Dancow milk, bottles of vinegar and boxes of candles. A barrel of pig snout stood in one corner, with a knife atop its shut lid. Next to it were boxes of Breeze detergent on which sat bars of Bess blue soap, arranged in the shape of a pyramid. On the floor were hundred pound bags of potatoes, onions, sugar, flour, all wedged tightly behind the counter. The rotating fan, as it came around, brought a welcomed rush of air, cooling Angus' face which was still smarting from his walk through the heat of the fierce afternoon sun.

Angus gazed at Mr. Julian's stock and thought that Ma Bazelique's shop was bare, in comparison.

As Julian stepped up to the counter and took off his soiled apron, Angus inquired, "Mr. Julian, you know I don't come here... this is my first time," he hesitated. "Make sure my sugar have no spit-lump in it. And my rice, check it for stones, okay?"

Julian, both hands on his counter, smiled at the boy, while shaking his head with regret.

"What happen to you son? Where you hear that about my sugar and rice? You been listening to propaganda? Who giving my shop this *mepuis*?"

Mepuis was what Julian had been getting since he opened up his shop.

They didn't tell you that I have a moose too?" Julian asked.

"No sir, I didn't hear about the moose part, but you have one? I can see it?" Angus, is hopping with excitement wanting to see.

That "moose" Julian was talking about was not the same as the four-legged mammal of northern climes. Rather, it was a mysterious part of local legend. Locals who thought that others had done too well often laid such success at the door of a moose: a mysterious little dynamo of a man spawned from a chicken egg laid at midnight and which had been held under the armpit of an obeah man from one Good Friday to the next. A moose was said to work all night and sleep all day. Allegedly a producer of great wealth, it had to be fed a lot of meat with pepper. If it ever got angry it could kill its owner, burn his store, jumble the numbers in his ledger, piss in his cask of rum, abuse his wife and scold his children. It had been said that if the owner of an angry moose had his shop near the beach, it could raise a big wave and flood the place. Many shopkeepers' wives who were too ashamed to admit that their husbands had heavy hands would blame bruises about their faces on an errant moose. People who failed in business were said to have fallen out of favor with their moose. Neighborhood know-it-alls would claim that some businessmen who burnt their shops to collect insurance sometimes were, really, the victims of a rebellious moose.

"No son. I don't have a moose. Our people believe in too much damn stupidness," he said with a sigh, swiping at a fly with his apron. Angus stared at a centipede like scar on the shining black skin of Julian's forehead and listened.

"You see son, I don't have a big new car. I don't waste my money on flashy clothes, gold teeth where I don't need it, big gold chain, running the street, drinking too much beers, that kind of thing. I don't gossip. I treat everybody fair. I give a little credit here and there, that's how I keep my money, that's how I get business."

This didn't sound too exciting to Angus.

"About the rice, I selling it as we get it from Guyana. Same thing with the sugar from Trinidad. Is the same sugar and rice Ma Bazelique have. Is the same as the Syrians have in town. I don't add nothing to it," he went on. In referring to Syrians he used the name that islanders called all traders of Arab origin.

"You know what, I'll bag some rice fresh for you, so you could see for yourself," Julian took a scoop and bent towards the open mouth of a bag of rice. He dug in and started filling a one pound bag he held in his other hand. It was not a busy afternoon and Angus followed Julian's every move. As he bagged the rice, weighed it and then closed the top off, Julian kept talking:

"But Dominicans like crabs in a barrel. They see one of theirs trying to crawl up, they do their best to drag him down! They never stop going to the Syrian because he have spit-lump in sugar or because they believe he have a moose. But, when is their people? Boy, we catching hell!"

Julian slammed his open palm down on the counter in disgust, jolting Angus upright and shaking the big jar that held the Extra-Strong brand of peppermint candy. Quickly, Julian dug his hand into the wide mouth of the candy bottle.

"Don't 'fraid boy, have an Extra Strong," Julian's smile and the Extra Strong candy in his open palm, reassured Angus.

"You see, what you have to do is invest in your business and not spend money wildly son. When you grow up, remember that. You know what? Soon, I'm going to have a cash and carry. You wouldn't have to stay behind the counter anymore. You will be able to come in my shop, take what you want and carry it away. Hah! But you must pay first!" Julian laughed and pointed to Angus. Angus smiled at him.

"What you mean by invest?" Angus inquired.

"Well, that mean you put your money into something that can make more money for you. It mean you don't believe in waiting around for any moose to work wonders for you and all that kind of tah-la-lah! You sell a bag of sugar, you buy two. You sell two bags of sugar, you buy four, and maybe some sardines and lard. You can buy a canoe and an outboard motor too; have somebody fish for you. That's how I have the fish I was frying back in there. You want some? Want a taste?"

Before Angus could accept his offer, Julian went behind the partition and was back in a flash. He offered Angus a hot piece of fried fish and some browned onion rings on a sheet of wax paper. He pulled a small loaf called a penny-bread out of a reed basket and slaps it on the fish.

"Go on boy, eat! Is good food. I fry it myself," Julian assured Angus. "Thank you sir," Angus answers with hesitation. His mother always told him not to take food from strangers, but Mr. Julian was not quite a stranger. And Angus liked the way he felt comfortable in the shop.

"Ma Bazelique made me shame about some back and neck sir. She say is that alone I does buy. Do you eat back and neck, sir?"

"Sure I do. Chicken is chicken, me son. Is protein it have in it, the same substance as the wings and legs does have. Eat your back and neck, it will make you strong. If that's what your mother can afford, that's what she can afford. Never try to hang your hat too high, where you cannot reach. Too many black people do that and they fail in business."

Angus was munching on his fish, chewing up the head and all. He listened intently.

"Is that why black people don't own a lot of big stores?" he asked.

"That's part of it son," he answered. "But it have to do with prejudice and slavery too. For instance, just the other day a black man like me couldn't approach the bank for a loan. But the other part is that black people don't teach their children enough about business. You see Syrians and them always have their children running things in the store. Not eating up the store like mad, but working the cash register, counting money. Going to the bank for their parents. Have you ever gone to the bank son?" He looked at Angus askance.

"Yes sir! I've been there, but just with my mother. She had gone to exchange some money she got from my uncle in England." Angus was happy that he was able to show he knew something.

"But did she tell you about how the bank does work? Interest? Savings?" He pressed Angus.

"Nope! All I know was that inside the bank was cold, cold, cold and it was hot outside. When I ask my mother she tell me that it's something called air conditioning is what they had in the bank," Angus mumbled.

"That is what I mean, we don't teach our children enough about things that are important. What you know about the bank? Air conditioning!!?? Hmmph!" he sighed.

"Look, Ma Bazelique with all her *mepuis*, none of her girls work in the shop. They too fresh and don't want to talk to their own people. They run customers away. So we must learn the customer is always right. You, too, can learn. You see you, if you want to come bag sugar and flour in the afternoons, I'll pay you. You can open a little account in the credit union, save your money. Don't spend it all on cinema and popsicle. I, self, have no children. If you want to learn, I'll teach you. Ask your mother about it. You can come after you do your homework in the week and Saturday, too." With that said, Julian pushed the rice and sugar into Angus' bag. He took his money and gave him his change.

"Check it to make sure it don't have spit-lump in the sugar or stones in the rice, " Julian grinned.

"I don't listen to propaganda, sir," Angus said with a laugh, as he turned for the door.

His new job offer had Angus ecstatic. As soon as he got home, he told his mother. She hesitated a bit about it and then consented. His father thought it was a great idea.

In the days, weeks and months that followed, Angus labored hard at Julian's shop. While many of his friends ran wild in the street, Angus was earning an income. More so, he was taking notes.

One day, when business was slow, he noticed that Mr. Julian had a little trouble reading an invoice that a salesman of a new deep freezer wanted him to sign.

"Read this for me son," he said. "My eyes seem to be messing around today. I can't see this." He rubbed the centipede-like scar on his forehead with one hand and pushed the document towards Angus, with the other.

"Oh, this just say the terms, sir. Here, it say that you agree to pay $110.00 per month to Astaphan's Wholesale Warehouse until paid in full. You can just sign here."

Julian, slowly, deliberately, scrawled his name in block letters in the space provided, while Angus held the paper for him. Afterwards, Angus looked at him and wondered. He had noticed that when things were not too busy in the shop Julian looked at magazines. He always went through them real fast. "Maybe he was just looking at the pictures," Angus muttered softly.

Angus started wondering that it was perhaps for
reasons of Mr. Julian's inability to read well, that Ma Julian
always came in to do the books. As if Julian was reading his
mind, he heard him say:

"Life is full of challenges me boy and you got to stand
up to them. But it's not all 'bout book knowledge, son. Some
people gone to high school, even university, and they have no
damn common sense. They don't know how to treat people,
they can't handle money. They don't own business. My
parents couldn't afford to send me to high school. In my day,
only well-off people kids could afford to go to high school.
But I have common sense. Common sense, Angus! That's the
key: Common sense!"

Not long after Julian closed his little cubbyhole of a
shop under the big step and opened a shop in a new, two story
concrete building that had gone up in a once deserted lot at
the end of the street. The bright new sign represented the
fulfillment of a promise made years ago: Julian's Cash &
Carry. Across, the way Ma Bazelique's store had failed. A
couple years back, one of the girls had crashed the shiny new

car while coming from a club and the family had migrated to Canada, shortly thereafter.

Meanwhile, Julian still kept his little Canpad exercise book for his regulars, but now he had a new cash register and the salesman who sold it to him had taught Angus how to run it. Though he bought a new van to deliver bread from his new bakery to his customers at other shops, he still ran around in his old van.

Angus was almost through with high school; taller, with a wispy moustache showing on his upper lip. He intended to attend university and go into business for himself as Julian had encouraged. Then one day, a little after the new store had opened, a young boy of about nine years old walked in.

As Angus checked his items, the boy blurted out, "My mother say that somebody tell her that Mr. Julian pass his hand in your face. He buy you. And that's why you working for him so long. You cannot leave. Is true?"

Angus wore a wry smile, "Who's spreading this propaganda son? Did they tell you that we have stones in our rice or spit-lumps in our brown sugar too?"

"No, I didn't hear that. But I hear it, from good source, that they really turn you into a moose. And that's why you cannot run with the fellas in the street, because they *mount* you on the store. All you can do is go from home, to school, to the shop," said the boy, wide eyed.

"Don't worry about that stupidness boy! Try reading a good book! Study hard! Knock some common sense into your head! And you know, you better stop being like a crab, trying to pull your own people down!"

Chastened, the little boy grabbed his bag and looked, quizzically, at Angus' wide smile.

"And here is a lollipop son, that's on me," Angus said. "Okay," said the little boy as he reached for the candy, hesitantly.

As he tumbled out the door, he examined the lollipop, surprised. Just before he disappeared, he turned around to look at Angus and his face lit up with a smile.

Traveling to the
Castle of Papi

His wrinkled face spoke of age and wisdom. More still, my memories of his presence are serenaded by sounds of the Caribbean Sea, the gurgling embroidery of which lulled me into sleep whenever I visited Papi.

Waves crashing against the rocks which strewn the beach a spittle's throw away from the back window of my Grandfather's wood-fired kitchen with its soot stained walls. My mother's childhood home: St. Joseph, a half mile strip of clustered houses squeezed between steep hills to the east and the frothing sea's edge to its west. St. Joseph named, as with all the island parishes, after the saints in the hope that good would come of it. A small village thick with brick ovens where bread was baked every day. A place where, even in the sixties, one could find - scattered here and there - a few gray thatch roofed street side huts. In St. Joseph life continued at its predictable pace if awakening brought with it the smell of freshly baked dough hanging in the dew drop heavy air of each rooster aroused morning.

The castle of Papi was the big wooden house by the sea with the stone steps that emptied on both sides. The yard paved with balled, fist-sized, shifting rocks. The house with an unpainted interior; at the ceiling, thickly cut rafters with a rusting two-man saw fastened along one side, from end to end. The all-wood windows with stoutly cut hurricane bars. Sepia colored photographs of my uncles in faraway England in their gilded frames on a small table: one, bareback and in boxing shorts had his gloved fists raised in a guarded position; the other, bundled enough for the weather, a worldly-wise smile creasing his face beneath a dapper hat. Above the table was a well thumbed bible on a shelf next to his two felt hats. The sleek hat was for church and the weather-beaten one for when Papi worked around the house or traversed the slanting track to his garden in the hills above the village. The castle of Papi meant all this and more.

Summer! And school is out. The town is hot, noisy and parents quail at the trouble spawned by listless youth. Summer: a time to bath in the sea or river all day.

It is a time to climb up and down the rusting deck of the beached oil tanker *Amelia* at Fond Cole bay, from which we would sometimes cast a fishing line in the hope of reeling in some sprats. The small sprats would be good base for a fish stew when pots and food could be pilfered from our unknowing parents.

Summer, a time to idle. Maybe, shoot air pellets into neighborhood cats? Better still, climb the numerous fruit trees at the Government Stock Farm up the hill, without permission. Beware the locks men, misty eyed with heady weed and rousing talk, our parents warned.

To keep busy we build tree houses, grow interested in girls. Or, congregate on the rough stumps of neighborhood trees, devouring mangos, oranges, grapefruit; our tongues blazing with rude talk of come-come-quickly manhood. Maybe, kick around grand ideas, while we scatter the assorted fruit peel piled at our bare feet. Restless, we would sit under the shade of the tamarind tree near the road and tease passerbys, hooting and hollering about those who were too fat or too thin, those who were too short or too tall. Argue the politics of the day, or ponder the great things in life such as:

Who's the best guitarist? Jimi Hendrix!

Who's the best boxer? Mohammed Ali!

Who's the best drummer? Buddy Miles!

Who's the best calypsonian? The Mighty Sparrow!

Who's the best footballer? Pele!

Who's the best cricketer? Sir Garfield Sobers!

Who's the best trumpet player? Louis Armstrong!

Fettered by our limited lives we wore the "best" of our kind on the lapels of our consciousness. Having the "best" be part of us, if only at a distance, signaled an early sense of arrival and belonging and such was pleasing. So we were into all that meaty substance while grown folk, on their way to work, would cast disparaging glances our way and call us the field hands of "Idle Hall Estate."

Escape from the noise and mischief of the city meant only one destination for me: A trip to see Papi.

The first year that I retained a memory of being sent alone, my mother sewed me a cloth bag with lots of pockets, secret hiding places, and a shoulder strap. I piled in some clothes, a limp toothbrush and Lux soap. A half-empty-borrowed-without-permission Dryad under arm roller deodorant. And some of my older brothers Old Spice, to insist on my "big city" ways. Then, hot, freshly baked city bread, wrapped in brown "paper-bag" paper. Some Tip-Top cheese, couple cans of sardines, a salami sausage roll. But, my mother had me repack this thing. First, before everything else, my church clothes--with pointed shoes must go in. No wrinkles must come that way. Then, I must repack the perishables on top. In the side pockets, glossy comics by *Marvel: The Mighty Thor*, *Fantastic Four*, *Submariner*, *Red Skull* and *Iron Man*, to impress my village cousins. Maybe a couple *Commando* comics too. And a four-cube pack of Max chewing gum, to keep my mouth busy. I couldn't speak much Creole. So, I would read my comics, chew and listen. Maybe I could improve on my city-bred Creole starved tongue.

A quick cheerio to laughing brothers and sisters who teased of jumbies, and the dark country nights, forbidding. They can't all come to Papi's because there are cousins there too and I will share the floor with them, wrapped in bedding. This is my first trip away from home, alone.

They will be happy to be rid of me, I thought. More space in the house. Now, a quick dash past the fire brigade to see daddy.

"Daddy I'm going to the country!"

I would shout before I got close. The other firemen would hear. Sagging under my shoulder bag, I flash a smile to all and wait around. Maybe daddy could dig into his pockets for a fifty cents piece. Big money in those days. Big money, especially in the country. With results, I begged excuse. I jingled the silver in my pocket. Bye, bye again. I must go to the truck stop now.

I was on my way. My mother had put me aboard one of the old lumbering British Bedfords. The trucks were made of imported frame and engine with cabs crafted out of local hardwood secured, sometimes tenuously, atop their creaking factory-made metal chassis. Handled with love by their owners who had to coax them up and down precarious places, the trucks had their own names, like people: *Lily of the Valley, Christ is Lord, Rocket, Abide with Me, Pay me or Vex With Me, Hold Tight, Who Die Must Bury.*

It is aboard the truck called *Hold Tight* that I made one such trip. A lumbering creature, it would carry little me: a reserved self atop tiny buttocks squashed between the ample rearguards of hardy women, who smelled different from city women and spoke differently too. Rocking from side to side on smoothed hard board seats, the creature of wood and metal had me well caged. Caged, as it careened round the deep corners of my island home's roads. Now and again, an unsold grapefruit, coconut or dasheen escaped its bag at the rear of the truck, to slide, aimlessly, around or under my dangling feet. Sometimes, with the mischievous delight of a new wonder, my face would go caroming into the bosom or belly of the two market ladies who were my seatmates with every violent, jarring turn of the truck.

Along the way, I smiled at how the people of Massacre and Mahaut village would scatter from their curb side seats. They never seemed to tire of chancing their lives by squatting at curbside, near the trucks huge roaring wheels.

Nearer Tareau and the Leper Home, my eyes darted from the stark cliff face to my right, and the gently, inviting, Caribbean Sea, a couple hundred yards down a precipice on my left. No chance for an error, in those twist and turns. No second chance. But then, by the time the flatlands of the Layou Estate and its ranks of coconut trees filed by, I was asleep. Only a ruffle at an ever awake sense would rouse me.

Such a ruffle would come, borne on the graceful wings of an aroma. It was an aroma of earth, wreathed in the fresh bouquet of a sea shore's breath. Perhaps, wood smoke wafting above the choir of village voices and noises is what did it. Not much metallic clang and beeping horns here. More the soothing gentility of unshod feet, flop, flopping on earthen paths, alongside the narrow streets. It was out-of-school fellas like me running alongside the truck. Quickly, now and again, they were trying to hitch a ride to nowhere by swinging themselves aboard the truck's tail-gate. They would suddenly let go and disappear in plumes of dust when the tailboard boy who collected fares, would make a lash at them with some gnarled stick.

Meanwhile, the press of street side chatter was seeping into the passenger box. Or, more stirring, the smell of rich cask rum escaping through the doorway of a rum shop was wagging a finger near my nose. Urging me...wake up!

But, in the box of the truck I tarry with sleep; head lolling against the big bosom villager to my left who my mother had told to cast an eye on me. Out of half closed eyes, I saw a thin line glisten from my puckered lips, drooling onto my lap. Soon, my senses would be stirred into more acute receptivity by the difference of arrival. The gears would down-shift, a distinctly different, lower, less hurried, mechanical whir. Soon would come more, abbreviated, stops. Folks would be unloading. Passengers began shifting in their seats. The chain reaction jostled me, ever so gently.

Touching on my ears and nose, before my eyes caught sight of a village framed by a sunset... a sensation of far away.

As little as I was, down the street is far away. Especially on an island where one grew up in miniature. The awesome depth and spread of distance, as exaggerated by youth beckoned. Sought to spring my dozing mind from rest.

Before I caught sight of the village, with its Catholic Church steeple and tin roofed, multicolored houses scrambling up the hillsides, I would catch that smell of the country. It's not a smell that one can ever capture and secret away in some bottle. Rather, it was a bashful freshness that had one giddy in its difference, its presence. An arrival at purity, perhaps? Then, I would feel the lightheadedness of a small place, which to me was always new. It was there. It was then. It was how the fragrances of Papi's came to greet me. And that, long before I heard his voice, saw his stooped outline at the top of the steps, or felt the pin-pricks of his grizzled face upon my cheeks as he hugged me a tight welcome.

Going to See Fire

Rosa had been having bad luck. First, she had failed the Common Entrance Exam last year. She had come out dead last on the list of those who had taken that all-so-important test. Disgusted, her mother had placed her in the typing section at The Christian Musical Class.

Like so many parents on the island, she thought the regimentation at Christian's would thwart her daughter's errant ways. But, now, even stern Mr. Christian had sent her home. He had asked Rosa to explain a bulge in her white shirt for two weeks straight. When Rosa's explanations changed from "indigestion," to "gas," to " I'm bloated from gas," to "I don't know, Sir," he had sent her home. Later that day, he called Ma Paris and explained that her daughter couldn't come back, as he believed she was pregnant.

He was right, Rosa was big pregnant. A street character by the name of Simbot had observed Rosa and told some schoolchildren next to The Christian Musical Class that

Rosa had been given, "*An everlasting stay-home dumpling in her female sector.*"

Simbot used big words. People said that he had been a famous head teacher but he had made the mistake of taking his whip to the buttocks of an obeah man's dense son. The obeah man had made a special trip to Haiti to "fix" Simbot. From that time, Simbot started drinking harsh cask rum, the kind of rum that frothed and hissed at the slightest disturbance. Simbot had gone mad with verbal diarrhea and lost his job in the civil service. But he still retained the smarts to comment on school children whom he noticed "slipping."

Soon, Rosa's mother found that her daughter had skillfully suppressed her expansion by binding her waist with bandages out of the first aid kit she still kept from her Junior Red Cross Society days. Rosa was a good girl in those days. But Rosa had, since, left the Brownie and Junior Red Cross Society days behind to roam the National Botanical Gardens after school. People said that she saw different guys from the high schools in town. Neighborhood wags had told her mother how someone had seen Rosa laying underneath a boy on a bench at the Gardens. Someone else said, that a good "source" had seen Rosa bathing at Silver Lake at high noon, and that a man was swimming around her legs and Rosa was only beating the water, laughing. All that time when she was supposed to be at typing class. But whomever brought such news to Ma Paris got a tongue-lashing. Meanwhile in her neighborhood of Leblance Lane, fellas would watch Rosa as she wagged her behind down the road and call out: "Rosa, force ripe!"

Ma Paris kept up a defiant front. She was a strong portal of the Roman Catholic Church. She firmly believed in taking everything to the Lord in prayer. She had tried to eke out information from Rosa as to where she had gotten this "everlasting gas" from, but Rosa remained tight-lipped.

One Sunday morning, after church, a prayer group from the St. Alphonsus Catholic Church accosted Ma Paris. They offered her prayers in her time of troubles. One of them promised to do a pilgrimage to the saint at La Salette for her. But Ma Paris puffed her chest and walked off in a huff.

"Not my Rosa!" She said. "All you think my daughter just like all you children who does roll themselves all over the place? No way! My daughter is class!"

But the reality of baby was approaching and no man had presented himself as the father yet, not even in the discrete preserve of an evening.

It was common for parents of means to ship children like Rosa away to the Virgin Islands, England, Canada. Some distant place where Ma Paris' child could escape the cruel scrutiny, slicing gossip and preying eyes which was closing in on her life like the thick prickle bush of the gluglu tree.

But things had tightened up, money and all. Ma Paris' husband had gone to New York, ten years now. People said that he had gotten married to a Yankee woman for papers and had forgotten his family. With her father absent, Rosa had grown hard of hearing. She had written letter after letter, hoping that her father would file papers for her. Frustrated, and now that she was wearing the same panty size as her mother, Rosa wouldn't take any correction. She was full of backchat.

To all of that, Ma Paris' younger brother had a theory. His name was Royo and he had gone to high school and had obtained a couple Cambridge, General Certificate of Education 'O' Level subjects. Between playing cricket and working as a customs clerk he read widely and had a penchant for doing analysis of why people were thinking of what they were thinking. Over a bakes and saltfish breakfast one Saturday morning he had told Ma Paris that Rosa had had a negative over-reaction to her father's inability to send for her. He had gone on to explain:

"You see, them kids like Rosa so, they living in America mentally, even though they in Dominica physically."

Ma Paris had only glowered at her younger brother and sucked her teeth, digging into the saltfish and cucumber dish before her. Her brother had kept at it.

"I know what I talking about Sis, all these girls and them looking at soap operas, even blue movies and thing... they not satisfied with what you and I used to like. In our day, a little cinema on a Sunday afternoon, some coconut ice cream, a snow cone now and again and we happy. Maybe, on a weekend we hit the beach and so on. Come Christmas, we get a new shoe at Bata and a cork gun or a doll by Fair Deal. The old queen would fix us some ginger beer or sorrel and we cool. But not these children. They want to move fast and live that big city lifestyle. All they want to eat is hamburgers and french fries night and day, chase it with all kinds of Sprite and

Pepsi, and play videos when their head should be in a book. And, if you don't look sharp, they get themselves in big people business too fast. I bet you her friends and them troubling her, because so long her father gone and he don't send for her yet. That breeds a resentment complexity in the girl's mentality!" With that said, Royo had grabbed the hot pepper bottle and shook some of its contents over his meal.

"So you is a brain doctor now, eh? Which medical school give you the psychology degree you believe you have? Boy, you reading too much damn big books! Just eat your saltfish and be thankful that I invited you here this morning. You know all those woman you have, none of them can cook," Ma Paris said, trying to get Royo off the subject.

"You talking about all the woman I running, but that's not the point. I trying to get you to analyze the situation," responded Royo, but Ma Paris interrupted him before he could finish.

"Is a good licking I don't give her for a long time, is why she behaving so slack. One of these days I giving her one thump when I catch her giving me backchat, she'll wonder where my hand come out!" Ma Paris' eyes were blazing as she looked towards the shut door of Rosa's bedroom from

behind which loud dance hall reggae music could be heard
blaring.

"Peace, sister! Peace! Don't be hasty, talk to the child,
make sure she focus on what is realistic." Royo's voice had
trailed off, as he shook his head. He had decided to end the
conversation before his sister exploded, as she had the last
time when he focused on her own loneliness. He had told her
that she suffered from "a denial complex based on the
delusion that her dashing Don Juan would return." That time
she had dashed a cup of water in his face. From now on, Royo
figured that he would keep his own counsel on what ailed
Rosa.

Meanwhile, in the neighborhood, people were
watching and waiting for the next move. It was then that Ma
Paris abandoned the high road. She decided to see Fire.

Fire was a middle-aged man with red eyes and
graying temples. He was black and stout. No one was sure
where he came from. Some said he was from Cayenne.
Others said he was from Martinique and had married a
Dominican huckster who sold vegetables to the French

islands. His wife was hardly ever home as her trading took her away often.

"Allo? What can I do for you?" said Fire, as he spotted Rosa and her daughter entering his yard. Only the "allo", instead of "hello" sounded French.

"Well... Mr. Fire, I need your help. You see... I have a problem. I think someone spoiled my child." Ma Paris was nervous and rubbed her hands in front of her lips as if guarding her words.

She held a clerk job for the city council and was a respectable enough lady. She felt embarrassed standing in Fire's hard scrabble dirt yard. It was in a poorer part of town from where she lived and she didn't want people to recognize her. For that reason she had a scarf which covered her head and was tied beneath her chin. As she looked around, a little breeze from the mountains jangled some tin ornaments of the horoscope hung off a red cord stretched across the yard.

Rosa hung behind her mother. She smiled coyly at Fire and rolled her eyes upward, whenever he turned his piercing red eyes at her. She surveyed the place and wondered how come it could look so meager if this "Fire" was any good at doing obeah.

"How you think they spoil her?" Fire asked.

"Well... I have been having strange dreams. Nine months ago, I killed a big bat on my front step. Not too long before, I believe someone may have put some foot powder near my back door... and you know, Rosa, my daughter here... since those things happen... she wouldn't listen to me! She gone wild!" Ma Paris looked at Rosa.

Rosa pouted her lips and looked down at the red nail polish on her big toes that stuck out the front of her black patent leather sandals. Her remaining toenails were painted yellow and green, but they were hidden under the sandal straps so her mother didn't know how psychedelic she was.

"Hmmph!" said Fire. "It looks like you have some enemies. I could look for you. I could find out who put a bad spirit on you or your child. That will cost you fifty dollars."

"That's fine," said Ma Paris.

She fished around in her purse. She seemed to have trouble finding the right amount of money. She whispered in

Rosa's ear. Rosa stuck her hand into her skirt pocket and took out a green bill. Not too long ago her father had sent her a birthday card with twenty U.S. dollars enclosed. She handed it to her mother.

"This is what I have," said Ma Paris as she held the bill forward. "Will you accept it? You don't need to give me change. I appreciate whatever you can do. You can hold the rest as a tip."

"You must give it to me in your left hand. And turn your eyes to the East. All wise men come from the East," Fire said. Ma Paris went through the paces as she was told and handed him the money.

When she looked back in Fire's direction he was gone. She had not even seen his departure out of the corner of her eyes. Soon he returned from the modest concrete square that was his house. He held a large piece of broken mirror between both hands. It had a black ribbon tied across it. He placed it on a cleared spot on the dirt and drew a ragged circle around where he stood with a crooked stick. He started to hum something unintelligible and stared hard at the mirror.

Rosa clutched at her mother's arm and peered at the mirror. Ma Paris looked too.

"Shut your eyes! You mustn't look. Depending on what you see it can blind you," Fire said. "In fact, you must step back a bit. If you not careful, when you looking for the person they could see you too. You can't be too near this. Some of these spirits real wicked, they can spit in your eyes and blind you. Sit on this bench over there." Fire pointed to a rickety looking bench in the corner of the yard. As Rosa followed her mother, Fire gauged the bulging outline of her blouse.

Mother and daughter hunched close to each other, closer than they had been in months. They shut their eyes as Fire had instructed.

In their shared darkness, mother and daughter heard Fire clap. He sang lustily for a while. Stamped his feet a couple times and then stopped. "Open sesame now. You may see," Fire said.

"What's that got to do with anything? Isn't that from a fairy tale? This sesame stuff?" Rosa whispered to her mother. She sounded skeptical. Sarcastic.

"Hush child! You hear you already? Your mouth always going further than your eyes can see. Look and listen! Look and learn!" Ma Paris said gravely.

"But Ma... the man didn't let us look..." Rosa said.

Fire stared at the mother and daughter as they went at each other.

"Oh spirits! Spirits running mad over your child Ma Paris. It have one, it looked really rude. It is a spirit of disobedience. It will cause Rosa to give you plenty backchat. But, when she do that, just slap on the left side of her face. But make sure you rub Alcolado or Limacol in your hand first. You must do that because your hands need cleansing. Someone dirty your hands too. Just slap her face though, don't touch her on the stomach. It look, it look... it look like your daughter.... she maybe in child or putting on too much weight. A bad spirit must have laid upon Rosa... That's why she spoil so." As Fire spoke, he looked serious and stared hard at Rosa with his red eyes.

"Also, there is a spirit of... of... travel. It is a bad spirit too, but it has good in it. Now and again you may get money from it. But don't depend on it because you could get disappointed. I..., I..., I also hear a baby crying. It mean Rosa need help." Fire was sweating.

"Yes..., yes Mr. Fire. That's what I really want to know, who give Rosa that belly, eh? Who is the father.., who is the father, eh?" Ma Paris was wringing her hands. She was trying to get to the bottom of the real purpose of her visit.

"Well... that would cost you some more money. I didn't look for that. I was more looking for things that spoil her, spoil her self, self, self! To get a particular person... I need more time. Especially where young people involve... it really...really... mess up. With young people... the spirits faces aren't really formed too well yet. Sometimes the spirit does hide its face so bad, I can't make it out. So I can't guarantee I will give you a name, but I will try." Fire was looking directly at Ma Paris' purse.

Ma Paris opened the purse and scrounged around some more. She came up with her fist clutching a crumple of red and green bills.

"It look like I have around twenty three dollars. Take it. It's all I have," said Ma Paris.

"I need a round number... something like twenty four. I will take coins too…" said Fire.

Ma Paris turned her purse upside down and poured some loose change into the palm of her hand. She handed it to Fire without counting. Rosa was increasingly irritable. She was watching her mother like a hawk, her mouth growing longer by the moment.

"Ma let us go…. since I come in this yard the fowl shit upsetting me," Rosa grumbled.

Fire did have loose yard fowl. Their droppings were all over the place and a scrawny rooster was kicking up dirt on the mirror.

"It getting a message... it getting a message. When it like that, I could see a face real good." Fire was looking at the rooster and weaving its dirt kicking into the scheme of things.

Right at that moment Rosa gagged and threw up. She screamed and clutched her stomach.

"My dou dou! Baby what happening to you?" Screamed Ma Paris. "The spirit is moving!" shouted Fire as he picked up a maracas in each hand and shook it to the heavens.

"Water! Water!" shouted Rosa. "I need water!"

Rosa's hands were now grabbing beneath her skirt, as she fell back on the bench. Ma Paris rushed to her side and hoisted the skirt, which had a spreading, wet blotch.

"Lordy! Lordy! Lordy! Is so you doing me Rosa? Is so you doing me? Is the baby that coming child! I didn't know you were so close. Fire, get us water!"

Ma Paris was beside herself. Just imagine! A good respectable church lady like her to have her first grandchild delivered in an obeah man's yard. "What would Father Felix and the ladies at the Legion of Mary say about that?" she thought.

Meanwhile, Fire had gone into his house. He returned with a white enamel basin filled with water and a towel. Dark circles were visible beneath the water surface from where dings had caused the enamel to flake off. He stood by, hopelessly.

Ma Paris had been in the Red Cross too. It was through her Rosa had joined the Junior Red Cross Society. Her training now came in handy.

A tiny voice pierced the air as Ma Paris, gingerly, extricated a squirming baby from between Rosa's legs. The sun still shone in the Western sky, bright enough to shine upon the baby's face. Fire pushed his face close, and narrowed his red eyes at the baby.

"The baby father, he dark, dark, but not real dark. Sometime, he could be light skin too. You know, life is funny. That could change. But... but, but by the hair... let me tell you. It look sort of fine... real fine. Like the father have Carib in him. But we have to wait and see... it could turn kinky too." Fire stood up and folded his arms.

Ma Paris looked to the heavens as she clasped the baby to her breast, shouting, "Holy Mary, Mother of God, pray for us sinners." She smothered the baby with kisses and bent over to Rosa, kissing her on the forehead for the first time in years.

"Don't worry child, we'll make it. You just need to listen to me when I talk to you. Let's go home," Ma Paris said, cuddling the baby in a towel as she busied herself in the direction of Fire's gate.

Exhausted, somewhat relieved, Rosa glared at Fire and sucked her teeth in disgust.

"I wish I could get my twenty dollars back," she muttered.

When Goodfoot
Was In Style

G oodfoot was a dance. It came right after the moonwalk. The moonwalk came right after Armstrong, Collins and Aldrin had landed on the moon, and my entire family had gone outside to look at the full moon to see if we could see anything walking up there. The moonwalk was a dance, where the dancer pretended he was in a world of zero gravity. Floating arms, moving with self imposed lethargy. It took a lot of sweat to mimic human movement in zero gravity. Especially, when wearing tight bell bottom jeans, made tighter by a thick wood handled Afro pick made of bicycle wheel spokes in ones back pocket.

When carnival and calypso wasn't rocking the place, popular music was mostly courtesy of: The Jackson Five, The Beatles, Donna Summer, Sly and the Family Stone, Osi Bisa, Led Zeppelin, Three Dog Night, Isaac Hayes, Billy Joel, Neil Diamond, Paul Anka, and James Brown. Otis Redding had his famous song about "...the bay," Diana Ross had The

Supremes, Gladys Knight had The Pips and the radio on Sundays had oldies but goodies, mostly overseas tunes.

The social culture was influenced by relatives and friends come visiting from up North, yanking. Or visitors with acquired British accents worn with: ankle-length boots, tight jeans, faded jeans, hole-in-the-bottoms-jeans, tie-dye t-shirts, mini-skirts with fancy studded shiny buckled belts, beads around visiting necks, gold rimmed sunshades and Afro-shirts. Plus, Chiclets to chew. This was a time of fusion kingdom come. An intermingling of local and foreign, which led to a profusion of local sound and new dance. Deep from the forested recesses of the thickly wooded island flared new talent, like a blazing hibiscus hedge at full rush.

Local bands proliferate, with daring names: Vibrators, Exile One, Gaylords Power Union, Swinging Stars, Family Reunion, Belles Combo, Black Affairs, De Boys and Dem, Midnight Groovers, Every Mothers Child and Wafrikai. This time, everything done make a big callaloo soup: calypso, rock, pop, rhythm and blues, jazz, salsa, nascent reggae and our very own cadance-lypso all bubbled around in close proximity. And in the midst of that the city suburb of Newtown hosted a Woodstock look-a-like called Harlem. For three days and three nights non-stop music blasted from the stage of the "Harlem" until some participants fell asleep on the savanna under the stars. It was then that The Goodfoot landed.

To do The Goodfoot, you jumped from side to side, one foot at a time touching the ground. Knees were to be arched at waist level and hands had to be clasped together, straight down, as if to protect the crotch.

It was still a decent country of nuns like Sister Borgia who walked in the hot, hot sun in full black habit - cape and all. Portly acolytes still swung incense-puffing metal balls at the end of chains, which breathed sweet images of heaven into the nostrils of pious parishioners at Sunday mass. It was still a place where, at night, rotund preacher men sallied forth. With sweaty faces glistening by light of hurricane lamp or blazing flambeau, they would scare attentive crowds about the blazing hell that awaited those with hellish ways.

Hellish or not, one had to be at a dance to do The Goodfoot. Clubs like The Cave, Manicou, Like-A-Fete Discotheque, or Palm Grove were late night affairs for big fellas. A little guy like me couldn't make the grade. I had tried and failed.

Once, I followed some fellas to Palm Grove. It was located in the Roseau River Valley. First, the late night winds swooshed from the darkened hills and chilled me, raising goose bumps on my skin. Little lights glinted ominously out of the forest that swaddled the club and did somersaults in the air, which were quite suspect. What I thought were the farts, belches, and whining of frogs, snakes, crickets, beetles, bush pigs, wild goats, and other nocturnal forest life gave off a cacophony which as-if wanted to drown out the music which wafted out from the band. All that time I couldn't go in. So, I hung around the entrance like some street boy, my face hidden beneath a big collar so no one could recognize me.

Overhead, the swaying palm and bamboo grove within which the club resided, groaned like a group of ample men collectively passing wind in a dark place. It was as if a strange darkness was grabbing at me. Suddenly, out of the corner of an eye, I thought I had seen a monster of a guy coming from behind me, shaking a stick in one hand. The shadow hovered, as I cringed. Thankfully, it turned out to be the exaggerated reflection of a sweating goodfooter who had just gone behind the club to catch some fresh air and ease of some piss. At that point, I was glad to run all the way home.

Clearly, at my stage, it was first communion or confirmation parties that would provide a stage. Maybe a school dance, if I could sneak in behind one of my bigger brothers. But, really, I wanted to do The Goodfoot with Portia who lived next door.

Portia lived across the street, a little down the way from my house. Her house was painted pink, with brown colored eaves. It sat at the foot of an incline, with a concrete porch that stood twelve feet off the road. Behind the incline, sat our island's solid blue-green mountains and a mostly blue sky. Below the brightly painted porch was the dark maw of a garage filled to overflowing with disemboweled British trucks and other mechanical bric-a-brac. Her father, Mr. Prentice, was a superb mechanic. A man who would hoist a foot on a bumper, reflect on the entrails of a recalcitrant engine and then attack it methodically; breathing life into it with his every finesse of a spanner or screwdriver. Her mother, a secretary, flitted in and out. A very social lady, with a round brown face, she kept Portia and her other brothers and sisters on a tight leash.

My house was pink with green eaves. Pink was in - at least in the 1970's when the concrete bungalows in my neighborhood were built. However, the house lay on the lower side of the road. We had a porch, but it mostly went unused. At my house we were always busy about school, the garden, the yard fowls, the yard pigs. Slop collection. Slop disposition. Go water the cattle. Bring them feed. Go to the garden; pick up provisions. But, that was before The Goodfoot put other things on my mind.

I started hanging out with partners down the street. I.P., Bentlee, Maurison, Baba, Clem, Hillery, Dave, Reid, Lennox, guys who could hold forth on issues of what was in and what was out. Talking of consciousness, our place in the world. Trading in our given names for that which seemed African: Ibu, Balawa, Pompees, Bubuus, and Momo. Tillee and Guinea Bissau. Now and again, I would try to bust in on the conversation with some war comic story or shout out some war comic German like *"Achtung! Himmel! Vowarts mein kameraden! Schnell, schnell, fraulein!"* Before the rise of our male hormones, that used to be cool. But, increasingly, the fellas would shake their heads, laugh and change the subject. I needed to change my comic-book focus and deal with pressing issues, I thought.

At Lennox's home the guys reigned supreme, as their parents never seemed to mind the ruckus of high philosophy and competing voices of teenagers. An Aiwa record player played coming music such as by Exile One and Bob Marley's and the Wailers. With our backs hardening under the onward march of biology the talk, more and more, shifted to girls. Talk of how one had to say it, when one wanted to say he wanted some and that type of thing.

In our shorts and cut-off jeans, we would prance some steps and try to be slick. Neighborhood girls didn't hang with us. So we had to try to look good in case we caught the eye of any passing schoolgirl. But I couldn't get Portia off my mind. She was quiet, looked smart and was pretty, to my mind.

Not long before, to entice the guys with my prowess, I had concocted some romantic escapades with Portia and noted them in a diary. Conveniently, I had "lost" the diary in a place where one of the guys could find it. When it was found, I protested loudly, making as if I didn't want it examined. With the inevitable examination, an uproar of teasing followed which had me glowing with feigned pride. But this creation of my daydreams left me unfulfilled. So I started plotting my real campaign.

School was from 8 a.m. to 1 p.m. In the afternoon, civil servants went back to work until 4 p.m. To those with parentless houses that meant one had three hours to get busy. At early afternoon, the sun would beat down mercilessly. The dogs would trot along the edge of the street to catch the last dregs of remaining shade. After lunch, it was somewhat like a siesta time, though most folks never really slept. It was an afternoon like that I chose to carry out my campaign.

Lunch over, I took an early bath. Lifebouy soap lather and cold water, a soothing cocoon for my feverish thoughts. Then my bath towel and a hasty wipe. Quickly now, some of my older brother's Old Spice under my beardless chin. I may just get close. You never know! My mother always said that life was full of surprises. On went my white P.E. shorts and T-shirt.

Oops! Almost forgot. I pulled up my T-shirt and pat on some Johnson's Baby Powder.

To the porch I must go. I grabbed one of the bigger books in our library: *Operation Overlord-The Allied Invasion of Normandy.* Feeling impressive, I strode onto my stage. I plumped myself on the wall of the porch, swung my feet up. I crossed my legs.

Ouch! It felt a little uncomfortable for my coming manhood. I crossed again, this time in reverse order. That was better. I flipped open to no place in the book in particular. I am facing Portia's porch. Soon she would come.

I am not disappointed. Portia walks up to the porch's wall. She does not look my way. She's making like a woman around her backside now. It's not flat anymore. It's starting to point. She rolls as she walks. She is sensual, a bit languorous. Is she bored? A slight wind ruffles her straightened hair, and she pats it down in place – absent-mindedly. Did she come out because she saw me mount my stage? I hold my head at an angle of exaggerated interest in my book, seemingly oblivious to the world.

Portia swung a leg over the wall. It was a brown leg. A leg where there was no differentiation between the portion behind the knee, down towards the heel. There was an absence of the curvature that comes with a muscled calf. That lack of a calf categorized you on such an island. Scrambling around in the streets, or up and down hills, with loads of bananas, yams, grapefruits, dasheens, plantains, or playing soccer, cricket, or netball compels calves. Maybe, carrying buckets of water from the public standpipe. But this is the leg of someone who is driven to the Convent High School in a Volvo. So, she lets her heel bump the outside of the wall with no rhythm in particular. I follow the heel up to her knees. Upward now, to her laps and the abbreviated edge of the shorts she fits. This a time of hot pants. Her hot pants put the heat in me and I feel that I raise a standard, but it's only momentary.

She now straddled the wall. The wall parted her buttocks, her back to me. I didn't want to see that. I wanted to see her face. I wanted her eyes my way, because I would soon put on some music to which I can do The Goodfoot. Ah! She turned. She was looking... but it seemed that she was gazing at some ship on the still Caribbean Sea, beyond where I sat. I turned to follow her gaze. And then I turned back.

Her eyes bored directly into mine. Her gaze seaward had been merely a diversionary tactic. Good generals use those. I was game. I connected and smile. Provocatively, she laid down on the narrow top of the porch wall. Her young breast squashing flat, her chest balancing on that edge.

"Child! You crazy!!??" I whispered.

My book is now closed on my lap. My mind raced and imagined the dramatic. Fly! Fly, I must fly! Really?

Must I fly to be there when she falls? I would do a good catch; some daring mid-flight grab as at cricket's mid-on boundary or silly mid-off. I thought of my stardom. "Boy Saves Girl In Daring Leap!" The New Chronicle headlines would blare forth my fame. I would be in. That would be cool. I would then be in control of my very own babe. Groovy man! The envy of the dudes in my lane.

I hopped off my perch. I was in and out of the drawing room in a flash. The old Panasonic was on, full blast. I caught Radio Antilles on Monsterrat in the middle of a James Brown rendition. Good timing. I had on no shoes. For this, what I was about to do, I needed none. I used my big toe to spread-out some of the talcum powder that I had- earlier - spread on the floor. I shout:

"Huh! I feel good!" I shouted. Did she hear that? That is James Brown... she must have heard something. I look at her, under eyes.

Quickly now, I pulled both my fists up to horizontal at my side, flapped them once - as I faked a funky chicken move - and got ready to blow Portia's mind. Louder then, as it must carry across the way, "HUH! I FEEEEEEL GOOD!!!"

I slid across from side to side. This was just a warm-up. I did a split. RRRRRRRRRRRRRRRRip!! There went my tight P.E. shorts. But I didn't think she could even see.

Portia's was now up, off her stomach where she had just been living dangerously. She had both feet outside the porch. Her face spoke of something funny, like... I'm not sure if it was amazement or amusement. I hopped into Goodfoot mode. Knees up. One foot down. Knees up. The other foot down. Jump from side to side. Hands clasped, down the center. Hands clasped, pressing down my excitement. An excitement which may protrude through the widening tear along the middle seam of my shorts.

Now, I am pushing some sweat. All eyes on Portia. Was I trying too hard? We would see. I smiled. Would she return it?

Lordy! Lordy! It looks like Portia was climbing back into her porch. Is this kingdom come? Was she going to sneak over and join me? It was as if we were alone in the lane. No one was home at my home, or so I thought. No one was home at hers.

Then,... no wait! Her lips curled downward. I went into slow motion, like in the pictures at the Carib cinema when the cowboys who are hit by a fusillade from John Wayne carom off a rotten saloon roof. Goodfoot up. Goodfoot down. Down with a thump! Was she saying... saying something?

"*Maco*! Yuh think I in your damn foolishness? Yuh cannot even dance!"

She had spoken loud enough to span the divide.

With that, and a long sucking of her teeth to underline her disgust, Portia retreated from the heat of the street and the unwelcome furnace of passion I had thrown her way.

Maco? Me? It hurt. It hurt like hell. To call someone maco on this island was to say that: one couldn't pitch stones well enough to down an idle pigeon at ten paces. One couldn't throw stones accurately enough to pick mangoes off a tree-without bruising the fruit into an unseemly pulp. That one couldn't, as a batsman, face a fast-paced cricket bowler galloping down with a delivery, which exceeded 75 miles per hour. That one could not climb to pick a tamarind pod, without falling off the tree. That ones ability to dribble on a soccer field was a bunch of *makakw*i. It meant that one held his hands akimbo too often, like some market woman caught in eternal gossip. Maco meant that even the pitch of ones voice was too high, suspect. To islanders, a maco was a man without manliness; one who could not run with the boys. Some weird masculine degeneration into effeminacy. To be maco was to be dismissed on all sides.

As if on cue, James Brown, was swallowed up by Big Ben's chimes and a bulletin of news from the BBC. Someone was at home after all. My older brother, Wello, came onto the porch. It was he who changed the dial.

"Man, you had the blooming radio on too loud! I was trying to get some shuteye. I've to study some "A" level chemistry tonight. You couldn't even hear me calling you?"

My head still swimming, I blurted out, "Man, I was peaceful here on the porch reading this history when Pinka's mad dog attacked me."

I was trying to pin the blame on one of my neighborhood partners, Pinka. His dog had pounced on me one dark night, a few weeks before.

"You know that mad dog of his...? The one that's blind in one eye? It got mad after someone fed it red peppers. I just had time to jump into the porch to escape! Man, as I was vaulting over, I even tear my pants. Next time I see it pass up the lane I will break a stick on its back." My explanations were jumping out my mouth in big gobs of freshly baked fairy tales.

Wello scratched his chin. He looked quizzically at the talcum powder on the porch tiles.

"So what's up with all that powder, now?"

"Oh...," I said "I just took a bath, man. I may have put on a little too much. You know, as I jump the wall there, some of it must've just shaken off me."

I glanced back at Portia's porch. It was empty of life. It was as if she had never been there, as if an afternoon of Goodfoot never happened. Behind her house, our blue green mountains and the powder blue sky looked the same. Perhaps this hurt could remain our secret. No one would know I had tried to come on and failed. Maybe, just maybe, I had another chance at a manly life yet.

❀

In A Time Of Weed

"Company !Compannnnyyy, 'tenshun!" Lieutenant Horace Richards gives the order and the Combined Drum & Bugle Corp of the high school army cadets stiffens; ramrod straight. Towards one end of the three ranks of khaki clad cadets, arrayed with their musical instruments and other martial impedimenta, are four Public Works Department dump trucks. It is a Friday afternoon, and students who returned for soccer or other extra-curricular activity mill about, gawking at the spectacle.

The lieutenant strides down the line swagger stick in hand.

"Listen up boys. Our destination is the village of LaPlaine. We are going on maneuvers with the police and defense force. Our job is to provide guard detail while the guys do their maneuvers out in the bush. Our band will provide the martial music for the church parade. Some senior government officials will take the march pass on Sunday morning. You will do your duty for God and country, understood?" Lieutenant Richard barks.

"Yes suh!" is the resounding answer.

"Company! Board in order of rank, march!" The first rank peels off into the dump trucks arrayed nearby.

The cadets gathered on the basketball court of the Dominica Grammar School are from that school and its main rival, the Roman Catholic run St. Mary's Academy. Their cadet corps are old and have a distinguished history; some members having fought and died fighting for the glory of the British Empire in World Wars I and II.

In the Grammar school's courtyard, a stark reminder of service to empire is memorialized by a squat chunk of weathered granite that bears a brass plate with the names of those who fell in the Battle of Britain and others who went to watery graves in the Battle of the Atlantic. The army cadet corp is a relic of such British military tradition. Now, it is under increasing assault as its relevance is questioned.

"Little babylonians, all you getting ready to rumble or what?" One of the upper classmen who sports some infant dreadlocks, calls out mockingly from beneath a shady flamboyant tree.

Several visiting girls from the Convent High school look at the cadets and laugh. They are clustered around several fifth formers who have woolen red, black and green tams pulled over their ears.

"Pay no attention to these weedies, gentlemen. They have nothing better to do," Lieutenant Richards assures his men.

"Shit,"Corporal Chasimuir hisses as he climbs, reluctantly, into the bed of the dumper. "I really don't feel like driving through town in this dumper. All these people looking at us funny... thinking we are babylon. We will be on big time display." Chasimuir is a fourth former and spots several of his friends among the group of spectators.

"Take it easy man, it will be fun," responds Private Registe.

"This is an opportunity to shoot some practice rounds for a change. How many of those guys over there ever shot a self loading rifle; an SLR? A sten gun? A bren? None of them. Not a one. They are bunch of lazy do-nothings, who talk a lot. Weedies. Weed heads. People like you and me will weed them out. We'll show them who is who, one day." Private Registe slaps Corporal Chasimuir on the back and reassures him.

"Yah, Registe. You talking big. You reading too many damn war comics. We are just going to guard, you hear me! Guard and then play music. If we lucky, they'll put a real rifle in the hands of some of our guards. Most likely they'll give you a baton. This is just going to be show, a show for the villagers." Chasimuir glares at Registe as he speaks. He is uncomfortable with this role.

"And you don't go around the village either, shooting off your mouth," he adds.

His response does not revel in the promise of any military grandeur this trip would bring. For people like Chasimuir, the camping, hiking, sharp-as-a-tack parades, are the reasons for the corp's existence. Self government and independence beckons and so the government had sought to insert the seed of self-reliance. Soon we would no longer be black Britishers. In the not too distant future we were expected to manage things on our island, we would be rowing our own canoe. Such led to talk of enrolling the cadets in a national service program. The idea had drawn howls of protest. The government proposal was met with a response that frowned on the idea of repairing schools and tending vegetable gardens. Many of the cadets were into the glitter of gleaming brass, fancy ribbons and other martial regalia. They thought national service not in keeping with the militaristic British lineage of the corp. All this discord, militaristic tradition aside, made Corporal Chasimuir's stomach churn at the thought of accompanying the defense force and police on weekend exercises.

The dumpers fill up and then rumble out from the basketball court area of the Grammar school. Some in the group under the flamboyant tree hoot and whistle at the departing cadets.

As the dumpers navigate the narrow intersection of the city called Four Corners, groups of locks men who loiter around that vicinity give the thumbs down and shoot the cadets poisoned looks. Most of the youngsters in the trucks remain grim.

Soon, the green countryside flashes by and a tranquility of spirit seem to settle among the men sitting and standing in the bed of the last truck; the one in which Corporal Chasimuir and Private Registe hold court.

As the truck barrels deep into the forested interior of the island, the convoy comes upon a dozen taxicabs parked along the grassy verge of the road near the Emerald Pool. The Emerald Pool is one of the choice locations for tourists visiting the island. A tight bundle of taxicab drivers form a beehive of activity around a half dozen, long-haired, back pack laden, bead-and-sandal-wearing tourists who seem intent on walking.

"Hmmp! Looks like the taximen out of luck today," reflects a cadet private as the truck whips past. "Those tourists look like a bunch of hippies anyway. They never have any money."

As the tourists and taximen recede in the distance, Private Registe grits his teeth, sputtering angrily: "Christ! Seem to be the only kind of tourists we getting these days: White dreads!"

"As my old man was telling me last night, the government needs to crack down on those dreads, man. They are killing the business. Look, the tourist ships eh coming anymore since that tourist fella Milasek got shot in '74." Registe's father ran a shop, taxi business and guesthouse. The senior Registe was also a staunch supporter of the current government.

"Yah, that's true. Them tourist not the only ones scared. Those fellas scaring people away from their gardens. My grandfather 'fraid to go into his garden. The other day, as he step behind a tree to piss, a big bongo locks man just appear. The man was looking so fierce, my grandfather almost died of fright," Lance Corporal Peterson, usually a taciturn guy, is adding his voice.

"And they thief too," chimes in Corporal Chasimuir.

"I 'fraid all you, pal," says Private Wiltshire. All you sound just like the police, man. What the hell wrong with you fellas? Just because you going to be rubbing shoulders with those guys, don't mean you have to sound like them. You mean people never use to steal in this country, before dreadlocks came in style? If anybody steal in a garden these days, everybody blaming dreads. That not fair, man. In everything it have in creation, you find good and bad. Don't forget, the police and them do wrong too, you know. Just the other day I see a policeman break a baton on a dread's head. It knock him out. The man hadn't done a thing.

"What? You mean those thick bongo locks didn't cushion the blow?" Registe feigns surprise, his voice dripping with sarcasm. He looks around, at the other cadets, for support.

"Man! Those fellas heads need softening. They hard of hearing, so their heads must be damn hard too! Same time, if it was my brother they do that wickedness to, is blood and sand in the place," Peterson says.

"Boy, some of the things I hearing sound like the same ignorance you get from the police and defense force guys," Wiltshire shouts, as he tries to keep his voice over the roar of the dump truck's engine. "Is this talk tailored for the company we going to keep? Look, this is just a one of a kind, weekend camp. Don't fall for all this propaganda you hearing, my brothers."

Wiltshire's budding Afro is beginning to peep out from beneath his regulation issued red beret, as the wind tugs at it. Lieutenant Richards had told him several times to cut his hair, but Richards hadn't forced the point. Enlistment in the cadet corp was voluntary and had dropped off. Lieutenant Richards knew that coming down on the popular Afro would send a chilling message, that the cadet corp was not cool. He did not want to strain the already tense situation at the school where the principal had already clashed with students over wearing tams and sporting dreadlocks.

A yellow, red and green, bead chain with a pendant in the shape of Africa can be seen at Wiltshire's open collar, where he has loosened two buttons. Wiltshire was a vocal student, active in the debating club and the student council. This was an awkward time at the school, in the country as a whole. Layers of tradition are being peeled back, scrutinized. Definition of country, culture, future, religion, self are argued endlessly in the schoolyard. The once staid school teetering on the cusp of an unknown, as if most everyone had imbibed some heady wine.

Wiltshire went on:

"And as for tourist afraid to come because of dreads, is people like them that start this marijuana business anyway. Peace Corp people, hippies, police never arrest any of them for smoking weed? Anyway, smoking weed is a symptom of the problems born of poverty and backwardness, it's not the problem itself."

"I think Willy have a point, you know guys," shouted Corporal Chasimuir over the din of the whipping wind commingled with engine noise.

"What point, corporal? Willy talking like he too smoking weed. He too like to encourage damn slackness. You notice he always fast to find excuse for fellas who don't want to stand at attention at class assembly. For a cadet, I find he not standing firm and disciplined enough about things in this country. He always busy talking of why things are how they are, instead of what *is*!"

"Registe, careful with where you going with this business about me and grass...," Wiltshire interjects, but Registe is on a roll and continues, anger rising in his voice.

"The other day I hear you grumbling on parade when Music Lovers Band was playing God Save the Queen. I had a good mind to report you to Lieutenant Richards. What you think people go think about our school, eh? Everything in the place going to grass and you only talking foolishness. You have no respect for discipline and tradition and that's why you're still a damn private after three years!" Registe spits out.

"Here you go again Registe, you are a real snake. Why you didn't report me to the lieutenant? Your report may have earned you that one stripe you've been slithering in the grass so long to get." Disdain in his voice, Wiltshire stares hard at Registe.

"Okay brother Tumba, we hear yuh!" Private Registe snickers in his response to Wiltshire. Tumba is a notorious dreadlocks in the hills who is on the run from police. Registe knows that associating Wiltshire with that name will stir up trouble.

"Okay, Prime Minister of assness, enough! I didn't start with you, so it let it stop there. I was making a general comment, I wasn't even talking to you. So, just put me down right there," Wiltshire splays his legs and looks like he is ready for anything Registe will try.

Registe raises his boot, as if to kick Wiltshire. Just then, the dumper hits a deep pothole and all the cadets fall into a tangled pile in the bed of the truck amidst their knapsacks and band instruments. The proximity forced by the sudden jolt defuses the tension some.

"Okay guys, enough politics. We have to remain united to ensure the weekend passes off good. Leave that fight for the defense force and police to sort out," Corporal Chasimuir is trying to assert his authority as the highest-ranking cadet in that dump truck. Lieutenant Richards is up ahead in the lead vehicle.

The convoy soon arrives at its destination and the trucks drive into the LaPlaine police compound. Men in khaki uniform from the Special Service Unit (SSU) of the Royal Dominica Police Force, lounge about, weapons in hand. Scattered about are the olive green clad soldiers of the Dominica Defense Force. The cadets disembark.

The cadets are assigned a place in the magistrate's court section of the police station, and the men immediately set up sleeping quarters on the bare floor. Outside, Sergeant Samson, the most muscled soldier on the island, is stirring a big pot of corned beef, into which he has just dumped a dozen or so onions he sliced with his bayonet. The pot rests on three blackened stones that seemed to have been in place for a long time. Nearby, a wiry soldier whose nickname is Piwi-Popsicle-Stick is brewing some cocoa over a wood fire.

Inside, Wiltshire's has laid his head on his pack, reading Frantz Fanon's *The Wretched of the Earth.* Registe has cooled off and has his head buried in a *Lion* comic, which features the exploits of Sergeant Hurricane and his faithful batman, Tisch. In the next room, Lieutenant Richards is working on the guard and parade arrangements with the senior police inspector and the major of the defense force.

"Pap-pa-rap-papa-rap! Paparap-papa!" It is Corporal Chasimuir bugle chow call. Before too long, everyone is in line, plates and cups, outstretched.

It is dark outside so the men return to the magistrate's court area to eat. LaPlaine was not completely electrified. So the darkness is almost total, but for the area around the police station.

As Wiltshire wipes the last bit of corned beef off his plate with a wad of white bread, he holds a book in one hand. Suddenly, a strong grasp turns the cover back, so that the bearer of the hand can read it.

"Must be an exciting cowboy novel," the voice is crisp. Businesslike.

"No, sir! It's rather political. Political science, really," answers Wiltshire.

As he cranes his neck upward to look, he spots a slight smile beneath the clipped moustache of Inspector Merit Jones. That inspector is a renowned marksman, bush tracker and head of the police SSU.

"What's your name, boy?" he asked.

"Private Wiltshire Lestrade, sir!" Wiltshire had jumped up, fixed his beret on his head, all of that in a flash, as he snapped a smart salute to the inspector.

"At ease, private. Just thought I would check on you guys before we leave for our night exercise. I didn't know we had illustrious political scientists among us?" The inspector smirks some as he looks at Wiltshire.

"Isn't that stuff a little too heavy for you? Don't you guys do Shakespeare or other stuff like that anymore?" Jones asks.

"No sir! Not really sir. Well, I mean yes, sir. We still do Shakespeare, but this is my personal reading, sir. It's just about the perspective of this brother, I mean doctor. Actually, he is from next door... a Martiniquan. He studied psychiatric medicine in France, was a French army doctor in Algeria. I just want to get his point of view, seeing he comes from so close. He talks about development of people like us and such. It makes interesting reading. It may have some bearing on things here in Dominica, I think sir..."

All the while Wiltshire is at attention, even though the inspector has told him to assume the "easy" position. Nervous, he searches the intelligent eyes of the inspector and is pleasantly surprised that he was spending this much time speaking to him, though he was doing most of the talking.

"What's with the hair son? In my day, guys at the Dominica Grammar school didn't walk around with this sort of bush on their heads." The inspector looks Wiltshire, up and down, suspiciously.

"Oh... well. It's just the times, sir. It's just a style, sir. I mean nothing by it." Wiltshire is uncomfortable now, sweating a little bit from the attention.

"Careful son. Carry on and have a good night," says the inspector as he walks away, a sten gun slung over his shoulder. There is a hint of menace in the inspector's voice, ever so perceptible to Wiltshire. As the inspector steps into the cool night, the last Wiltshire sees of him is the tail of his camouflage bush jacket flapping in the light wind.

Tense, Registe springs up from the floor from where he had paid rapt attention to Wiltshire's encounter with the inspector.

"Boy, you okay?" Registe pushes his face near Wiltshire's.

"I hope these guys don't stop inviting us out to camp. I mean, if they feel we look like dreads they wont want to associate with us. Dammit man Wiltshire! Lieutenant Richards spoke to you about that Afro already. You had better chop it off, or you will never get anywhere. Look what happen now. On top of it, you reading all kind of subversive books. The inspector didn't say that, but you think he stupid, eh? You think he don't know?"

"Oh piss off, Registe. You too like to kiss *boom boom*. The man asked me a question, I answer him. We had a regular dialogue. You see anything wrong with that? Don't worry about me, worry about your brainwashed behind," Wiltshire pulls back from Registe and turns away.

"And go brush your teeth, your mouth smelling!" Wiltshire's parting shot goes straight to Registe's solar plexus. Everyone knew about Registe's breath in the corp.

Registe was about to say a bad word to Wiltshire, but was interrupted by the entrance of Lieutenant Richards.

"Company! Company, 'tenshun!" It was Lieutenant Richards, and everyone flies into the upright position from the various bedpiles that they had arranged.

"Listen up! I am going to read the guard assignments. Each detail of ten guards will patrol the perimeter as directed. You will each have a Lee Enfield 303 rifle and five rounds. This is real! No messing around! Understood?" Barks the lieutenant. "Yes sir!" The cadets roar excitedly. Real rifles, with rounds? That was rare.

Wiltshire drew a 0100 hours guard detail. As luck would have it, Private Registe is on the same route as Wiltshire. As he walks the perimeter with his rifle at port arms, Wiltshire spots Registe.

Registe's eyes are as wide as saucers, as he peers into the darkness. Registe is walking on the edge of his boots, crouching, spinning around. He hoists the rifle over his head and jumps in place. He, twists and turns, mimicking a soldier in the assault. Now and again, he points his gun, horizontally, into the woods. Wiltshire tries to steer clear of him.

Someone approaches. It looks like a defense force soldier. Wiltshire goes through the motions of asking the approaching officer the code: "Halt! Who goes? Password?" The defense force officer rudely shoves him aside and says, "f- - off!" It is Lieutenant Freed.

Two hours earlier a company of defense force soldiers had headed in one direction and a company of the police SSU in another. Defense force Lieutenant Marty Freed had forgotten his luminous compass and returned to the station for it. Earlier in the evening, Freed had walked around the compound with exaggerated swank and swagger; his every step evoked a come-and-get-me-if-you-dare cowboy at high noon.

Wiltshire stepped aside. He shook his head in wonder at how little the officer paid attention to the rules. How he was so cavalier with his language, to a cadet no less. Nonetheless, Wiltshire returned to his duties and kept his eyes peeled, his senses keen.

"Brat-tat-tat-tat!" A burst of machine gun fire rips the night. Registe drops to the ground, his gun pointing towards the bush. Wiltshire jumps behind a tree, and takes aim in the general direction of the woods.

"*Oui Mondieu*! *Oui Mondieu*! Dreads! Dreads!" Without warning, Registe works the bolt of his rifle and discharges two rounds into the woods.

Before he can chamber a third round, Lieutenant Richards jumps on his back and grabs the rifle away.

"What the heck are you doing, private? Are you crazy? Do you think you are in a war zone? Who the hell, gave you an order to fire? For all you know, what you just heard might have been blanks fired by the guys on exercise." The lieutenant was livid.

"But, sir. The thing sounded real. I... I... thought maybe Tumba found out we were here and that only cadets were in camp... I... I... I," Registe was shaking, both hands clasped in front of him.

"Get back to your sleeping quarters and remain there until I deal with you," the lieutenant cuts him off. Registe lifted a trembling salute and then slinked back to the station house.

The entire camp is now roused and the lieutenant stays on the perimeter for a while, checking things. Suddenly, there is a rustle in the nearby bushes and a police officer bursts through like a rocket.

"O lawd me God! Someone's, been shot. We need an ambulance!" he screams at no one in particular, as he heads for the guard desk.

Behind the speeding policeman, a cluster of soldiers and policemen come up slowly. They are stooped by the weight that they share between them, as the dark forest looms ominously in the background. Wiltshire slings the rifle over his shoulder by its strap and rushes to help.

When he gets close he is waved away, but not before he sees a face bathed by the dull glow of the bare bulb which dangles off a pole at the police compound's entrance. In that dull of light, Wiltshire sees Inspector Merit's face. It is contorted with pain and several of the policemen are in tears.

"Oh no! Look at what the dreads gone and do now!" shouted Registe. In the excitement he had escaped his confinement to quarters and had just peered over Wiltshire's shoulder at the bloodied inspector.

"Is blood for blood! Is blade for blade! Is hand grenade for hand grenade, we go have to give them something to feel, now. No mercy! No pity!" The incendiary words of Registe pour forth like a raging torrent from a breached dam. He is waving his hands and stomping his feet.

Lieutenant Richard spins around from where he went to assist the policemen with the inspector and flings a fierce look at Registe. He shuts up.

"Dammit! Dammit, it is my fault," cries Didier, a young inspector who brings up the rear of the procession. He is one of the best thought of police inspectors. Someone who was once a cadet officer and who seems poised to make police chief in a few years.

Now, he seems distraught and flings his sten gun into the roots of a nearby dwarf coconut tree. He buries his face in his hands. Everyone is puzzled. His fault?

Before, anyone can ask more questions, a Land Rover tears out from the compound, headed for the city. Several police officers are at the back attending to the wounded inspector.

It comes out that the night exercise had gone awry. While tracking the defense force unit, the police SSU had split in two; they had tried trapping the soldiers in a pincer movement. However, in the bustle of the bush, Inspector Didier's sten gun had gone off. It was thought that it was the errant rounds from his gun that had riddled Inspector Merit in the groin. In the dark, some police officers had gone to ground, in the belief that they were under attack by dreads. The shot from the direction of the camp didn't help any. It had scared the group even more and delayed them from seeking help sooner.

The excitement following the horrible blunder leaves the compound in turmoil. After a while the weekend warriors turn in for a fitful sleep.

❀   ❀   ❀

It is a morning of gray clouds and a nagging wind that moans through the trees around the compound. A light drizzle sweeps by, which stamps a veil of dampness upon the place. With it comes news that Inspector Merit hadn't made it. His loss of blood had been too severe. His wounds too grievous. It was over. They break camp.

"Company! Company, board the trucks in order of rank, march!" Lieutenant Richards does not have any martial sparkle to his voice. Having been up all night, he was tired. On the ridge behind the police station, some villagers who had heard the news stare down into the compound, concerned, dazed. A few, youthful, locks men among them wear barely concealed smiles.

In the corner of the last dumper, Registe sits silent, red eyed. His sense of bravado gone, Registe now looks broken, speechless.

Corporal Chasimuir is chewing on a stump of sugar cane and seems to want to get his mind off the present and memories of the dreadful night.

"Cheer up guys. We tried to help," says Wiltshire.

He goes on, "A great man once said, what is to be must be! There is nothing we could have done. Anyway this violence thing is getting serious. I really can't understand what's going on in this country. I think we should all ask ourselves a question, as to what this corp means. Who are we anyway? Who are we fighting to protect? Are we some pawns in a power play by great principalities and powers? Or are we really here to serve our people? I, for one, don't really know anymore. When I get back to school, I am out of this uniform and I'm out of the corp."

Registe looks at Wiltshire and doesn't say a word.

Many More
Fishes In The Sea

Joey Mitchell is running down the steep rocky hill from the village school. He keeps his upper body bent backward, to make sure that the gravitational pull of the precipitous descent does not have the better of him. His brown, ankle length, suede boots raise a plume of dust as he skids to a halt at the bottom of the hill.

The swoosh of the just completed run causes the strap of his olive green knapsack to, almost, slip off his left shoulder. He hoists up the strap a bit and pats his knapsack as if to make sure that the folded wad of hurriedly scribbled notes, names of new comrades, political tracts and an event program are still there. Then, he spins on his heel and looks in the direction of the rusting St. Joseph Bridge. With his right hand, he absented-mindedly jingles some coins in the front pocket of his blue jeans.

Beyond the bridge, the main street wound between a jumbled mix of brown, pink, green and bareboard wooden houses. Two wooden lamp poles at the road's edge, separated by a stout mango tree, lean forward precariously. Clusters of stray goats nibble at a clump of grass at the base of the nearest pole. Between the poles, loosely hung electric cables swing to and fro in the gentle breeze. Beyond the poles, the road takes a sharp curve and disappears into the bowels of the settlement. It's from that direction that one of the Toyota buses will come to take Joey back to the city.

At Joey's back a splendid orange orb of sun, dissected by the many branches of a flamboyant tree, is descending into a lavish sunset of yellow and magenta streaks radiating outward. The glistening sea, at its horizon, shimmers in the reflection of the multi-colored sky.

It is 1977, and the new National Youth Council (NYC) has just completed its first national conference. The organization is the officially recognized umbrella for youth organizations in the country. Two months ago, youth groups, which pushed socialist ideals, swept to a surprise electoral victory. The new chair of the NYC is Egbert Macheaux, a young teacher from the distant mountain village of Grandbay;

the part of that village called Lalay. He wears an Afro and sports a goatee like Lenin. His easy manner gives him a good feel for the masses. Clad in jeans and white T-shirt he speaks rapidly; shifting from his proper grammar school English to French Creole. Joey has been part of that surge for self determination and cheered on Macheaux, pumping the air with his fist at every opportunity. Brother Macheaux had addressed a hall packed with the faithful, the newly radical, and the simply awed. His delivery was high flown as well as spiced with street slang. He had told the gathering of victories in Vietnam, and Guinea-Bissau, how, just the other day, Cuban troops had chased the hated apartheid South African army out of Angola, that down trodden folk in Africa, all over, were dusting off their shame and raising their heads high. Locals could do the same thing, he said. He had gone on about how imperialism was being put under heavy manners and that we had a rendezvous with destiny. Many people clapped at that.

Joey was thrilled, but still thought that such talk wasn't concrete enough. That Macheaux needed more analysis. For instance, that we needed to be more serious about reading or that comrades couldn't argue by repeating hearsay or wasting their time reading *Hardy Boy or* cowboy novels. But, maybe, the comrade had come out too strong on imperialism. Maybe such talk would frighten away the church groups, like the one of St. Alphonsus. Then, too, nobody wanted to upset the nearby United States of America. The ruddy faced, brown haired, Peace Corp volunteer guy in the front didn't clap either. Rather, he just kept whispering to comrade Liza, for whom everybody knew he had a hard on.

When the turn of Joey's panel discussion came, he had gone on to contribute a piece on "The Role of Women in the National Liberation Struggle." To support his point, he had exhibited some posters of Mozambican women, babies wrapped to their backs, mashing manioc with a mortar and pestle; some Angolan women carrying Kalashnikov rifles while tramping through thick jungle; and another of Angela Davis, shackled wrists aloft, one hand raised in a clenched fist salute. That last poster had the crowded classroom of the St. Joseph government school whooping with satisfaction. Joey hadn't been too controversial or slammed the government too hard. He had to make sure word didn't get back to his parents that he was fanning the flames of rebellion in the countryside. Joey was anxious that his parents not cramp his style. Yes, sister Angela was beautiful. Everybody, especially the guys, loved Sister Angela. People could deal with that and what was going on in faraway Africa.

Yet Joey knows that, politically, the island is still an associated state of Britain, really a colony by another name. The local government was talking strongly of independence from Britain. At his school, students were taking sides and socialist talk flourishes. It is a time when rubber tire soled sandals are made in several backyard city shops and the pass-along Cuban newspaper *Granma* is popular with many high school students. Among Joey's friends the red, green and black bead necklaces, black bracelets of rubber or metal and woolen knit tams of all colors proliferate, even while he can't wear much of that stuff around his own home.

But with this conference over Joey felt lifted, eager to go forth and further the liberation struggle against what Macheaux had called, babylon system.

In the descending darkness, Joey glanced at some members of a dance troupe from the Portsmouth Secondary School coming down the hill, all girls. They looked like fourth and fifth formers; fifteen to seventeen year olds. Taking up the rear is Comrade Liza, accompanied by her Peace Corp volunteer suitor. The Peace Corp, as all the volunteers are called, teaches biology at Liza's school. He is a young guy, perhaps just out of college himself. Liza Duncan is a senior and will sit for her Cambridge University General Certificate of Education (GCE) "O" Level exams this year. She comes from a politically powerful family in the town of Portsmouth and is allowed to drive her fathers' Land Rover. Her father, Robert Duncan, owns a grocery store, a guesthouse, a cinema, plus a large coconut estate where a coconut falls off a tree each minute. Mr. Duncan is a staunch conservative of the of the old school but he indulges Liza's radicalism. He refers to it merely as incipient "radicalitis", a pestilence of youth, which will soon pass. Joey and his comrades have heard that Liza's father is to ship her off to London or Toronto as soon as she is through with her exams. He had been heard to say: "The cold up north will cool her itch to communize my estate."

"Peace to you my brother!" Liza said to Joey in greeting and grasps his outstretched right palm, with her right palm, in a power shake. In her left she twirled the keys to her father's jeep. She does not even pause, as she sweeps by Joey. Their palms wrapped and unwrapped swiftly. Joey's appreciative gaze followed Liza. His thoughts bubble as Liza's healthy behind bounces with her each stride. He caught himself and averted his eyes. That kind of feeling is for backward brothers with one-track minds, Joey mused. Meanwhile, the volunteer is hitching a ride with Liza tonight, and he hustles to keep up. He is a short, roly-poly hippie type in a tie-dye T-shirt and his arms flail about like he is engaged in some serious analysis with Liza.

"Hi!" A nice, velvety, voice intruded. Joey's head swings away from the departing Liza.

"Hi to you too," he responds. His eyes ached for a fix in the fast fading light. A slender girl walked up. Her skin is more like a light tan. She is one of those people with the blood of Africa, Carib Indians and Europe, fighting within her veins. Joey remembers her as one of the more graceful dancers. Her group had closed the event with song and dance. Her complexion was light enough for her cheeks to show red from the just concluded exertion. Her oval shaped face wore a mischievous grin and her full lips parted ever so slightly to show a row of nicely arrayed teeth.

"My name's Joey. Joey Mitchell," he offered.

" I go to the Sixth Form College," he added.

"I know already," she said. "I listened to you speak. You gave up some positive vibes. Keep it up." She smiled and Joey smiled back.

"Dawn! You coming with me or you taking the bus?" Liza shouted, somewhat impatiently. A little distance away, under the flamboyant tree, she was vigorously revving the engine of the jeep. The spinning tires pitched up gravel. A few children who stood gawking at this schoolgirl behind the wheel of the large jeep backed off as the gravel flew in their direction.

"Hold on for me Liza, I coming," she replied.

"So your name is Dawn? Dawn what?" Joey tried making some quick sweet talk.

"Just call me Dawn, for now" she teased.

"Look, your group was bad! Really bad!" By that Joey really meant good.

"Yah. Your song, it made the ending real groovy! *Forward March Against Imperialism!* That's a nice song. I mean.... it's good to tie culture with the politics. If not, people will get bored. Don't you think?" Joey's words were rolling, nervously, off his tongue at high speed. His stomach churned as he struggled to stifle an impending poom. He sized up the girl as he spoke.

First, he looked at her feet. He didn't like girls with feet the same size as his. He wore a size twelve. From what he saw, she couldn't be more than a size nine. Then he checked her legs. Her knees were a little knobby, but they were fleshed out enough. Her calves were strong looking, her thighs taut and athletic. Waist? A little thick, but the curve was discernible. All in all, she stood about five feet, seven inches but he couldn't see what she looked like from behind.

"Well, I got to go. We've got a long ride to Portsmouth ahead of us." Dawn spoke in a disappointed tone.

"Look! Grab this number. You can call me here. Do you have a phone at home?" Joey was thrusting a piece of paper at Dawn.

"Yah," she said. "But you call me first. Call me tomorrow." Dawn slapped Joey's right palm, as to give fives, and ran to the waiting jeep. Joey's eyes followed her in the subdued light brought on by the half moon that had just climbed over the hill behind the school.

Joey felt hot in the face. This girl had his heart beating fast. His mind was racing.

"I wonder if she could be a good revolutionary?" he muttered softly. Soon the bus came up, its stereo thumping out Lord Kitchener's "Sugar Boom Boom." The song sounded good and it seemed as if it would be a road march hit in the coming carnival. The sensual lilt of that calypso tune put more heat in Joey and he fantasized all the way back to his home in the city suburbs on how he could put some serious analytical rap on Dawn and really make it with her.

That night Joey tossed and turned in bed as he thought of Liza. He didn't have a girlfriend. Between the rigors of sixth form studies, household chores and the work he was putting into the struggle he had no spare time to fool around with girls. Dawn seemed conscious, though. Just the kind of partner with whom one could discuss *real* issues, besides "I love you," he figured. He pictured her at his side at demonstrations, on a podium, helping the struggle for a more relevant school curriculum and scholarships for university study, trampling through the woods in olive green if need be. She could be his equal partner in liberating the masses from mental slavery and remaking this colony into a land of the free. Joey's mind was rushing headlong into the world of dreams-come-true as he fought the sleep which, eventually, locked him in its embrace.

The next day, he confided in Tony who attended the same English Literature class with him. They met in the Convent Library Reading Room. The Sixth Form College Joey attended was still a work in progress and did not yet have its own building. The girls only Convent was a favorite spot where the Sixth Form College students had the privilege of using the library.

"Man! Tony! I met this sister at the St. Joseph conference yesterday. One beautiful daughter. I believe that this is it." Tony smiled, as he listened to Joey's use of all fancy superlatives to describe Dawn.

"Hold it man? What wrong with you eh?" Tony responded finally.

"You just meet the woman and you ready to marry her? You are a real romantic!" Tony cocked his head back, and looked at Joey like he wasn't serious.

"You making joke right? I mean, you didn't go down to St. Joseph to fish for woman did you? I thought you went there on a mission?" Tony asked.

"Nah man! Seriously. The program was already over. I was on my way home, minding my own business when this daughter steps up to me. She looked nice and fit. What you expect me to do?" Joey responded.

Before Tony could respond Joey quickly added, " And, from what I see, she moving in a progressive direction...I mean she hanging with sister Liza. She sang that song against imperialism...you know. If we could hook up, I could get her to be more concrete, more analytical, more involved. I self have no time for these *Mills and Boones* women around here." Joey was talking of a romance novel series popular among young women, especially high school students. With a slight sneer marking his lips, Joey surveyed some of the tidily uniformed female students who occupied the reading lounge. The students were on recess, and were sitting around in various poses, casually flipping through *Time, National Geographic, Newsweek* and *Readers Digest* magazines. A severe looking Belgian nun, looked over at Joey and Tony and motioned to them, a finger to her lips.

"Hush!" She whispered.

The nun's call to observe library etiquette was acknowledged, but the talk continued.

"Did you *lanng* it?

"Nope! Not so fast man, you think I am some exploiter or what? I'm surprised you would ask me such a reactionary question! Dammit Tony, I can't make the woman believe that is all I'm about. And I tired tell you Tony, don't call sisters *it*. That word, *it*, have a backward, feudalistic, connotation when you use it to describe a sister!" Joey hissed between gritted teeth, struggling to keep down his volume.

"Okay, okay! I hear you. It's true, you have to be careful. You cannot be careless and just think of sucking tongue in these times. I just joking man, you know I'm a feminist anyway. We have to be more conscious, show a better way." Tony whispered in Joey's ear.

"I know. You know me better than that. I'm not into practicing petty bourgeois love," Joey whispered back.

"Now, say you try to do anything that I, myself, would not do, make sure you put on your crash helmet. You cannot afford to plug the person child. You know how reactionaries are already. They will give all leftists the blame. Even me will pass in it. All the nuns will come down on us. The church will come down on us. I don't even think the nuns would allow us to come to their reading lounge anymore. Our organizational drive will be crippled. So, be careful," Tony intoned gravely, his earlier frivolity lessened.

Tony was a serious struggler. Like so many serious strugglers, he was from Grandbay, a village that grew out of an old plantation settlement. In the days of sugar and slavery, an insurrection at Grandbay is all it usually took to set the whole island ablaze. As to who controlled the land, things had not changed that much since those dark days. So even after a hundred plus years, the embers still glowed.

Grandbay, alone, produced about a half dozen broadsheets on left wing politics every week, of which Joey was a voracious reader. The Grandbay bus to the south of the city was where progressives went to buy their alternative newspapers. The only radical public library on the island, with books by Frantz Fanon, Che Guevara, or about the Black Panthers was at Grandbay. In the main hall of the library proper were posters of guerrillas fighting for independence in Portuguese Guinea Bissau, Angola, Mozambique and others of Fidel Castro and Malcolm X. On the wall fronting the entrance to the library, a big poster of Chairman Mao stared, serenely, at all who came in search of the truth.

At the same time Tony knew about girls. He ran track and had some serious muscle on his arms and legs. On sports day, the girls would go crazy whenever Tony took the baton for the final leg of the 4x100 relay. In fact Tony was the fastest running socialist around, considering that most of the sports guys didn't have any time for politics.

"So, when you call the girl tonight, don't go too fast. Also, never say you love her first. That might put her off. Make a lot of small talk. Just tell her you like her. If you start talking about love too soon, it will make you weak. It will put her on top, and you will never be able to extricate yourself from that position. " With that said, Tony gathered his books to go. Joey, absorbed in what Tony had imparted, followed.

This Tony was good, Joey thought. While Tony was hot with the girls, Joey was more bookish. On more than one occasion Joey had saved Tony's tail in Professor Henry Rodney's European History class. By encouraging Tony to rely on his encyclopedic knowledge of history, Joey was able to coax Tony into the struggle. He had also assisted him in Geography, dissecting for him the intricacies of the inter-tropical convergence zone, and how it related to hurricane formation. He had only, recently, encouraged him to attend meetings of the Cadre, a socialist study cell. Nowadays, Tony carried around a copy of Lenin's *What Is To Be Done*, and made sure the dust cover jacket with Lenin's photo was always visible if it lay on his desk or when he carried it around. It made him look serious.

While hanging around the corridor at school, and if a group of ladies were to pass by, Tony would change his subject from sports or sex and start talking about Angela Davis or the infrastructure of colonialism. Waving his hands, like he was engaged in serious debate, Tony would tell of how women were the primary means of production in a semi-feudal society, all of that loudly. When with the fellas, however, he would joke about treating all women equally, in his words, "Giving all of them equality of opportunity."

Joey had warned him about being an impressionist and a sexist. He had told him how important it was for him to say that women were prime producers *not* means of production. But when they were in big public discussions, especially when surrounded by loads of ladies, Tony had the nasty habit of brushing him off, paying him no mind. However, where it concerned the tactics of romancing women, Tony seemed to have a solid grip. Joey would try his advice.

"Hello. Can I speak to Dawn please?" It was now nighttime, and Joey was calling. He had gotten the number in the slim directory, which covered all phones on the island.

"Who is it?" asked a mature male voice, with a country accent.

"Joe, Joey Mitchell. A friend of Dawn's," Joey's voice trembled a little. This was his first call and her father, of all people, just had to pick up the phone, Joey thought.

"Hold on," the voice said, grating like a saw.

"Damn! What poor timing," Joey muttered, as he heard the dull thud of the receiver being placed down on some table or something. His stomach emitted an anxious growl, as the shit boiled within him.

"Hi!" The word came across, unsteady. It was Dawn.

"I was waiting for your call," she said.

"I couldn't wait to call you too," Joey fumbled. All that time Joey is wetting his lips that are rough against each other like dried banana leaf. Quickly, he swallowed half a dozen times, searching desperately for some rap.

"Ah, listen. I...really would like to write you and you write me. How about that," he offered.

"That's fine." Said Dawn. "But what about you? Tell me about you, your family, where you live?"

With that opening Joey started about himself and his family from Genesis to Revelation, then he launched into his father and father's family. Then onto his mother, his mothers family and all its generations. Then, before Dawn could get a word in edgewise, he started talking about politics; local and global.

All that time Joey mad to tell Dawn he really loves, or, rather, *likes* her. But he was mindful of Tony's admonition, and so he played for time. After the monologue, Joey surfaced for some air. Quickly, Dawn snapped up her chance to cut in.

"Anyway, ...I have to go now. I've got some geography homework to finish up. Maybe, I'll call you tomorrow." Dawn sounds somewhat faint as if she must have rested on a sofa, hands under her chin throughout Joey's soliloquy and sleep was now beating a path to her eyes.

"Goodnight..." whispers Dawn

"Goodnight, don't let the bed bugs bite," Joey states excitedly, thinking that he is cool.

"What was that you said?" asks Dawn. But Joey has spoken fast, and Dawn misses the part about the bugs.

He had spoken so fast, told so much, Joey had even forgotten to get Dawn's full name and address.

That night is one of fitful sleep.

The next day passed in a flash of daydreams, lectures that pass straight above Joey's head, and almost frenzied reporting to Tony. Tony, meanwhile, is simply nodding approval and saying "Hold up the side. Hold up the side."

That night, Joey is hovering near the phone, picking up the receiver on the first ring. None are his until, finally...

"Hail! Joey? This is Liza. What's going on?" The emphatic manner of Liza Duncan is unmistakable.

"Ah, nothing. Just waiting to hear from a sister. Dawn was suppose to hail me," he responded.

Forget about it for tonight," Liza says. Before Joey can respond, she goes on:

"Her father was angry she was on the phone for two hours last night. He got upset. You think Portsmouth people like that own shares in Cable & Wireless? Don't expect her to call you, if is so you tying up the phone. Hold your horses my brother, Rome wasn't built in a day. Take it easy on the phone thing for now, Dawn wants you to write her. She wants you to write her father too, "Liza was curt. It was obvious that she had spoken to Dawn.

The news is like a solid "Whap!" of a clout to the back of Joey's head. "Okay, but what happened ...", he trailed off.

"Don't worry man. Just do as I tell you. This is my territory and I know the people in this part. Is respectable people Dawn come from. Her father is the main assistant to the manager at Geest's Picard estate. He is really strict and petty bourgeois. Just write her a letter as I tell you. Introduce yourself. Her father's first name is Oswald. Oswald Anderson".

"What's the address," Joey asked.

"Oswald Anderson, Glanvillia, Portsmouth." That's all you need. It will get to him" Liza responded.

"Now, don't screw this up Joey," Liza stresses.

"Dawn is a star on the netball team. She is a star in the culture club. She is not too clear, politically, but she is generally progressive; moving in the right direction. She is in the Bible Club too, so you better not bring up any heavy stuff about dialectical materialism and evolution. That would just chill your rap right there. You understand?" Liza said.

"Yah, I understand," said Joey. "I hadn't gotten to that part yet."

"Well, don't bother to go there then! If Dawn's father hear about that kind of talk, *crapaud* smoke your pipe, *oui!*" Liza went on.

She went on, "You come from good people yourself, so why don't you focus on that when you write Mr. Anderson. Dawn is his first girl, his favorite, so you got to impress the man. When Geest paying the farmers on banana shipment day, her father even allows her to count the cash. Dawn is a big fish in these parts, man."

"Okay, Liza," said Joey.

" I can dig it! I understand what you're saying. But what about you? What's up," he went on.

"Irie" said Liza. "Not much on this side. That Peace Corp fella always want to give me extra lessons after class over. When sun going down is then his rap picking up speed. He think I in some *commess* with him *oui.*"

"Don't bother with him Liza. Perhaps you can enlighten him on the struggle," Joey said. 'But be safe, you never know…," he trailed off.

"I Alright man Joey, I can control that. Just mind what I tell you about Dawn, okay. I'll talk to you later," Liza said.

As he hung up the phone, ideas came to Joey a thousand a second. He would have to start writing right away.

Joey retreated to his basement room. On his desk, in front of him, lay a pile of English literature by Jane Austen and Chaucer, along with geography and history textbooks. He brushed them aside and cleared some space. He got his sister's manual typewriter and laid it on the table. He wanted the letter to Mr. Anderson to look professional. It was the first time he was going to try using the machine. Earlier, he had deflected every urging by his mother and father to learn to use the machine with some lame excuse. He thought that typing was for ladies and he was too much into revolutionary struggle to worry about such things. When typing of the pamphlets publicizing the NYC Conference had to be done for the old stencil machine, hadn't Tony been able to round up sisters to do that kind of work? Now, he had to bite the bullet.

He couldn't bring another woman to assist him in rendering his innermost thoughts. Involving another woman in this meant that before one could say "Jack Robinson" the news would be all over town. This had to be a "Top Secret" mission. He had to type it himself.

By four in the morning, Joey was almost burnt out. In the glow of his desk lamp he surveyed his twelfth futile effort at getting the paper to feed into the typewriter straight enough so that his lines could be level. The paper kept dropping too far left or too far right. Some of the lines were ascending and some were descending. Some words started off in black type and others were in red, from where he had accidentally hit the wrong key. At his feet were the crumpled remains of his eleven earlier attempts. He gave up and grabbed his best pen, a Parker, and started off in his best script....

He spoke of his parents, and how they both worked and were church going people. That he was a good student, a former cub scout and army cadet. That he studied hard, had never been in trouble with the law, attended college and intended to be a history professor or diplomat. In closing,

Joey said he looked forward "...with the keenest appreciation and desire to establish the appropriate level of rapport. Most Truly Yours, Joey Mitchell", etc. And "P.S., I may grace Portsmouth with my presence for this year's carnival and it would my distinct pleasure to make your acquaintance."

With that, Joey casted about for the most impressive envelope he could find. He set his eyes on one of the civil service envelopes that his mother had brought home. Since the place was still under British rule, the envelope was embossed with the Royal seal and read "On Her Majesty's Service" on the front. Joey licked the flap voraciously and made sure he had a hermetic seal. The letter was on its way.

A couple days passed. Then a week. Nothing from Dawn. Joey tries the phone once. The person who answered sounded like her mother. She said Dawn was at choir practice and that his message would be passed on. She did not respond. He attempted to contact comrade Liza. But nothing comes from Liza. Meanwhile, carnival is approaching.

Things looked bleak. Joey began to lose some weight. He left more food on his plate than usual. He is distracted in class. He loses sleep and shambles around the house with bags beneath his eyes. His mother noticed and asks of him the reason. Fitfully, he explains. She laughed it off and told him not to worry. That it is always like that the first time and that it would soon pass.

At school, Joey again confided in Tony.

"A real revolutionary must seize the time!" Tony spits out.

Joey nodded his head in agreement and fiddled with his pen.

"If the mountain will not come to Mohammed, Mohammed must go to the mountain," Tony stresses.

Joey rubbed his chin and stared hard at Tony.

"Who have cocoa drying in sun, must look for rain," Tony blurted out, waving his hand to the ceiling for emphasis.

Joey stared upward; following the path of Tony's every gesticulation. He is in a classroom at the Extra Mural Center of the University of the West Indies, temporary home of the Sixth Form College's main lecture rooms. He is in between Mrs. Speevy's English Literature discussion on Chaucer's *A Franklyn's Tale* and Professor Rodney's presentation on the place of Cardinal Richelieu in the history of European diplomacy. He had not done any advance reading for the next class. Time is moving on and he must be soon gone. Perhaps he can squeeze in a few paragraphs before the next class. He stares at the afternoon haze shimmering off the asphalt street nearby.

Nodding his head in agreement, he still waited for Tony to get more specific.

"I mean, you must seize the bull by the horns!" Tony added.

"But what are you really trying to say, comrade Tony? Be more concrete," Joey pleaded.

"I mean, haul your ass right quick man. Go to the carnival in Portsmouth... Liza can put you up at her father's guesthouse. Or, perhaps you can even stay at the fire station down there. Isn't your father one of the big boys in the fire brigade?" Tony gets with the program and is issuing a specific plan of action.

"That's what I really like about you comrade. You can really get with it," Joey said. "I'll do that."

"Remember, if you go down there don't play like you begging her. Don't just burst out wit' this love business. Pretend that you in Portsmouth 'cause Liza ask you to come down to assess the terrain, check some comrades. After that, if she still after you, you can deal her." Tony lays out his advice in a deliberate way.

In a hop and a skip Joey had it organized. It is the Sunday before carnival: *dimanch gwa*. His friends couldn't believe he was leaving town at this most festive time. But Portsmouth has its own carnival, Joey insists. Further, that he has some political work to do. Soon enough, he is on a swift mini bus to Portsmouth and the country scenery sweeps by his window in a flash. He had made plans to sleep at a spare room at the fire station. A plea to his father, had him intercede. He wanted to surprise Dawn, so he did not want to involve Liza and ask about any guest house space.

Upon arrival at the station house, there is much hugging and backslapping. He has known these firemen all his life and they are happy to see how he has grown up. He carries along a good supply of war and spy novels to distribute among the four guys who man the station house. They are so close to him, that he lets them in on his real mission. They all "Oooh" and Aaaah" about how Joey is a "...big man now and trying to run woman." With that they suggest places that he could have privacy with Dawn. Pedro mentions a beach shack made of coconut palms. Officer Corbett mentions a dark grove at the back of the Savannah. At night, he says, ones sole companions are the fireflies that dance harmlessly about.

In the midst of all this, Station Officer Hilaire steps into the room. He is an older officer; a stern man. He has overheard the conversation.

"Don't listen to these hardbacks, Joey," he says. "Better not be a scamp on my watch. You're here. Don't shame your father. Enjoy yourself. Have some clean fun."

He rapped a folded newspaper against his right thigh, and looks at Joey with a wry grin.

"Aye, aye sir!" Joey responded in an effort at the lighthearted.

The starch in his freshly pressed khakis crackling, Station Officer Hilaire spun on the heels of his gleaming black boots and went into the darkness of the station garage.

With his departure, Pedro kept on about the shack on Purple Turtle beach. He insisted that it would be free on carnival Monday and Tuesday as everyone would be running masquerade. The other firemen laugh at Pedro and ask him how he knows about the shack so well, and whether he pays rent on the place. Pedro only smiled, knowingly. Joey got up, stretched and cupped his hand at his mouth as he stifled a yawn. He retires to the spare room assigned him.

A quick rest and then Joey is up. It is about eight in the evening. The *dimanch gwa* show will start in a half hour at the Duncan Cinema. Joey lathers himself with some Dial soap and is out the bathroom in a heartbeat. He splashed on some Brut cologne, squeezes into his tight Lee jeans and his trusty suede boots. He has on a green and white polo shirt, and he has cuffed the sleeves to accentuate his, increasingly manly, arms. Before he dashed off, he grabbed a bite of some thick turtle stew, along with rice and red beans that the firemen have cooked up. As he chews rapidly, some of the firemen still chatter last minute advice. The meal quickly disposed of, he is now out of the station house.

Joey is bounding along to the cinema as the sweet tang of the sea breeze whips past his nostrils. Above, the inky night sky twinkles with the glow of a million stars. Upon arrival at the cinema a huge crowd was bubbling with all the excitement common to the Sunday before carnival Monday. In front of the cinema he negotiated the knot of crowd, gets in and finds a seat.

All the while, Joey's eyes darted back and forth. No movies here tonight. The wide white screen was a mere backdrop for the colored floodlights. Glittering streamers and tinsel adorned the stage.

The lights dimmed. The show is an all in one carnival production, began. In the main city, Roseau, all the different shows for the queen of the carnival or the calypso shows are split up. But here, this is queen show, wrapped up with a calypso king competition and an outrageous mockery of a matrimonial ceremony called a "pappy show wedding" at the end.

Joey had a Heineken beer. And then another. A flurry of acts hurried the night along and there was still no sign of Dawn. He started to sweat and was anxious that, perhaps, Dawn was grounded for the night. But, again, half the people in cinema are his age, some a little younger. Such provided hope.

The curtain was raised for another act. There! The Peace Corp guy is in a sweat, as he furiously beats some conga drums on the stage. He looked like he was under his waters and half the time his hands missed the conga drum tops. Now, who is that behind him? It looks like Liza in a red and white leotard was behind him. A line of similarly clad ladies, all kicking high, joins her. Dawn was at the end of that line.

Joey took a grateful, last, swig from his second beer. He went back to the bar and ordered a rum, chased by coke.

Joey is no drinker and the first gulp seared his throat and warmed his belly. The chaser soon soothed his heated gullet. Joey, a tingling feeling coursing through his frame, needed all the courage of his convictions. He strode up near the stage and waved at Dawn. Liza saw him first. She motioned to Dawn with her chin, between her leaps and bounds. Finally, Dawn got the message and spotted Joey. She hesitated, searched Joey's eyes with hers. Then she smiled. Afterwards, she flitted about the stage as if she was a woman possessed, dancing as if to Joey's heartbeat.

Soon, the stage lights dim and the dancers receded as the curtain drops and the show closes with some rousing steel band music. Everybody in the hall started to jump up, hands in the air, as the infectious carnival spirit spread. Joey, shaking his normally stiff waist in tune with the music, made for outside. He planned to circle around and head for the back of the cinema. It was dark. The Savannah is nearby.

"Joey!" she cried. Dawn was in Joey's arms in a flash. She buried her face in his chest. Her hair was all around his chin, in his mouth. He took the taste of one of the two thick plaits in which she has styled her hair. It tastes of sweat and coconut oil. He was a tall guy, and his clumsy effort at trying to crane his neck lower to peck at her face, search for those lips, ends up with his mouth on top her head.

"Boy! I missed you. My father thought your letter was too serious...he put a ban on me. He said I should forget about you. That you were a troublemaker; one of those radicals. In fact, I overheard Liza's father talking to him at the store. Liza's father told him, that you would spoil me. You would cause me to smoke marijuana and put dread locks in my hair."

"Ahh, dou dou, he didn't say that," Joey chuckled and cooed.

Joey was feeling big inside. The drink had put some backbone into him. His nervousness was gone, almost. He stroked Dawn's back with the flat of his hand.

"You know I am not about dread locks. I wear my revolutionary locks in my brains, I don't have to wear it on my head. I am a bald head rasta," Joey smiled, tipsily.

As he spoke the fumes of the rum and coke wafted out.

"Joey, did you drink?" Dawn asked with concern.

"A big revolutionary like you and you drinking eh? I'll tell the comrades on you," she spoke jokingly.

Dawn warmed to him. She stroked his breast, twirling around her delicate fingers the silver chain with the razor blade pendant, which he wears around his neck.

"You know Joey, the thing that hurt me most was what my father said after he read your letter. He said that I was still young. That I had plenty time ahead of me yet. That I shouldn't worry about you. That there were still many fishes in the sea," Dawn spoke softly.

"What? What's that? That's what he said?" Joey cried.

Her words bit into him. He shook his head and threw his right arm over Dawn's shoulder. He hugged her close to him. She slung her left hand along his waist.

"What is this? Fishes? I am not some rascal casting line all over the place. We are not faceless fishes swirling around in some sea, waiting for a blind hook or net of fate to snare us. The revolution, I mean love, waits for no one..." he stumbles, searching for words in his defiance. For a moment the effect of strong drink confounds that synapse between thought and his tongue and his words are slurred in a sloppy tangle. Dawn looks at him with concern.

Joey paused, bringing his left hand down his young moustache; strumming his lips with the forefinger of his left hand. Easy now, he desperately wanted to be analytical. He was collecting his thoughts for this offensive...desperately trying not to let down the side. He must win Dawn over to the cause and not just let this be an opportunity to make a lash.

"The way I see it," he went on, "we are beating, living hearts. Individual, feeling, loving creations at the apex of our evolution. As for you Dawn, you are my one singular sensation in this universe...and I...,"

Joey paused and strained against the leash of Tony's advice not to say the word unless Dawn had said it first. What was first: the passionate love that was bursting at his heart wanting to get out or Dawn's role in the struggle, maybe as a student leader? He didn't want to mess it up. Maybe he could weave together the two passions that now sought to tear him apart in indecision. He looked up at the stars and took a deep breath. God is my only witness, apart from Dawn, he thought. In for a penny, in for a pound, he figured.

"Well, I am not like these other guys who limit what women mean to them to just one thing. We have to go beyond that. In fact, I wrote this for you the other day. I hope you like it," Joey blurted out.

Joey whipped out a folded piece of exercise book paper from his back pocket and opened it. He urged Dawn towards the glow cast by a street side lamp post. He paused, took a deep breath and started to read:

To you my girl,

I cannot say that you an orange

and that I want to peel you back,

flap by flap.

Nor do I want to simply eat

of your curvaceous segments,

beneath the yawning tent of open sky.

No! I will not be the sterile one

who still embraces a macho ego.

Because if I go that way,

wouldn't I just fall?

Fall, when I realize that I have clutched

a barren stone for an idea

and led astray, my pearl?

Finished, Joey beamed at Dawn. Dawn's face broke into a smile that was lit by traces of moonlight filtered through the leaves of a nearby mango tree.

"That's great! You wrote that for me? Nobody has ever written me a poem. All I've ever gotten is a whole bunch of rap," she gushed, her words wrapped in the syrup of glee; her eyes making one with Joey's.

This was the moment, Joey thought. It was now or never.

"And I love you," Joey said.

Joey's words escaped the clutches of the frog in his throat before he could pull them back. The raspy words, parched by the heat he had swallowed at that bar, sailed out into the Portsmouth night.

"I love you too, Joey Mitchell," Dawn whispered eagerly as she looked up into his eyes.

"I know that you are a cool brother...just slow down for me, okay? You know how things are in this country already," she said.

"No problem," Joey said, as he returned the folded square of his poem to his back pocket, "And you're positive sister too, all set for the cause."

The night was cool and inviting. As Joey ambled off in direction of the dark grove beyond the Savannah, Dawn did not resist.

❀

My Friend the Sergeant Major and the Coup d'etat

In the time just after President Kennedy's assassination, the Queen of England had caused a stir among her island subjects by passing through a place called Balaw Town in a plain-Jane pink dress in an open top Vauxhall. All the grown ups who had been fed on the milk of empire were crestfallen. They had lined up for hours in the scorching sun to see the mother from the mother country. When she swept past in a fuzzy pink blur, I remember glimpsing something human waving. That was all. For me it had been exciting enough to be in a big crowd, balanced on my mother's shoulder, but for the older folk I sensed a disappointment. A lot of people had sucked their teeth in disgust, *cheupsing* as we called it. They did not appreciate this swift ride-by. This had not been grand enough, after what had been a life's wait for mostly all of them. The last royal visit could not be remembered. They had grumbled about not seeing the queen's crown, the medallions and the ermine ornamented cape that she wore in the picture which graced the cover of the school exercise books used on the island. It was amidst the controversy of that time I made a friend.

He was a bigger guy than I was too. But he would always wave to me, friendly, friendly like and pushing a round-faced smile. Me? Just a kid, but I liked making friends with strangers and others passing through our yard.

We lived in a little wooden bungalow, with a big yard shaded by a mango tree. Next door was Ma Antoine's house. Ma Antoine was from the country, but she kept a house in town. Really, she was a professional market lady.

Every Friday, the day before market day, she would put down a big basket of produce in the yard.

"Heeeft!" she would sigh. Oranges, grapefruit, bananas, plantains, spinach, chives and dasheen would fill the plaited reed basket to the brim.

"Dou dou, you want a ripe fig?", she would ask me with a smile. Looking out of my bedroom window, no shirt on, and round faced, I would respond by stretching out my hand. Soon, she would reach out and a nice long banana would be in my tight grasp.

"Thank you Ma Antoine!" I would shout.

On other occasions, she would step-up, and reach over the rusting corrugate iron fence which separated our yards to hand me a nice mango, fat poke or some other natural, tasty, wonder.

"Little dou dou happy? Little dou dou is a good boy? Little dou dou is my boyfriend?" She would ask. Dou dou was a local namby-pamby term of affection. And all that time, I would be nodding in the affirmative, my mouth filled with fruit. Her son was my friend. Ashton was his name. Ashton Benjamin. Everybody called him Benjy. He would quickly follow his mother into the yard. His muscles rippling beneath his tight garden-stained khaki shirt, he would swing the jute sacks with more produce, like yams and tannia, onto the ground. He would be unloading a big Bedford truck across the street, the idling engine of which would rasp in my ear.

Early that morning they would have traveled down from the blue-green highlands of Cochrane village; down dizzying, single lane roads, aboard trucks with creaking home-made passenger cabs and shifting bench seats which pinched one's butt.

MY FRIEND THE SERGEANT MAJOR AND THE COUP D'ETAT

Benjy would sometimes, watch me. Smile. Wipe his brow. If his mother wasn't there, he would light my eyes with amazement whenever he lit a little clump of cream gommier wax wrapped in banana leaf. That wax came from the gommier tree deep in the forest. It was a fire starter for coal pots and firewood. A native version of kerosene. It would fizzle, crackle and pop, setting off an aromatic cloud of smoke which permeated everything in the yard. Every time Benjy did the wax trick, it would blow my little mind. Hanging out the window, I fancied the wax a toy. Sometimes, he would give me a little piece and I would carry it back to Mama to show-off. As he was older than I was there wasn't much that we could talk about. But he would look out for me all the time and mark his passing through the yard with his smile or more.

Such was a childhood in Balaw Town which had got its name after a eight inch, dark blue fish with a pointed beak and which had a lot of bones. The town was near the sea, and fishing was its main source of income. Come to think of it, it wasn't even really a full-blown town. It was more like a suburb or appendage of Roseau-the capital of Dominica. You had to pass through Balaw Town and cross the Old Bridge over the Roseau River to get into the city proper.

The balaw itself wasn't a fat fish. If I remember correctly, it was usually no more than three inches in width. However, it was a common catch with an affordable price. Balaw Town fish vendors would wend their way through the narrow streets of pastel colored wooden bungalows, some mere two roomed affairs. Perpetually opened doors, with flapping cloth curtain entrances, allowed for the occupants to eavesdrop on each other and so ensure a constant tie-in with the street side gossip, noises, and quarrels. The opened doors and windows allowed the voices of itinerant salesmen of snow cones, mangos, avocados, rough cakes or fish to carry through. But the boisterous fish ladies gave Balaw Town its signature.

"Balaw Fway! Balaw fway!," they would cry out in French Creole; announcing the freshness of their catch. Balancing their loads of glistening fish atop their heads in enamel basins, the vendors would wend their way through the narrow tarred streets and beaten-earth alleyways of Balaw Town. After a sale, usually accompanied by boisterous haggling, the balaw would end up on some table, fried dry, fried in a gravy of onions, tomatoes and coconut milk, or boiled into a broth of dasheens, yams, green bananas, cabbage,

hot peppers and dumplings. But one day we left Balaw Town and that scenery of Benjy and Ma Antoine passed away.

Soon my family moved to Cat Lady's house. We were on the ground floor, while the landlord with her multitude of multicolored cats, lived above us. Hence, the name "Cat Lady". We had a flushing toilet and all, with an inside bathroom. We were still renting. Then it was onto the city: Roseau. A house with a long veranda, a flushing toilet, but our bathroom in the yard.

All that time I was growing. I no longer hung around windows, waiting for fruit to be tossed to me by a strange friend from the country like Benjy. The fire starter wax with its aromatic cloud, no longer regaled me with wonder. We had moved on from using a coal pot, then kerosene stoves, and finally a propane-fueled range. Through those years Benjy had disappeared like some childhood dream.

Then one Queen's Birthday Parade, I saw Benjy. He was with the soldiers of our local defense force. He swept by me in olive green, a big black gun on his shoulder. The rousing martial beat of the Dominica Defense Force's Drum &

Bugle Corp had me skipping and jumping alongside the marching ranks of soldiers for a while.

"Benjy, Benjy, I see you!" I shouted. "Remember me?" I asked, as I ran alongside breathlessly.

Benjy winked and smiled. What did I believe, eh? After all, the man was a big soldier now, with a green beret, steel-heeled boots, a gun, everything. I didn't really expect him to shout back some recognition. The man was a busy big-shot now. But with that wink, he acknowledged our past: The fire-starting gommier wax; the early morning carnivals of fruit. A childhood spent in the yard with a big shady mango tree. But I was getting older.

"Stand still, the front rank!" I am now an army cadet and I stiffen as Benjy's fierce gaze swings my way. He is now the Sergeant Major of the defense force.

It's Benjy dressing the island's military on parade. The Royal Dominica Police Force in resplendent whites, the serious olive green of the Dominica Defense Force, the khaki of the Army Cadet Corps of the Dominica Grammar School and St. Mary's Academy. Stern, Benjy strode the line. Three green and white wool chevrons were on his right shoulder. A red sash slashes diagonally across his puffed-up chest, tassels at its end near his left hip. Swagger stick tucked firmly beneath his arm, Benjy barks out the orders, and I respond. It's nineteen seventy something and Benjy has the job of making sure the National Day Parade passes off well. That the lines are straight.

"Eeeeeeeyyyyyyes front!" He barks his commands by stretching the words. His voice builds to the final word in each command like from the pit of his belly and ends in a crash like musketry ablaze. A couple hundred military heads snap to the front in unison.

This day was called Empire Day in my father and mother's childhood. In my boyhood, it was called Discovery Day, in remembrance of Columbus. Now, I am a high schooler and we are an associated state of Britain. Now we consider ourselves. It is national themes we sing of. Places we have seen, places we have been. The Queen is now more distant. Our national parrot and a native Carib canoe adorns our flag.

Like the Australian and New Zealand flags, the Union Jack only occupies the upper left-hand corner of our flag. Soon, we will be independent, and even that much smaller quadrant of Union jack will disappear. It will be all ours.

"Are you lonesome tonight..." The Music Lovers Government Band played a martial version of Elvis Presley's love song for the inspection march. Our Governor is a local now; a dutiful relic of the old colonial civil service. He shuffled through the troop review, his dazzling white pith helmet aswirl with peacock feathers, and a thin sword tucked-imperiously-at his side. Benjy kept the appropriate distance behind Zong, as the Governor is fondly nicknamed.

Soon Zong's speech wafted over the gathered crowd, slurred, haltingly. People are distracted. You see, at carnival we look upon the governor amusingly as he follows the frolicking bands in his casual whites, walking stick in hand. It is said that his walking stick is hollow and secrets a section out of which he draws upon his favorite island rum. Considering how his voice waffles over the crowd, we think that such refreshment is not restricted to carnival.

There are many more parades. But then the troops begin to march up and down the hills and valleys of the land for deadly serious reasons.   Lives are lost.   Soon, the pageantry of the parades sour. With the masses, there is now an alienation from the soldiers. But I hear no one accuse Benjy of being one of the uniformed desperadoes. In a couple years, independence comes. Turbulent voices become locked in the contest over which path to progress - so long denied - that our new country should follow.   Meanwhile, the atmosphere surrounding our little army has worsened. The men in green assume less ceremonial tasks.   The facade of splendid ceremony will flicker, soon fade.   The once amusingly long commands will cease to amuse. With the innocence of my youth stripped away, the ways of the real world intrudes. I leave the cadet corp and Benjy remains my, now distant, friend the sergeant major.

Soon, the quietness of my island ceases.   And we make world news for the wrong reason.

❀   ❀   ❀

It was early Saturday morning, just before the Christmas of 1981. Earlier that night I had trawled around for some action, but nothing had been really kicking so I had come home to my bed.

In our backyard, we have dripping sections of freshly slaughtered beef hanging off hooks. This period of hanging is prelude to next morning sales. We had slaughtered one of our biggest bulls that previous afternoon up at the live stock farm, near the national jail. I participated, even whipping out a .22 special and administering a coup de grace to the quite alive head of this noble bull I had helped feed into such a fine specimen. My act scattered the unsuspecting assistants who had not expected such an explosive flourish from me.

I had blown away the blue smoke curling upward from the barrel of my revolver and had glanced at the nearby jail complex. The jail was closely guarded as it housed the former Prime Minister and some of his colleagues, imprisoned for plotting an overthrow of the government. No guards had come looking.

At this time, what of was the local defense force? Well, things had changed. A few weeks before I had spotted Benjy in civilian clothes. He had been demonstrating outside the Prime Minister's office, lobbying to get his job back. Like so many others in the force he lost his position when it had been disbanded recently by the new government. A couple weeks ago the FBI had captured a squad of American Nazi Party members along with some Louisiana Klansmen. They had been aboard the ship *Manana*, heavily armed, heading out of a New Orleans port and bound for Dominica. It was a coup plot against the new government of the Dominica Liberty Party and the country's first head of state, Prime Minister, Dame Maria Centurion. The plot had been foiled when *Manana's* captain alerted the F.B.I The suspects were a sordid bunch: Grand Wizard David DeButt and Ku Klux Klan operatives from as far away as Canada, recently dethroned local politicians, South African money. It was an invasion forestalled. The Dominica Defense Force had been implicated, then disbanded. Benjy, my friend was without a job for the first time in almost fifteen years.

He desperately wanted back in. I bought him a beer and said that I would speak to a few people to explore his options. There was not much I could say or do. In recent times, the soldiers had acted in a manner that distanced them from the population. It was tough getting sympathy now.

But my mind is on tomorrow. The butchering over, I know our house will be all hustle and bustle with the selling of meat and the making of *bouden* - our homemade blood sausage. I am tired and soon drift into sleep atop my bed in the basement apartment of our concrete bungalow.

Bow! Bow!

I am rudely roused. A glance at my watch showed it was early morning. This could be bullets or bandits. Bandits aren't people in Dominica. Rather, here, bandits is the local name given to serious German-made firecrackers that can blow-off a finger. It's Christmas time and I believe that late night revelers make the sounds. But I fear that the bad news, which is commonplace elsewhere, has just found a local home.

Bow! Bow! Bow!

Single-spaced reports! I doubted they were bandits. I am now alert, my torso raised.

Brrrrrrttt! Brrrrrtt! Boooshooom!

"Christ, no!" I hissed. Though distant, it sounded like an SMG to me. Automatic weapons fire? A grenade exploding too?

I twisted out of bed and hit the floor. It was the army cadet training in me come to action now as I slither along the bedroom floor, through a door, to my older brother. He has barely stirred.

"Wake-up, Wello! Wake-up! They're shooting!" I shouted, but in a sort of hushed way, as I pulled at my brother's bed sheets from my position on the floor.

"What the hell happen to you, eh man? You don't see I sleeping then?" Wello isn't pleased.

"Listen. I think it's real shots. Bullets," I whispered.

He raised himself, rubbed his eyes. My brother is a professional civil servant type. A recent veterinary college graduate. A man schooled in faraway India. While away, he had been to big places, been a witness to many perturbations and strange scenes. A cool guy, slow to panic.

The night was now still. The stillness betrayed me. We both listened carefully. I am still in a prone position on the cold concrete floor. Wello is raised partially, on his bed. We heard nothing more, but the "Woof-woof" of a quarreling dog in the distance. He peered out through his room's glass louvers. No wail of sirens. No screams of neighbors. No scampering feet. From upstairs, where our sisters and parents sleep, all was still.

"Just damned bandits, man! Christmas coming you know," Wello muttered, assuredly. He shot a disgusted look in my direction. His reference is to the same notorious fireworks; something which had already crossed my mind. He flopped down on his bed, draws his sheets up to his chin. Serene.

I got up off my stomach and stumble back to my room. The dejection of one who seems to have falsely alarmed shames me. But the morning has not yet come.

When the morning comes, I find out how chilling it can be when someone shouts a whisper.

"Slade! Slade! Come upstairs quick!" My sister Elizabeth called.

She is calling me from the upstairs window. Striving to speak softly, her failed attempt at restraining the normal pitch of her voice makes for a mockery of her attempt at a whisper.

I felt in my belly that something was up. It is strange that they ever call me like that. I vault out the room, out to the outside stairs, into the upstairs lodging, all in a flash.

"What happen?" I asked, breathless after my rush.

There has been a coup!" They all whispered loudly, in unison. Eyes wide, faces agonized, everybody was trying to speak at the same time: Mama, Daddy, my sisters Elizabeth and Hilo. My oldest sister, Catho, was a mostly silent witness and she laughs unknowingly. Her cheerful smile evincing, sadly, the limitations imposed by a mental handicap she has carried from young. Otherwise, the ladies of the house all hold their nightclothes tight to their bodies, as if like protective shrouds. They speak in whispers, as if the walls have ears.

"The Chief of Police has been shot. The prison was attacked last night, so too the police headquarters. Radio Dominica is off the air and nobody knows what's going on." Mama is speaking with authority. She goes on, "We just got a special call a while ago. You are to stay inside, because they are perhaps moving around."

"But who is they?" I asked. "Who the f-- is making a coup, eh." I curse before my parents. I am astounded by my own rudeness, but do not seem to care. That is not normal, but neither are these times. It was the first time in my life that I had used such a "bad" word in their presence. It's like that when things seem to fall apart. My scalp creeps with the intensity of the moment. The calm shroud of a morning usually swaddled with a cooling dew is ripped to shreds by this foul drama. Coups happen via reports from the BBC, in other places. Dominica is, well, ...behind God's back, as Daddy liked to say. A place where you would least expect a coup to take place.

"Anyway boy, stay inside! This thing sounds serious. I heard the bullets last night. I smelled cordite," my father intones gravely.

Furtively, he paced from one window to the next. He parted the curtains, peeped out. He was in World War II; an infantryman in the British Army's South Caribbean Command. He knew the crack and smell occasioned by the use of old Lee Enfield rifles. He would know cordite if he smelled it.

"It must be those f--ing ass holes! They've paid mercenaries to coup their own f--ing country." I am shrill.

My mind swiftly focused on the some of the recently unemployed politicians who consorted with South Africa and the Ku Klux Klan while in power. Too many of them in the Dominica Unionist Party - a party which once championed the poor and downtrodden - had strayed from that noble past. Adrift, some in leadership had cast about for exotic fixes to problems of cash flow which bedevil small, vulnerable, ex-colonies. Bereft of ideas, lacking faith in their own native intelligence, distrusting their own supporters, the scurrilous among them had connived at fronting for South Africa and its operatives in the international right wing. Their plan was to help that pariah state circumvent the oil embargoes and other boycotts from anti-apartheid countries. A BBC news program, *Panorama*, had broken the story. Astounded, people could not understand why a party, which had brought poor blacks to power, would stoop so low. Why the first political party on the island to have women ministers in government and a Carib in parliament could forget its roots. Why the party and leader who had brought much welcomed political independence could go so wrong. Why? Why? Why?

So confronted, the government was dumbstruck; speechless in its inability to explain the inexplicable, the inexcusable. In its alienation, the government tried passing new repressive laws on May 29, 1979. A riot had ensued. Many were wounded. The only person killed by gunfire was Phillip Timothy.

Of all people, Phillip! A humble teenager from society's roots. A young man whose father, at the moment of his son's slaying, was bending his back under a ferocious sun, tending the garden of the Prime Minister who was commander-in-chief of the troops; the same troops who had fired into the crowd.

Phillip, my boyhood friend from the street where I had gone to my first funeral and my inner-tube ship mate on so many trips to Under Power and the foaming rapids of the Roseau River. Phillip, my frequent soccer partner at the Windsor Park. Phillip, my sometime movie companion at the Arawak Cinema. The guy with whom I once took turns looking through a rotted crevice of an Arawak Cinema door at a sliver of screen for the showing of the movie, *The Charge of the Light Brigade*; I related to him what I had seen and he did the same. Between us we were confident that we had gotten most of the movie. Then the bloody end.

On May 30, 1979, in only my second funeral ever on Boyd's Avenue, adjacent to the everlasting fire station, I had accompanied Phillip's funeral cortege to the overburied Catholic cemetery. The D-Special Steel Orchestra, led by Pancho, had played. No hot calypso tunes that day. Rather, cold hymns flowing from the mournful steel pan. Flowing through the city streets a seething mass, marching;

determined. So, I had joined the outraged crowds. After tenacious protest, with students in the lead, the government had collapsed. Now this! Perhaps the past was trying to get back into the driver's seat, I thought.

To me it seemed war had come. I jump into my jeans. I pack my .22 special. Since the heady days of student political activism, I walk loaded. I bark out what sounds like a last testament.

"Look! After they've gotten the government, they're bound to come for us."

"Us" meant all those who constituted the radical political element in the country. All those who had spoken out for black and Carib dignity. Human rights for all. More local control of the economy. Real independence. Those who stood for difference. I had gone away in myself, since the days of catching ripe figs through windows and smiling at Benjy and Ma Antoine. Change had come to my mind since the days of the aromatic gommier fire-starter wax. I now thought that our people could be more than mere banana tenders or porters. No one was going to steal this mountainous jewel wreathed in the green of warmth and belonging. I had buried my hopes into the innermost crevices of my island's soul; laced tight my destiny into the arms of those who sought to spring her free.   No coupmaker brandishing the pliers-of-death could dare attempt such a violent extraction of that rootedness.   So, a fire burnt deep....deep within me. Now that fire sprang from my eyes, lashing out in defiance.

"But they won't win! We will retreat to the hills, and put licks in their ass. Grenada will help us!" My spirit was bolstered by the example of nearby Grenada's revolution; a change which had just cast off the chains of colonial despotism in black face.

"So this it. This is where we are in Dominica now, eh? Making coups? I must go. I need to be able to contact the cadres...be out in the open, be able to maneuver," I said.

I spoke my plans aloud, as I paced the living room. Muttering one moment, dashing to the back bedroom window to catch an outside view, the next. I snatched up my black diary with code-writing, names, locations, and key phone numbers. Couldn't allow such crucial data to fall into enemy hands.   Elizabeth and Hildreth, my sisters, were snatching glances out their bedroom windows, whispering excitedly to each other.

"Yes! We will struggle! Now we'll find out who are the real revolutionaries," I shouted in sing-song paraphrase of Bob Marley's *Zimbabwe;* an ode to the recent guerilla triumph in former Rhodesia.

Quickly, I searched for those boots. The same Vietnam era US army combat boots that I had my brother Sami bring me when he went to study in Georgia. I always knew I would really need them one day. Not merely to jump-up with in the local toe-stomping carnival this time. Rather, perhaps, soon to traverse the dark green mountains of my country.

I kicked-off my sandals and began pulling on the dusty combat boots which I had retrieved from beneath a bed.

Wello followed me upstairs. He had taken his own good time to come up. Now he stood in the dining room, arms folded, solemn.

"Cool it man. Where the ass you going, eh? You wanna get shot?" This is big brother to little brother bullshit, and I hate to hear it--even though his advice is usually good.

Mama and Daddy would let him do the talking. They thought him more persuasive with cantankerous me.

You see, when he had gone away to study I was no more than a little boy. On his return, he found me to be a man around town.

"Shit!" I muttered darkly. In my befuddled anger, I wanted to accuse him of being some soft petty bourgeois, but I didn't.

"We will fight in the hills. We will get help from our overseas comrades. We will never f--ing surrender! The Klan can kiss my *boom-boom*!" I brushed passed him and entered the bathroom.

In times like these, ones piss is slow to come. It's easier when you cringe your face and close your eyes though. So I did. I tightened my stomach to work my bladder loose. The hot yellow line shot straight down the center of the gleaming white porcelain toilet bowl.

Hurriedly, I washed my face. Passed a comb through my hair. Grabbed a toothbrush. I spat out the morning blah and Colgate mixture in my mouth and exited the bathroom, brushing past Wello again who, with his arms folded, was following me around like all the others. I know they are worried.

"But hell, if we have to die let us die fighting like men. I am not going to wait around at home,... waiting, for them to arrest my ass." I was talking loud enough for Wello to hear as he stood behind me as if to block my way.

Unconcerned about his brotherly concern, my mind raced ahead to figure out where we could get arms, ammunition, stuff for molotov cocktails, where I would have to sleep that night. It was like 1979 all over again.

But now, I was still thinking Louisiana, South Africa.

"Lousiana! That's where the treacherous lice must have crawled from to enslave us this morning!" I shouted, as if speaking to a crowd of comrades. Now back at a bedroom window I peered out. I pushed the curtain aside ever so lightly so I could see, my toothbrush in the other hand working my teeth. Over the banana trees in the neighboring yard, next to the External Trade Bureau warehouse, I spied a caravan of three yellow Public Works Department jeeps. Inside were black people with guns. On their heads, old World War II British Army helmets: The round type, which resembled an upside-down soup bowl. Pointing upwards were several old Lee Enfield 303 rifles from 1914-1918 or maybe 1939-1945. I knew the kind. The same type I drilled with as an army cadet.

"Yes!" I shouted to the rest of the family who were pressing me from behind, anxious to hear what I had to say.

"Yes! We still in control. That is police over there. Our police." What I said stirred a collective sigh of relief.

"You sure?" Daddy asked. "Those fellas aboard there, could have captured those jeeps," he wondered aloud.

He came around my shoulder, as I eased off the window sill to allow him a view. I pointed to the three jeep caravan. It was standard practice for the government to use Public Works Department vehicles when there was any trouble. The police were always smashing their own vehicles, so in a pinch they were always short and Public Works would have to bale them out.

I spun around. Things didn't seem that bad.

"Boy! Where you going, eh? Why you don't wait for at least the news to come on the radio?" Mama implores.

News on radio? I thought. Whose news would they report anyway, if they had seized control? I ran out the door before another word could be said. I grabbed the keys to the family Nissan pick-up truck too.

Outside, I looked towards the Princess Margaret Hospital on the hill in the distance. The very place I had taken my first gulp of air twenty years prior. The sun was just climbing over the emerald hills in the hospital's background. However against the white backdrop of that building a teeming multitude of humanity had gathered. I now knew that last night had brought death and injury. I jumped into the pick-up truck and sped off.

Along the way, people were peeping out their houses, faces, fearful. Most, still in their nighties.

First, I sped by the Chief of Police's residence. He lived in the lane next to ours. I knew him from boyhood. The family was absent, the house empty. Only strangers, their faces blank with shock, milled about its entrance. I could not see any of his boys, my friends.

Leaving burnt tire rubber in my wake, I sped to the hospital next, leapt out the cab and head for the Casualty department. I part the thick knot of onlookers with difficulty. Off to one side of the drive leading to the Casualty people are taking turns to look at a camouflaged uniformed body lying on a stretcher. I walk over to the body.

"It's Piper!" someone mentions in a hushed tone.

Yes, it was Piper. I recognized him. A local soldier of some daring notoriety. A brash man from the village of Cochrane. A defense force member in his French army camo pants and combat boots. This was certainly no South African or Louisiana Klans man.

Piper's glazed eyes were locked at half-open, with a little blood still trickling from his side. He was dead alright, but otherwise quite composed and neat in appearance. Just a few flecks of mud on parts of his body betrayed any evidence of the struggle associated with the early morning combat.

"Hah! Piper, eh?" Snorts a plainclothes police superintendent who had just walked over to look at the body.

"You think you was a commando, eh? You were too damned troublesome! We showed you commando in your ass, didn't we?" His arms akimbo, the officer harangues the voiceless corpse, cursing its mother in the process. The crowd hangs onto every word, some nodding their assent. Most in shock, mouths agape.

Abuzz with descriptions of fierce combat the onlookers were eager for more. Yet, even in this sober moment born of fright, the fissures that mar the land colored the commentary of bystanders.

"That woman too hard, man. Since she come in power, she squeezing everybody. If she hadn't caused those guys to lose their jobs, all this would have never happen. As for me self, I don't want no damn woman to rule me nuh!" The angry words seep out the mouth of a middle-aged female fish vendor who is locked into conversation with an old night watchman. She spoke in muffled tones, but loud enough to wear her sympathies on her sleeve.

I recognize the watchman to whom she speaks as an employee from the port, a man who owed his job to the displaced regime.

"Yes, is true. I self don't want no woman to humbug me, nuh!" says the night watchman. "God put everything in its place and only trouble will come of it when we disrupt his laws. Since this lady come prime minister, is a whole bunch of calamity in the place. Is she self that encourage people to overthrow the last government by tossing stones on people roof at night. Right after that, a big hurricane hit the place. More dreads running wild in the bush these days and now look at this mess, eh? God punishing us for putting those *boojwa* back in power. Now, they getting theirs. The fire they'll get in their tail, I hope they can take it!" As the words tumble from his mouth, he raises his hands to his lips to muffle his volume, casting his eyes about wildly, hoping that no one from across the divide heard him.

"Aw shut up! All you old people too backward. All you want Klu Klux Klan to rule here?" It was a young woman responding. She had caught the gist of the comments made by the fish vendor and the night watchman.

"Unionist party dead and gone now, you better believe it. We Libertarians here to stay and is the lady's time to rule and rule she must! You better watch out! As a matter of fact, see if you have a job tomorrow!" With that said, the young woman - pink curlers thick in her hair - jumped into her late model car parked nearby and sped off.

The watchman, eyes now bulging with fear, grips the vendor by the arm and hurries away. As he does, he sputters in the vendors ear, "Mildred, is the same thing I was telling you... you talking in this place and you don't know who listening to who. Anyway, what is this about the koon klang klang that fresh woman was talking about, eh? Is a new party they trying to bring in Domincan, nuh?"

Meanwhile, around the hospital entrance, armed policemen are scattered about, along with some government ministers who are tied-up in several knots of excited chatter. The presence of some semblance of authority in a time of flux made the hospital a natural haven for news and assurance. The crowd kept growing, as people stuck around to glean what they could of the early morning action which had led to this commotion.

The officer who had been hovering around the corpse of Piper turned around and walked away. A little revolver stuck out of his back pocket, menacingly.

More casualties streamed into the area, all policemen. I sped off for the city center. I had heard that the police national headquarters was still under siege. In the distance, I could hear gunshots.

I am at the national headquarters - after a mad dash across the Roseau River. The city is quiet. It's early morning, no more than six a.m. I spotted a long line of policemen creeping alongside the walls of the headquarters, guns in all directions. I remain discrete, as I park off a side road and take up a strategic position near the fire station.

Nearby, the ambushed car of the police chief is still lodged at an awkward angle into the living room of Mr. Boston's street-side house where it crashed after the chief was shot. As I edge closer, the ghastly sight of the blood splattered car unfolds in stark relief. Dried blood is splashed next to gaping bullet holes, which have peeled back the flimsy tin of the white Mazda 626. Certainly, high-powered rifle bullets at work. But I am pulled out of my meditation on the carnage, by the racing gears of a huge army truck, which has just exited the police headquarters.

Aboard are policemen in a variety of camouflaged uniforms. Some still have on sport shirts, necks open showing dainty gold chains; nightclub wear from the night before. One or two officers packed tightly in the open bed of the truck have on pajama tops. They have taken back the headquarters and seem ready for battle. On top of the cab, I noticed Brother

Lala. Lala is a boyhood friend too. But his face was grim, a belt of machine gun bullets flowing behind his shoulder in the swift slipstream of the speeding truck. In his grasp, a long dark metal and wood contraption; some sort of vicious looking machine gun which looks like it has more than done its fiendish time in some conflict of another era. I couldn't discern the make. However, fear is in the air and the officers have unearthed strange pieces from the deepest recesses of their arsenal. Everything will be made to spit fire. The officers brandish weapons of all makes and calibers and fire off fierce gazes to onlookers. There will be little mercy shown this day.

By eight in the morning, things had calmed down. The radio crackles back to life and the usual announcer comes on. I have already been back home to assure them. We now realize that this coup was a local production. The defense force had gone on the offensive. An offensive within its own country.

Quickly, I went back to town to observe the fall-out. I've unloaded my earlier anxiety and now seek a status report. A while ago I picked up Pablo, Stan and Jane, the chief's children. They were alright and their father would live. I had dropped them home.

Back in town, I grab a Heineken malt at Param's Paradise, a bar that sits right next to Param's Ford auto dealership. The sweetness of this early morning malt, along with the excitement of the morning, causes my stomach to emit a growl. I am not a beer man, unless it's really a festive affair. So, I nurse my malt, staring hard at the dark-colored drink. A sober reflection, with an elongated skew to my face, stares back from the side of the dark brown bottle facing me. My mind drifts on and I fear for what all this will bring.

The chorus of competing voices, within what is a tight space, soar as bar regulars came off the street to quench their thirst. With my head bent, I do not spin around on my stool to listen to the exotic chatter of "Why-try-this-coup?" theories.

A fireman stopped by for a drink. His wide eyes and twitching lips bespeaks a man who has just navigated great peril. He must have been a virtual eyewitness, considering that the fire station adjoins the police headquarters. Out the corner of one eye I noted that all eyes trailed him, expectantly, as he made his way to the counter. I turned to face him.

"Man, these guys came in, guns blazing," he said.

"They took over the guard room. From there, they shot every officer who came off his beat and was unaware that the guard room was occupied. They shot a couple guys and piled them up in a corner, but they weren't all dead. They laid there with seeping wounds, eyes half-cocked, seeing faces, listening."

He went on.

"Boy, the Major, Major Hutton, he was something else. He said things like, 'volley to the left! Forward my boys! Don't panic, we must make it! Shoot a volley to the right!' But, they didn't have much ammunition. Ms. Centurion had sized them up long time, man. Lucky for her, she had stripped them of their powerful weapons, early in her term. All their serious guns were locked in the police armory. All they were carrying around were personal pow-pows they begged or borrowed off friends. You talking .38's, 45's; nothing really serious. They were supposed to have gotten a key to the armory, but the guy let them down. He didn't show up. They tried to bust-open the armory gate with a sledge hammer. They took turns slamming the locks. But I heard Ms. Centurion had put some real fat padlocks on that too. She had sent all the way in England for those locks. Unfortunately for them, the locks held and the sun came up. So, they had to split. Before that, they got one serious rifle and that's how Piper got to attack the prison.

The place is struck still and everybody is fixated on the fireman, some shaking their heads in disbelief. He goes on.

"Piper shouted at the guards that all the policemen in town were dead or captured. However, when Piper tried advancing on the prison to free politicians like small Dove and the others, he got shot with an SLR . That bugger was such a commando that he was able to jump back into his jeep and take off. He went half a mile, parked his jeep and went to the house of Painter. He asked Painter for water and bandages, because the bullet was burning him up by that time. He told Painter that if he knew he would have gotten shot, he would never have gotten involved. Then, he drops dead, right in Painter's yard with his gun still in hand. Boy, what a night," with that said, the fireman downs a stiff one.

"Man! These guys messed up. They couldn't even have asked around for an acetylene torch? Shit! I would have lent them mine." So speaks a burly mechanic in overalls, as he raises a beer to his lips. With that he cuts eyes at all in the bar and not a dog barks.

"They pepper Benjy by the New Bridge, man!" That resounding voice brought a hush to the bar. At that, I swung on my barstool to face the bearer of the dreadful news.

"Brrrrrtt! A set of lead from a sten gun. Brrrdap , bap, bap! Another set of hot lead from forty fives, SLR's, bren guns, everything!"

It's the bar-owner speaking; Hiram Param, a Dominican of Lebanese descent. His family owned a slew of businesses on the same street as the bar within which I sat. His family had been in business with the old regime, but now all the old Unionist bunting and portraits of its leaders had come down off the walls of the different businesses they owned. Param's father has been heard to jokingly say that he belongs only to the P.I.P: the **P**arty **I**n **P**ower. A stark neutrality embracing every word, Param describes Benjy's end by mouthing the sound of automatic weapons fire, accompanied by his simulation of Benjy's collapse, both hands clutching his throat. He went on:

"Benjy wanted to surrender, you know. He wanted to give up. But those fellas weren't taking prisoners so early in the day, man. No way! Not after those fellas had to tear their ass jumping over barbed wire fence, when bullets start flying last night. I think alot of people are going to be positively screwed by all this. In fact I just heard they picked up Major Hutton. Poor man had his pajamas on. He came out of his bedroom stretching and yawning when the police arrived. He said he had been in all night. Only problem, his pajamas were crisp and still had the price tag attached to the collar. Inspector Star Black asked to smell his breathe to check to see if it was really true he was sleeping all night. I hear that the man's breathe wasn't even kicking...the way that morning breath can really kick. Hmmmp! They put so much rifle butt on the poor man, it wasn't fair. Anyway, enough pal. I ain't calling no names."

Most of the bar patrons take in the delivery, wide eyed. Some civil servant looking types give high-fives, coupled with nervous laughter. A few grizzled mechanics from the dealership next door, veins twisting like cord around their thick arms, are locked solid to their seats, daggers in their eyes. Beneath their breath, they curse the news. The mechanic who would have lent his torch stomps off without paying. A teenage locks man flicks his head back, defiantly, and downs some orange juice. He slams his closed fist on the burnished counter and deposits a crumpled, red-colored, Eastern Caribbean dollar in payment. With a parting flourish, he shakes his locks and shouts:

> *When the kingdom falls,*
>
> *I and I say,*
>
> *Babylon go kill Babylon*

That remark was a paraphrase of a popular 1970's anti-establishment calypso.

"Haul your ass!" shouted one of the civil servant types with a goatee beard, as he followed the youngster out the door. "You want yours too, eh? We'll give you yours! Is fellas like you that spoiling the place. Police should put some heavy manners on your tail!"

"Okay fellas! Okay fellas! Not today. Not in here," pleads Param, as he waved his hand over his head. He went over to goatee beard and tugged him back inside, towards the counter.

A little more nervous laughter here and there. The patrons returned to their drinks, but whatever ease had existed had evaporated. An unseen chasm divides this small space and patrons steal furtive glances at each other.

Reeling, I grapple with what I have just heard. This is a betrayal within a betrayal. At this instant, I am swept with a twisted, angry, ambivalence, which plays havoc with my feelings. Benjy? Not the same Benjy? Sadly, I concede that it must be him. Anybody who knew anything about Roseau and parades etc., knew Benjy. Over time, he had become a local military parade staple. Now, he was dead?

The thoughts through my mind, come fast and furious. Benjy? Benjy, gone? Dead? For what? He hadn't been known to be a brutish soldier. Hutton? He seemed a cerebral guy. I thought the man had some sense. These were guys I knew, or thought I knew. Benjy, most of all.

Yes, the new government had fired all of them. I know that the action had spurred resentment. Indeed, some officers had been in on the Klan plot, which had been foiled earlier. But discharging the whole army had seemed too drastic, like having Peter pay for Paul. Was this about families who no longer had a father to bring home a pay check? I shook my head and stumbled over my feelings like a blindfold has darkened any attempt at clarity in this macabre blind-man's buff of a moment. I restrain my feelings, as I transported myself back to another time and place.

Outside, it looked like it was going to be a bright morning. It was Saturday, market day; a few days before Christmas. The trucks from the country were already streaming into town, heaped with fruit and ground provisions. The early morning action had been so abrupt and brief, most of the peasants from the hills would only know of it once they got to the market. For now, they were oblivious to the tensions in this troubled place; a place where the harshness of the outside world would now be more common.

We had the meat hanging in the backyard and Joe, our butcher, would start the chopping and selling soon. At our house, they would soon need the pick-up truck to drop meat off to close family, to do groceries for Christmas, to get on with life. I paid for my malt and left.

On my way to home in the concrete bungalow suburbs, I passed through Balaw Town. It was like a clash with another time, flooding me with feeling as I whipped past the small wooden houses with curtains flap-flapping at their open, inviting doors. The spicy aroma of a multitude of lunches cooking atop back yard coal pots rushed by my cab window.

Memories of another time flashed by: the rippling muscles of a peasant, smiling as he laid down his load, ready for the next morning's market day. A kid hanging out a window, catching ripe fruit in mid-air. The crackle and pop of the gommier tree wax fire-starter. Benjy, Ma Antoine, the yard, and what could have been, drifting away in a puff of aromatic wind.

❈

How Is It, Man?
How Is It?

"Why you put this wool in your head, eh? How you make it come so?" Ibrahim asks as he is passing his hand through my low-cut hair.

Ibrahim is Pakistani. He is the head cook at the Newsroom Cafe at Connecticut Avenue and S Street, Northwest, Washington, D.C. A couple months ago I came aboard as a sandwich chef, something necessary to support my college tuition in my junior year at the University of the District of Columbia. Now, in the stickiness and hubbub of a steaming dishwasher, humming microwave oven, sizzling grill and the half a dozen waffle machines which pack this kitchen, I grow tired of his wonderment.

"Shucks man, Ibrahim. Leave my blasted hair alone! That's how Allah made I and I. You never see a black man before?" I flap both arms to shake him off me.

"No! No! No! I never seen a black man or a white man or a China man or a woman man...oh, oh no!" Ibrahim is doing a jig, saucepan in hand. He is grinning, making light of everything I say.

I look at Ibrahim and shake my head in resignation. His sparkling eyes are sunk deep into a well creased face, a face which often cracks into smiles which smooth the rough edges of this unending kitchen hassle. The kitchen help is all foreign born, the waiters are local. The orders keep coming and coming and the waiters and waitresses scream, cajole and try to bribe us with tips to get their orders out first. All the while the unceasing orders have some in the kitchen wondering - aloud - as to whether Americans ever cook at their homes. In an attempt at illustration Ibrahim laughs and tells me of his American roommate who can't even boil an egg without imposing a fire hazard every time he tries. Ibrahim exaggerates, but so too is the frantic pace exaggerated by the constant interruptions of near-abusive waiters.

Ibrahim says he is from near the Khyber Pass and he listens to my strange island stories of going to the sea, crystal clear rivers, calypso and carnival, on and on. He is old enough to be my father, but we have become fast friends. This is a solitary existence for Ibrahim. He left his wife behind in Pakistan, and mourns their apartness.

"Ibrahim, what about that woman you bought? Tell us!" I am teasing Ibrahim about the plastic blow-up doll he mail-ordered from a flesh magazine.

"Every night, all the time, I give her," he responds.

I laugh. Jennifer, the white waitress with a female for a boyfriend, laughs too. Even Jose Duarte, the exiled student activist from El Salvador who wears the psychic scars of civil war on his ever-serious face, pauses from his bussing of the nearby tables and cracks a smile. All eyes on him, Ibrahim gets his cue to sing:

They say that she is too young,

too young,

too young for me to give her

He is singing his own sick version of one of my favorite songs by Gregory Isaacs, the Jamaican reggae crooner. The real thing goes like this:

They say that you are too young

too young,

too young to be my lover.

Gregory's songs salvage warm memories of island romance from the icy grasp of cold D.C. nights. His tunes are my whistled delight as I hustle this restaurant kitchen job and clean up as a janitor at the group house I call home.

The group house where the refrigerator cannot be trusted, forcing me to secure my perishable food by burying it in snow-packed trash bags on my balcony. A place without a phone and which is too poor to let anyone but my brother Sam, his lady June and my two closest friends in. An almost tomb, where I fear the well muscled rats which climb my chest of drawers to try lunge at my groceries dangling from the ceiling rafters to which I secured them with rope and a plastic shopping bag. Alas, a place where the brothers leave scum in the bath tub so thick that one can cut it with a knife. All this, while carrying eighteen college credit hours. Through it all I dream of my woman, reminisce about the green grass of home.

It has been several years since our eyes have met and it seems like an eternity. I dash off frenzied letters to my island home and dread the emptiness of months without a response. Initially, a letter per week would grace my palm, as I would tear ravenously through the blue air mail envelopes to savor her every word. Once, she asked me about how I was doing, "over there in America, eating all that good food, driving all those nice cars and sleeping like a log." Then, I smiled, sadness clouding my eyes: If only she knew.

My movements were always fast. But, in this city, survival meant that I had to move faster. The hustle between school and work was via a crowded metro bus, which groaned up and down Georgia Avenue at rush hour. It was an existence unparalleled in my personal history. No more being dropped off to school or work by mother in the Singer Vogue

Sedan or double cab Datsun. No more, the spicy home cooked meals. No more the dazzling sunshine. No more the week end outing to beaches at the sea or river side. No more dancing the night away at Warehouse Disco, that once derelict sugar mill rescued from its dark history and hoisted into its new perch as Saturday night make-out-heaven. No more, dew drop-aplenty, soothing, mornings. No more the melodious wonder of dogs barking at night, their canine vocality carrying across the valley, answered from yard to yard. No more the sweet mountain breeze caressing my face and lulling me to sleep. Or the pitter-patter of a rain lullaby on my tin roof. No more the crowing rooster rousing one from sleep. No more sleep-as late-as-you-want Sunday mornings. Then, to wake up and find breakfast made.

Going away meant change. The glossy magazine imparted glamour of "away" was a lie. Beneath the sheen of "away" was a harshness, unrecognizable at a distance. But even then, some cream will always float and bright spots give off an effervescence of good: The nobility of so many of the downtrodden of my neighborhood, who strive to build a new day, holding their heads high. The increased access to better now afforded to those of my hue - a reality spawned by those who cared enough to march, struggle and win in the sixties. The fabulous museums with the knowledge of ages stored within. Lavish libraries with pleasingly late hours and the humanity of those who overlook that you are foreign, welcome you and dispense a smile and sometimes *a freeness* burger and fries or more.

So, there is no heaven stateside. Rather, sirens wailing-out the nightly woes of a city gashed down the center by class and color. Many of my brothers, trapped and unseeing, at the throats of each other. Come Sundays, there is the cleavage inflicted by the alternating pull of the churches and liquor stores along my littered block, with stern preachers who try to rescue their oftentimes errant flock by draping them in flowery sermons and hopeful songs. But, so often, that hope is assaulted by the sound of gunshots born of tragic history and denial. And then more sirens. To be followed - sometimes - by choppers with piercing searchlights bringing daylight to my neighborhood at midnight, while they whirl away in hot-pursuit on high. And, many a night, the girl upstairs screams for murder when her boyfriend slaps her around from wall to wall.

Yet this moment, the here and now, is about an endless quest in a vast space where the possibility of opportunity exist, but at costs unexpected and unforeseen in gentler island times. All the while the sharp edges of home which had started to shred my hopes for better, mutates into the smooth mirage of carefully selected memory. A nostalgia encroaches. A nostalgia which revises history and paints most everything - prior - as beautiful as a blazing island sunset. It is a nostalgia that forgot the clamp of academic opportunity denied for many like me. A feeling of solitary confinement for those with aborted hopes for that scholarship to study at university. Dreams of better constipated within the rigid bowels of political victimization. Opportunity denied by the prejudice against those who were not for the way things should remain. A prejudice, which like some venomous prickle bush, had pressed me into a corner until I had to fly away to create my space. So, I had gone away. Now, I was feeling the call of home.

After several years of trying, I had scraped enough money together to buy an airline ticket from Eastern Airlines. I would be going home on a vacation. I made a call to my girl, Tessa. She is distant. But she tries to connect; a forced joviality.

"Yank for me," she says. "So long you in America, I find you not yanking enough."

"Whazup? Whazup? Are you going be down and be ready to give up some snatch when I touch base wit' you or what? Don't you jive me baby?" I struggled to imitate the lingual lilt and vocabulary of my present.

She giggles. But, I knew that I didn't seem convincing. Here, I had held my accent close to my breast, striving to retain a rootedness. Maybe, when I drew near to her, I'd try to "Yank" again.

So now, at the Newsroom, I hurry through my last order of a Daily Lux: A bagel with cream cheese and a strip of almost raw smoked salmon. Soon my apron is off and a quick farewell to Ibrahim and company is over. I will be home again, soon.

❀   ❀   ❀

Up and away from DC's National Airport and the metropolitan sprawl unfurls below and then fades. Later, I transfer in Antigua from an Eastern Airlines' 727 and enter a Leeward Island Air Transport (LIAT) turbo prop, at a crouch, squeezing through the plane's narrow entrance.

As I settle into my tight seat, I smell that plastic, which reek of the imported plastic Christmas toys of my childhood. The islanders jokingly say that LIAT stands for "Leave Island Any Time" and I fear that I will have to suffer in the stuffy cabin for a while, but today is different. Soon enough, we are off and the plane rocks gently from side to side as it ascends. Guadeloupe comes up quickly, the linear patterns of highways and well-manicured sugar plantations speeding by below.

Suddenly, a fierce band of rain clouds swallows the aircraft and darkness edges out the sun. The fuselage shudders, and my stomach churns. The burger I had consumed on Eastern creeps up my throat and tries to peep between my teeth. It is a small plane. If I spewed, I would easily slather both sides of the cabin. The well complexioned air stewardess wobbles down the narrow aisle on high heels, her knuckles are white as she grips the sides of the plastic rail below the overhead bins. She shoots me a well rehearsed smile that does not disguise the precarious nature of our circumstance. But I take heart and my Adam's apple works the bolus of burger meat back to its proper place in the coils of my tummy.

An ample lady, her bosom pouring out of her scant bra, moans softly to my right. Tightly wedged about her feet are well stuffed shopping bags. Maybe she was one of those who made quick trips to the US Virgin Islands to buy consumer goods for resale on Dominica. She smells of a perfume that went by the name of Atom Bomb. It was an affordable perfume with a pointed red cap and projectile-shaped bottle. A popular sales tray item among hucksters in the 1960's, it gave off a hardy scent. That scent would hover around the pious ladies who attended early morning mass at the Roseau Cathedral. By the time I would have gotten there for the children's mass, the cloying vapor would have sunk itself into the hymnals and the grain of the wooden pews.

She stirs and begins to fan herself with an open, dazzling gold ring adorned, hand. She looks at me with bloodshot eyes and forces a grin. I acknowledge her presence and try to impart that all will be well.

As we burst through the clouds, Dominica soars up from a clear blue sea towards the aircraft. A warming tumble of green ridges, peaks, and valleys bisected by winding, glistening, streams flow by. I think of how the cultivation of this steep land with bananas, coconuts, yams, plantains, is a heroic task. None of the linear patterns of the nearby sugar islands is replayed here. The history of our islands is sticky with sugar. Because of our terrain we had never been big with sugar. Thus, we had retained some semblance of difference.

The aircraft is descending steeply now, the once sparse settlements coming into better view. As we approach the capital, Roseau, houses are spilling out of valleys in a colorful rabble, marching towards the frothing edge of beach that girded the land. At Canefield, a more orderly quilt of the new housing estate and industrial park unfurls. Nearby, are big houses atop the hill, which seem as if they are preening. The aircraft's fuselage is now reverberating as it slows its descent. My ears pop. A screeching, grinding, touch down on the narrow strip of asphalt causes an uncertain swaying, and I am grateful when all is still.

As I exit, the blast of warm sea air jostles me welcome. Outside the terminal building, taxi men are already eyeing their picks as they hop off the plane. They focus on those who seem to have been away the longest and, perhaps, have lost their stride of the place.

You can tell those who have lost their stride. They are suited, scarves twisted in delicate knots around their, now sweaty, necks. Spanking new suits and expensive American Tourister and Samsonite suitcases crowd their feet and they look around, as if dazed. A sweat-streaked face middle aged man is wiping away at his neck and chin in elaborate motions, as a taxi driver makes a pitch to him. Flashy watch on his wrist, a thick gold chain around his neck, the heat already has him defrosting.

Me? Dressed in jeans and colored cotton shirt, I avoid the tightening knot of taxi men and "been-away-a-long-time-to-see-the Queen" Dominican visitors from the United Kingdom. Some are from the US and Canada too. The "long-time-no-see" types are easier to tell as they are dressed to impress.

As I dodge the last taxi man who seeks to nudge me towards his car, a familiar voice grabs me.

"Aye Slade, so you back in the country then?"

I spin around. It was Mano Peltier talking, his jheri curls bouncing and glinting as he jogs towards me.

"Yah man. I'm just here for the summer. Catch up on my folks. Check my woman. How 're doing, bud?" I ask.

"Bud?" he answers. "Budweisers? I'm not a beer, man! Anyway, is strictly Heineken and Kubuli I drinking."

"Come off it Mano, I was only kidding."

"*Ca ka fait, bouge?*" I try out my Creole that has been in cold storage for some time and ask him how he's doing.

Mano could be ignorant when he was ready. I didn't want him to believe that I had come to show-off or anything. When I say "ignorant", I really meant hot-tempered. When Mano was young, he would thump anybody who messed with him real fast. In fact he didn't finish high school, because he had gotten vexed with a fella and pricked him with a compass from his geometry set. He had been expelled the same day.

"But, your Creole rusty man? All you fellas go to 'Merica and overnight forget everything. What happen to all you, eh? Anyway boy, for a fella who was in 'Merica I find you looking plain, *oui?* Where your sun shades, eh?" Mano looks at me up and down, his eyes finally coming to rest at my feet.

"You mean, you not even wearing a jigger boots, man?" He was talking of those ankle length leather boots with the zipper on the side. They were popular among returning Dominicans of my earlier years. Mano's words had a sneering edge. His attitude was already sticking in my craw.

"Alright, man, you know I was never an impressionist. I am a struggling student, man. I eh have no reason to show off! Come on, let's not start like that," I countered.

"Anyway, I know about Heineken, but what is this Kubuli?" I ask. I was trying to change the subject, dodge his verbal jabs.

"Well, is Dominica's first and only local beer. Of course, except the ginger beer the old queens and them does make at Christmas time. Some Dominican guy who use to live in New York managing the factory. They doing well...."

Mano was already piling my luggage into the boot of his car. It was a Honda Accord. I got in and sat up front with him.

"I noticed, the little time I left, you guys into a lot more Japanese cars!"

"That's right dude. Got to move wit' the times my man." Mano looked at me and smiled. He put on his sunglasses and turned on his stereo's volume full blast. Prince's song, Purple Rain was playing.

Soon, we are speeding along the winding road beneath Morne Daniel's sheer cliffs. To my right, the narrow two-lane highway gives way to waves crashing against black boulders. Strewn amongst the rocks are the signs of an encroaching modernity: Empty tin cans, floating plastic grocery bags, bobbing plastic soda bottles in the surf, and the rusting carcasses of several British made Humbers and Bedford trucks so common on the island roads of my childhood. Going in the other direction, towards the countryside, are Japanese made trucks, some with gleaming white refrigerators lashed to their rear beds.

"So how is it, Mano? Tell me what's happening in the country?"

He smiles at my question from beneath his gold rimmed sunglasses.

"Man, you into business? You come with enough money to set up?"

He is dead serious, staring at the curving road ahead.

"No big wad of dollars," I say.

"But in terms of plans, I think I have what it takes. I do have a few ideas on compatible technology, though. Maybe a few things we could do to secure environmentally friendly development. We need to get our people to appreciate our culture. Development without raping the land... making use of what we have, wisely. For instance, solar energy is something I want to specialize in when I get done with college," I added.

"Yah! All that sound nice, but you gotta do business my man. Business, that's what you have to do. Here, everybody is a business man today. You got to walk with a briefcase in your hand. Maybe, you could buy a used Cessna. Get a pilot to back you. Grow some anthurium lilies, fly those to Miami. Fly-in late, customs guys gone home...you get the picture. Negotiate a little 'caine. A little nose powder never hurt anybody, you know." He looks at me and smiles a mischievous, knowing smile.

"Culture?" He went on. Culture can feed you? You better not come, with this history of roots shit! People don't want to hear about roots, man. People want branches. The kind of green paper branches that can fit in a wallet. The kind that can set up your woman; grease your wheels; put a satellite dish in your yard; buy you nice threads. That's the kind of branches we need to shelter from this hot sun down here, the greener the better. The dollar talks."

Mano is excited, and as he talked some of his spittle splattered on my arm, as it rests across the back of his seat.

I feign a smile. I want to get off the subject, for this discussion is already grating me the wrong way.

"Where are the boys, I ask?"

"Hmmped!" Mano grunts. "Boys? Which boys? Well, every man for himself, Jack! Your remember Polydore? Man, he gone off with a German botanist chick who was here on some project to study our forest. I hear he is a head fork lift man for Lufthansa now."

"You lie, you damn well lying," I say. Polydore was the shyest guy in creation, the man couldn't open his mouth to breathe in front of a woman even if his life depended on it.

"Stag? What about Stag?" I poke Mano in the ribs and smile.

I expected to be amused by a retelling of one of Stag's latest capers. Stag had been a real sweet man. Always in the latest fashions. A guy who prowled around parties, knew all the girls; glinting gold teeth, chains dangling from his neck and thing.

"What? You in America and you didn't hear?" Mano whips off his shades and stares at me for a split, bewildered, second. The smile dies on my lips, slowly.

"Stag died in Bronx, man. He died of AIDS. They just shipped his ashes home not too long ago. His mother didn't even want to touch the urn. She 'fraid she catch it too. It was bad, really bad. People saw him wasting away...he told them he was on a diet. Shame, shame, shame on his family. With all his woman, I never knew the man was backing up all the time."

The macho prejudice of Mano was oozing from him. He slips back on his shades. I am stunned. Growth, meant change. Change was unpredictable.

"What about Marcus?" I ask, speaking softly now.

"Marcus okay. He studied in Havana... did medicine. Government wouldn't let him work for a while. You know how they victimize people for politics down here. The government thought that he was mixing socialism with medicine. But, finally, he took some medical board tests and passed. He is at the hospital now. He pretty much top ranking now. He even doing a little something on the side, running a clinic for fat ladies to lose weight out of his basement. Lose weight... if you know what I mean. The man have a Toyota Celica and a Camry. The Celica is for his clubbing on the weekends, the Camry is for work. He must be doing good."

I understood his comment about women "losing weight". It was still a Catholic country, and abortions were illegal. As we sped on, the huge mansions which now occupied the hillside where cattle once grazed and mango trees grew, took my mind away from Mano's status reports. One building was particularly garish and obese.

"Who's building this Beverly Hills look-alike- up there?" I ask Mano.

"Oh, that's one of the young businessmen. This thing not tall now. You should have seen it last year. He must have been trying to beat the Tower of Babel. The government had him take out the penthouse. It was blocking the approach of planes coming in at Canefield Airport." He smiles.

The city is fast coming up and I wanted to hear about what I had dared not yet ask.

"How's my woman doing?" My question was pregnant with apprehension.

"What? You not asking me that, right? Boy, I not touching that one! We grow up together... I know you before you even know yourself. In fact, lemme hush me mout! For that matter, I eh know nothing. I don't want to spoil your holiday." Mano is shaking his head. He avoids my eyes.

He had said enough.

Before I know it, the car is hurtling up my narrow lane. The tires of the taxi grounds on the gravel in front the house. Daddy is on the porch sweeping, doing his "fatigue" as he liked to say. He smiles.

"Boy, Slade, good to see you, boy! Your old man holding the fort! But what the hell you wearing this kind of clothes for, eh? Where your three piece suit?" He backs off and looks at me.

"I'm alright Daddy," I respond. "The sun too hot for that kind of outfit."

I know he wanted to be proud of me. He was into the status signaled by suits and the like. I was coming from America and had to look the part. I was some trophy he wanted to show off to the neighbors. I wasn't into that. I wanted my re-entry to be subtle, quiet. Mano quickly tossed my one piece of luggage onto the porch.

"Careful man, careful! I've got some sensitive electronics in there..." I caution.

"I've got some taping to do: *Days of Our Lives.* If I don't get that done, my woman will leave me. See you at the club tonight... a little later, alligator," he said.

"In a while, crocodile," I responded, trying to be cool.

Soap operas? Mano? I couldn't believe it.

A wet kiss, flour covered hands about my face, "Slade, darling boy. How you doing? So long..."

It is Mama. She looks well. The rich aroma of a coconut oil based fish stew flows out the door to meet my nostrils.

Quickly, I survey the house. Some new furniture, a new television, refrigerator and stove, otherwise it all looked the same. My parents have maintained themselves well and I am pleased that aging has not dampened the sparkle in their smiles. I grab a bite, spitting out stories about school, big city life, between every gulp of the stew Mama had made. Daddy is busy asking me the price of everything in the states and converting it into E.C. in his head. Boasting how we have everything in Dominica nowadays and how, dollar for dollar "we eh doing too bad."

After, I unwind a bit and then ask to borrow the car. I had to go see my lady.

A dash to town and I am outside Tessa's yard. The knock-abouts next to Boyzee's Grocery recognize me and follow me with their eyes. I wave to the guys clustered around the door leading to the bar section, where hard drinks are sold. An ex-policeman by the name of Catch-A-Fly shakes his head at me.

"If you go into that yard, I'll knock you out!" Fly said good naturedly, but with a slight edge of disgust to his voice.

"Whatcha mean?" I ask, as he approaches me with a rolled up New Chronicle newspaper in his hand. With one hand, he pounds the newspaper in his other open palm to make the point.

"I like you boy. Since you small, I like you. I like you even before you like yourself. But since you gone away all kind of male crab trying to get into that hole. If I were you, I would disabuse myself of any grand ideas of jumping back in.

Anyhow, enough of this. I know you just come from away, so make some beers for the boys, nuh?" Fly licks his lips and sweeps his hands towards the men who loiter around the entrance to the rum shop.

"Nah man, I don't have money for that. Is studies I hustling up in the states, I eh loaded with cash," I quickly respond and walk away.

But this inference about my lady is almost too much to hear. It seems as if all my countrymen have been keeping faithful watch for me. Nonetheless, I must face my fate. I grit my teeth and plunge along the winding path of well trod yard dirt, which leads to Tessa's house.

I knock on her door. She opens it and her jaw drops. She clasps her hands to her throat. I don't know whether I must laugh or cry. She hugs me tightly. All seems well. Her scent is a little different from what I remembered. But, perhaps, it's me.

I step up and try to enter the dining room. She is slow in retreating. The back door slams. Out of the corner of my eye a male form goes dashing by and disappears behind a galvanized tin fence into another yard.

"Who was that?" I ask.

"Oh, one of my brother's friends. He was here keeping me company. I told him you might have been expected today, but, I guess he is kinda shy. I wanted him to meet you..."

"So, why couldn't he meet with me?" I shake my head and my scalp is tingling. This holiday is short. It has been so long. Must I deal with this now? Can I just be here? Just for the here and now? There is so much I want to accomplish and I feel I could take her just so, right there on the doorstep. But there is an anger that flares.

"You know how damn hard I worked sending every little thing to you, eh? You know the plan is for you to come and study too. Why you messing it up? " I was angry. "Is study I studying to make things better for us, ...I must be able to walk with my head up in this place, you know. You know how Dominica small already. Girl, you promise me, promise me you'll protect our thing, but I not in the island a day yet and all I hearing is that you give it up? What kind of *jouboum* you putting me in, girl?

I held her hands tightly.

"But Slade you only taking what people say as gospel, eh? You don't how our people too *maco*? Everywhere I go they say some man trying to check me. When they cannot get me, they lying on me. Is jealousy, man. All them neighbors spying on me too. If I stand up by a lamp post too long, they'll say it checking me too.....but I didn't roll myself in the street like they say...they lying on me. Don't believe them Slade, I not no *salop*." Tears come to Tessa's eyes and my eyes started watering too.

I bite my lower lip and my hurt and anger dissipates. I can't stand to see a woman cry. I release my grasp.

"Is alright babe, is alright. I know times crucial. Let's just play it cool," I say in resignation.

I sit in the drawing room my eyes growing accustom to the subdued light. Her mother is out. My loins tingle and my excitement causes me to pull a root. Tessa disappears momentarily and returns with a drink of Ju-C. As I raise the fizzing cup to my lips, I drink of her face. I lay the glass down and, before I know it, we have our way with each other on the couch.

My exertions over, I lay on my back. Tessa's head nestles in the crook of my arm. As I gaze at the bare rafters of the small room, all seems right now. I think that just this morning I woke up to the stale breath of a big city. The suddenness of return has my head spinning. While I drift, Tessa gives me a status report on what's gone on, where she's been. Slowly, I appreciate that there is hurt on both sides. I reflect that distance is a dagger which snips the bonds of our familiar and slits open an entrance so strangers may enter.

I remain mostly silent, respond some. But this moment is too overwhelming for me to say much. I'll take it slow. So much is tied-up inside of me. So much repressed passion to unload. But I'll bear this weight. The hustle of big city life and the harshness of separation has made me strong, accustomed to the fact that things are not always what they appear to be. Conscious that a promise is just that, and nothing more. Fretful, that I will be a stranger here too - as well as in Ibrahim's kitchen. After quick kisses, promises to take her clubbing tonight surround our parting. I will see her later.

When I leave Tessa's door, it is already dark. At home, I find Daddy ensconced on his faithful couch in front of the TV looking at CNN. Mama is out to some National Women's Council meeting. I return to the porch.

Outside, the street is empty. A few cars whiz by at breakneck speed. The days of street soccer and cricket seem so far away. In any case, the guys aren't even around anymore. Whole streets of friends have migrated. The neighbors are all new. For the most part, there is no one to talk to. I'd have to regain my rhythm, fall in step, or fall aside; behind perhaps? The place was on a different track, careening down some rather twisted rails, from what I could surmise. The right track? The wrong track, I didn't know. Couldn't tell yet.

I look up at the stars. I search around for the Big Dipper and other familiar patterns. Below, in the distance, I see the darkened outline of the green mountains which loomed over me in my early days. The lights of new houses dot their once virgin foothills.

I swing my gaze back toward the heavens. The absence of light pollution given off by the city magnifies our stars a hundredfold. They seem real close in a way I never appreciated before. As I gaze in wonder, they twinkle, as if winking me a welcome home. Maybe they remembered the little guy with cut-off shorts, bareback, who once scrambled the hills of this land - big ideas knocking about in his head. But now, my eyes grow misty, my Adam's apple begins pumping again, this time for a different reason. I swallow hard, emotion sweeping me. The twinkling stars in that inky sky seem to want to know where I've been, where I am going.

They seem to be asking: "How is it man? How is it?"

❀

Glossary

Word	Definition
Bakes	A flour pastry with a salty taste fried in oil.
Bekay Layvyē	White man of the river or river white man. Used to refer to people whose skin becomes pale from being in the river for an extended period of time.
Blasay	To cripple with blows.
Blēsē	To wound; to hurt.
Boojwa	Someone of the upper class, usually with a light complexion.
Boom Boom	Backside or butt.
Bouden	Blood sausage made from spiced vegetables, rice or bread crumbs stuffed into pig or cow intestines and boiled.
Boum-boum	Piece of hollow bamboo.
Ca bon!	That's Good!
Ca ka fait bouge?	How are you doing man?

Carib	An original Inhabitant of the Island encountered by colonizers.
Cheupsing	To suck ones teeth in disgust.
Chien Lawen	King's dogs or public dogs. Used to refer to police during the colonial period.
Chip Chip	To dance behind a carnival band in a slow pace.
Country bookie	An unsophisticated person from the countryside.
Crapaud	Local edible frog.
Dasheen	Local root crop similar to yam.
Daybah	Trouble
Demijohn	Narrow neck glass bottle used to store rum.
Diable	Devil
Dimanch gwa	Sunday before Ash Wednesday.
Farine	Flour
Fou	Mad
Fway	Fresh
Gommier Tree	Local hardwood tree.
Gramoxone	A weed killer used in the banana industry.
Jook	To prick.
Jouboum	Confusion
Kaka/Caca	Excreta; feces

Kaka Rubber	Very soft rubber; likened to being as soft as excreta.
Kalōt	To rap someone over the head with the back of ones fingers.
Kawant	Street urchin; vagabond.
Kenip	Local grape size fruit.
Kochi	Crooked
Kochonni	Garbage; stupidness.
Konmēs or Commess	A big mess, or an untidy situation.
Kwēvē	To beat up badly.
Ladjablēs	A she devil.
Lanng	Tongue
Lapli	Rain
Lougawou	Werewolf
Maco	A man who gossips; is overly clumsy or effeminate; a homosexual.
Makakwi	Foolishness
Manicou	A local wild life specie similar to the opossum.
Mepuis	Slanderous remark.
Mondieu	My God.
Mort	Dead

Mounted	To have some object be used as a source of ones strength or prosperity; as in a gold chain or silver ring. One would be *mounted* on the object after a ceremony performed by an obeah man or woman.
Obeah Man/ Woman	A magician or someone who, by dealing with the devil, is capable of healing, prophesying or doing great evil.
Oui	Yes
Pied Jaune	Used to refer to people of mixed African, European, and Carib descent; generally people of light complexion.
Poom	A fart.
Salōp	Nasty
Sea Poom	A loose woman; a woman of easy virtue.
Sensay	Carnival Costume made from combed rope, which is highly flammable.
Soosoon-clayway	Rayon or silk cloth. However, commonly used to refer to cheap or poorly made cloth.
Soukouyan	A witch of local folklore who flies at night in a ball of fire, and leaves her skin behind.
Tate	To touch up someone in a sexually suggestive manner.
Toeless	A black rubber sandal commonly used by school children in the 1960's.

Toutouni	Naked
Vert- t- vert	Roadside reed used to make baskets.
Zuuti	A local bush, which irritates the skin when touched.